WITHDRAWN

the
IMMEASURABLE
DEPTH of
YOU

Published by Peachtree Teen
An imprint of PEACHTREE PUBLISHING COMPANY INC.
1700 Chattahoochee Avenue
Atlanta, Georgia 30318-2112
PeachtreeBooks.com

Text © 2023 by Maria Ingrande Mora
Jacket illustration © 2023 by J.A.W. Cooper

Edited by Ashley Hearn
Design by Lily Steele
Composition by Amnet Contentsource Private Limited

Printed and bound in January 2023 at Lake Book Manufacturing,
Melrose Park, IL, USA.
10 9 8 7 6 5 4 3 2 1
First Edition
ISBN: 978-1-68263-542-1

Cataloging-in-Publication Data is available from the Library of Congress.

the IMMEASURABLE DEPTH *of* YOU

MARIA INGRANDE MORA

PEACHTREE *Teen*

LETTER FROM THE AUTHOR

As a semi-professional doom scroller, I can't say I'm the best at setting boundaries between myself and the content I'm in the wrong headspace for. However, I encourage you to reflect on what kind of story you're ready to read before you set off with Brynn into the weird wilds of Florida.

This book contains depictions of anxiety, depression, intrusive thoughts, internalized ableism, grief, suicidal ideation, panic attacks, and homophobia from teen peers. It also deals with the description of and aftermath of suicide.

If your gut says it's not time to read, trust your intuition. The book isn't going anywhere.

I also want to share with you that I have anxiety, depression, and ADHD. Most of the time I'm okay. I'm so fortunate to have access to counseling, psychiatric care, and folks who support and affirm me.

If you see yourself in Brynn, please know you're not alone. I'm giving you a psychic high five. (My hands are always cold, sorry.)

With love,
Maria

National Suicide Prevention Lifeline
1-800-273-8255 or dial 988

For everyone who's ever felt like they're too much.
You're perfect.

CHAPTER ONE

SUMMER BEGAN WITH A lurch of deceleration.

We pulled up to the terminal, and when it was finally my turn to deboard, the gap between the plane and the walkway coughed musty, hot air that smelled like fuel and roadkill.

Florida felt like an armpit.

I trudged up the incline, avoiding eye contact with the passengers who'd been too close for comfort for the past three hours. Half my body was asleep, and I mistook the pins and needles for the buzzing of my phone. I reached for my back pocket and came up empty.

Nothing to see here. Just me touching my own butt.

My phone was normally an extension of my whole being. An instant connection to my best friend. A way to document my life and make beautiful things. Without it, I was naked. And pissed.

My empty hand ached like the ghost of a bruise.

A little kid skipped ahead of me, the arms of their fuzzy Paw Patrol backpack bouncing manically. I didn't have that kind of energy anymore. At least, not today. Not when I was walking away from my perfectly acceptable life in Cincinnati toward someone I hadn't seen in five years.

I kept my head down and nearly barged into a man standing in my way. When I looked up, my face heated and my heart started jumping around. He wasn't supposed to be right here. I wasn't ready. But there he was, arms open and furry beard split by a big grin. His eyes were like mine—so dark they were nearly black. His sparkled with excitement while mine were probably radiating dread.

"Dad." I took a small, shuffling step toward him.

He pulled me into a hug. "Brynn. You're all grown up!"

It was a nice gesture. But the truth was, I hadn't grown an inch since he'd last seen me in fifth grade (unless you counted my enormous boobs).

I ducked out of his arms and adjusted my backpack. "You didn't have to come all the way to the gate to get me. I know how to find baggage claim. There are signs . . . everywhere."

We stood right in the path of the people deplaning. Since I couldn't moonwalk back onto the plane and make my escape, I lingered stubbornly, taking a good look at the next three months of my life. People muttered and bumped into me, but I held my ground, curling my toes in my shoes.

I'd expected him to have a shirt with a big jumping fish on it, or rubber boots, or overalls. Especially since even his name was rugged: *Hunter*. But he looked like a normal guy. Beardy, suntanned cheeks. A little bit of gray peppered his curly, black hair. He wore rumpled jeans and a Star Wars shirt. Was that something he genuinely liked, or was he trying to awkwardly connect with me by co-opting geekiness?

Despite the grays, his thirty-seven looked a lot younger than my mom's forty-two.

On her Instagram, Mom blamed her wrinkles on single parenting, bitterness buzzing between the lines. Hashtag blessed. I couldn't really blame her for being pissed when Dad had spent the last five years living on a houseboat in a vacation town. Meanwhile, Mom put up with a daily commute and a daughter with a growing list of diagnoses.

My banishment from the state of Ohio for the summer was supposed to be about my mental health, but I couldn't help wondering if it had more to do with Mom needing a break.

From me.

A sick emptiness spread behind my ribs.

"Ready to get your bags, sweetie-girl?" my dad asked. The familiar/forgotten nickname roused a small flutter of uncertain butterflies in my stomach. I willed my body to stop freaking out. He offered his hand, and when I did nothing but stare at it, he shoved it in his pocket and nodded toward the airport shuttle.

"I only have one." My whole life in a single bag. Everything but my computer and phone, which were back in Cincinnati collecting dust thanks to an ill-timed Tumblr post. Syrupy regret caught in my throat. If I'd left it as a draft, I'd be at home right now.

If Jordan hadn't messaged my mom about the post, we'd be having a watch party or chatting on a three-hour Discord call. I wasn't angry with Jordan. I'd have done the same thing if I'd been worried about them. I was angry at myself for being naive enough to be honest.

Dad and I shuffled along, a thick space between us. Other families chatted and walked arm in arm, probably arriving for beach vacations and quality time. I didn't come from the kind of family that traveled together. Or lived together. Or stayed married.

When my parents had finally thrown in the towel just after my tenth birthday, they'd taken me out for pizza to drop the D-word. We'd sat in a back corner booth, where my thighs stuck to the vinyl seat. I'd shredded a paper napkin to pieces in my lap and gritted my teeth until they squeaked. Anything to keep from crying in front of the waitress, who kept coming over to refill our waters and fill the silence with chirping questions about breadsticks and parmesan cheese.

I still hated pizza.

Even though I occasionally got pissed that they'd quit trying to be married, their breakup made sense. I couldn't remember a single time they'd acted like a normal romantic couple—cuddling or kissing or talking like people who liked each other. They had nothing in common except me. Mom worked in financial planning, and Dad was a groundskeeper at a public golf course. Mom liked keeping her house clutter-free and carefully curated, and Dad lived on a freaking houseboat.

Airports were a buzzing reminder that my family was different.

"What do you think?" Dad asked. "Pretty cool place, huh?"

I'd expected a Floridian airport to look like a tropical resort. But it looked like every other airport, with horrible geometric-print carpets and big, bland murals on the walls:

Vintage airplanes soaring in front of sunsets.

Huge ads for the beach.

Giant, horrible stingrays.

Dad caught me looking. "Those are cow-nose eagle rays."

"They look like sea monsters."

"They're not dangerous." He stepped onto the shuttle and let me take the seat by the front window. One of my butterflies half-heartedly twitched. "They only kill one or two people a decade."

I shuddered, imagining a scaly barb piercing the softness of my middle. If I'd had my phone, I would have taken a picture of it to post about the horrors of Florida. "You just said they're not dangerous."

"They don't sting you like the ones at the beach. But once in a while they leap out of the water at the wrong moment."

The shuttle took off, and a cheerful voice on the intercom welcomed us to the Tampa Bay area. I held the rail tightly, wondering how recently the brakes had been checked. "The leaping kills people?"

"Only the people they land on." Dad shrugged.

Normally, I would immediately look it up online. But the pathetic flip phone tucked in my backpack wasn't going to sift through Dad's bullshit for me. Without evidence of Dad making stuff up, I had no choice but to accept his words as the truth. I was stuck with the graphic mental picture of a helpless boater squashed and suffocating under a slimy stingray.

"Well, it's a good thing we're living on a boat where giant cow rays can destroy us at any second." I'd promised my mom I'd give Florida a chance, but we were already on strike one and we weren't even out of the airport.

Dad laughed, evidently thinking I was joking. I stewed about it until we got to the baggage claim belt, where I got distracted by considering how fun it would be to ride on top of the huge suitcases. My vigilant brain quickly reminded me that the baggage belt's metal plates were just waiting to chop off fingers.

The bags from my flight started flowing down the slide and onto the belt, but I had to pee. Mom and I normally joked about how we both had tiny hamster bladders, but that wasn't a Dad-friendly topic of conversation. "Gotta wash my hands. Bag's pink," I blurted, darting to the bathroom.

In the stall, I dropped my red face into my hands. He was my *dad*, not a total stranger. Why was I being so weird?

"Maybe because you only talk to him once a year," I muttered, bitterness swirling under my skin. One time Mom had tried to explain that he didn't know how to parent long-distance, so his insecurity turned into avoidance. To me, that sounded like a good reason to move back to Ohio and get a therapist. Not a good reason to avoid calling your daughter.

At the same time, I understood. I was *a lot*.

The toilet beside me flushed, and another wave of embarrassment washed over me. At least it was a total stranger hearing me talk to myself.

At the line of sinks, I squirted pale-pink, hospital-smelling soap onto my hands and stared into the mirror, more keenly aware than ever that I looked a lot like my dad. Curly black hair, dark eyes, and moles all over my body, like splashes of ink. Back at home, people asked me all the time if I was adopted. My mom has strawberry-blond hair, a slender swimmer's body, and pale-brown eyes. She's gorgeous, stress-induced crow's-feet and all. The only thing I'd inherited from her was her height, all five feet even of it.

I dried my hands on my shorts and wove my way back through the crowd hovering around the baggage belt like vultures. "Still no bag?"

"Not yet. Any good movies on the flight?" Dad asked.

"I did trivia." My final, blissful moments of screen time. I regretted not stroking the smooth glass for longer. "I kicked some old lady's butt. Oh—I think that's it."

Dad wrenched a hot-pink suitcase off the belt. I checked for the charms hanging from the handle—Viktor and Yuri from *Yuri!!! on Ice*. My favorite shows were just more things I'd be isolated from in a purgatory with no Internet access.

The wheels of my suitcase hummed softly as we left the baggage claim area. A wall of touch-screen computers blinked at me, beckoning. My palms went sweaty at the thought of dashing away from Dad and checking to see if the consoles offered free Internet access. What would I do with a few seconds? Email Jordan to let them know I was okay? Check my inbox?

It didn't matter. I didn't have the guts to sneak online—not when I was haunted by the memory of Mom's voice breaking with helpless fear.

Shame gurgling in my belly, I stomped ahead of my dad and blinked until my eyes quit burning. I didn't want to have sympathy for her. She could have stopped herself from overreacting and saved me from a summer in swampy hell. Instead, she'd doomed me to feeling bad for no reason. Isolated from my friends. My fandoms. My voice.

My whole support system.

Automated doors opened to the parking garage, and I fought the urge to cast my arms over my face and hiss like a vampire. The heat grabbed and shook me. I started sweating instantaneously, and by the time we got to my dad's beat-up Jeep I was already sticky in places that weren't meant to be sticky.

"Sunglasses?" Dad asked, handing me a pair with a hideous neon sports strap. I put them on to hide my horror and buckled my seat belt as he pulled out of the garage. The exit ramp spiraled down and down and down, and Dad turned to me with a grin.

"Dare me?"

"I'm not supposed to dare someone driving me to do anything. That's how teenagers die in horrible car accidents." I'd gone down a deep rabbit hole on Reddit reading AMAs by first responders, and I knew exactly what would happen to my soft body in a mangled wreck.

"Good thing I'm not a teenager." Dad gunned it, and the Jeep jumped forward and hugged the tight curve.

I grabbed onto the door, the swooping tickle forcing a whooping laugh from my belly. A sick rush of anger wrenched the happy sound away. "Dad!"

We only slowed down when we reached the payment booth. My fingers ached from gripping the seat belt, but a tiny, traitorous part of me had loved the thrill.

The woman at the booth shook her head, but once Dad grinned, her stern expression melted away. I rolled my eyes as we followed winding airport roads that curved and tilted like roller-coaster tracks. The warm air smelled like hot machines, diesel, and salt. I stretched my hand out the window, just a little, to feel the air curl around my fingers. I knew better than to reach out too far. One unexpected side-swipe and I'd lose a limb.

When we merged onto the interstate, the whipping wind made it impossible to talk. I didn't mind. The blissful rush of loud white noise put a barrier between me and my dad.

We roared under an overpass and emerged on a long, flat bridge that went on and on across a wide, flat bay. I'd never seen anything like it, and my skin lit up with goose bumps.

Late-afternoon sun glinted on the rippling water, gleaming white against dark blue. Speedboats soared across the surface, leaving froth behind them like the contrails that crisscrossed the clear blue sky. I could see forever, all the way to the horizon.

Dad glanced at me. A small smile tickled at my lips.

"This isn't the worst," I murmured, letting the wind carry it away.

Florida was hot and stupid, but it was really pretty—at least here in Tampa Bay, far from the gator-infested swamps I'd seen online.

"Look for dolphins!" Dad shouted over the sound of the wind.

I held my backpack in my lap and scanned the surface of the water, picturing dolphins doing flips and tricks. My hair flapped in my face, blown free of my ponytail and making my nose itch. It was going to be hell getting the tangles out after this.

A shiny fin broke the surface in the distance, rolling gently and leaving a ripple where it had been.

"Dolphin!" I yelled. "Holy crap! It was right there!"

Hating my scary-unfamiliar-no-Internet fate with every fiber of my being didn't make me immune to actual dolphins. I watched the surface for the rest of the speeding trip across the long bridge, but I didn't see any more polished-gray fins peeking out from the waves.

Disappointment formed a hollow pocket in my chest when we reached the other side of the bridge and slowed down, and Florida looked like a regular, boring place again. At a red light, I tried to fix my ponytail. A terrible thought occurred to me. "How do you tell if it's a dolphin or a shark?"

Dad made a curving shape with his hand. "Dolphins come up for a breath like this. Sharks come directly at you, and they make a different sound."

I frowned. "What kind of sound?"

He looked at me very seriously. "Dun-dun. Dun-dun. Dun-dun."

Acute cringe made the hair on my arms stand on end. "Very funny," I deadpanned.

How was I supposed to survive here if my dad joked about how to spot apex predators? He was going to feel really bad when his dad jokes got me devoured by a hammerhead in my own backyard.

"Mom let me look this stuff up, you know. Even she told me to be careful. Alligators. Hurricanes. Poisonous spiders. Incredibly poisonous snakes. Crocodiles. Bears. Panthers. Fire ants. Wild boars. Giant fish. *Dozens* of species of shark. And, apparently, leaping stingrays."

"If it helps, we don't have many sharks in our little bayou." Dad's voice went serious and gentle, and I turned my head away so he wouldn't be able to read my fear.

The flight had been turbulence-free, so I'd made it three hours feeling like a rock star who wasn't afraid of anything. Now the fear was back. It curdled, whispering that I'd be dead someday, maybe violently, and definitely forever. Maybe even soon—someone might T-bone our car right now. We'd end up as smears on the pavement, blobs of smashed organs and shattered bones.

Intrusive thoughts. My therapist suggested coming up with an alternative vision when the terrifying thoughts surfaced. Something warm and happy. Something that wouldn't make my lungs freeze over. A shield. A guiding power.

So far I sucked at conjuring alternative visions. I could only manage acknowledgment of intrusive thoughts. Every time I tried to imagine a protector, my mind went blank. A blank slate to fill with terror.

I wasn't very good at therapy.

"Brynn."

"Not many sharks means *some* sharks." My voice got wheezy. Were they big sharks? Small sharks? Nurse sharks supposedly don't eat people. I'd learned that in second grade, imagining them wearing little hats and stethoscopes. Which hadn't made much sense. "Sharks don't even have necks."

"Brynn." My dad pulled over into the dirt on the side of the winding road. I made myself look at him, knowing exactly what I'd see—the pity-worry face adults gave me when they expected me to unravel right before their eyes. His gaze was warm and concerned, a mirror of my mom's every time she looked at me and didn't understand how my broken brain worked. They probably regretted combining their DNA to make the perfect cocktail of crazy.

I braced for him to tell me to calm down. Or worse, for him to somehow read my mind and know I was using ugly words about myself to double down on the hurt.

"A guy got eaten by a shark here about four years ago," Dad said. "But he lived on the Intracoastal. He went swimming where he usually chummed for fish. That was a huge risk factor." He yanked his thumb toward the brown, algae-covered ditch beside the road. "We're in the shallows. It's flats and canals. It's where sharks have their babies, and none of them are big enough to hurt people. If we're ever out in shark-infested waters, I'll let you know. And I'll keep you safe."

My nose itched as I tried to force tears back into my eyes with willpower alone. "Okay." I didn't mind Dad talking to me like I was five, not right now, when I was acting like a child.

I had a lot of different coping mechanisms for the spiral of doom. *Catastrophic thinking*, my therapist called it. It sounded like the title of a summer blockbuster. Catastrophic thinking and intrusive thoughts were my brain's idea of an OTP. But right now, none of my coping mechanisms came to mind except doing a breathing exercise that involved pressing one nostril at a time. And I wasn't going to do that in front of my dad.

The water in the ditch beside the road moved sluggishly, like a spill creeping across a paper towel. A cloud of bugs hovered over it, thick as smoke, and dragonflies flitted around, wings iridescent green. Now that we weren't moving, the sun blasted the top of my head and my pale thighs.

I forced a smile, and when Dad smiled back at me, it didn't feel as artificial. My anxiety was just another passenger in the car now, unwanted and unwilling to take a hike.

"It's a moon tide today." Dad pulled back onto the road and stayed in the right lane this time, driving under the speed limit.

The wind wasn't so bad that way. I put my hand out the window and made it surf in the resistance. He was driving slowly for me, to help me chill out. The gesture made me feel warm, but I couldn't tell if it was a good kind of heat or the bad kind of heat, like an angry wound.

"A moon tide?" If I didn't say anything, he'd keep watching me. He'd used the same tactics when I fought with him over my homework or lied about cleaning my room. His dark, calm gaze had a way of pinning me down until I forgot how to be full of crap.

I'd missed it. Mom was too easy to lie to.

Sadness crept toward me like the water in the ditch, thick and ugly. I wasn't little anymore. And he hadn't been there.

He'd left.

"It doesn't really affect us, but I think it's cool," he said. "The tide gets higher than any other time when the moon pulls it."

I scanned the cloudless sky and found the pale full moon. Did it pull me too? I'd always been drawn to moon imagery, to the thought of the solitary heavenly body orbiting our wild planet. The moon didn't seem to mind being alone. What a badass.

Dad turned onto a bigger road lined with industrial buildings. Water shone behind the buildings on one side.

The color wasn't the same as the big, wide bay we'd driven over. Here it was darker, brown and blue at the same time, with a glassy surface.

We drove into a gravel lot, the Jeep shuddering over dips and bumps. I had to pee again after chugging water on the plane to prevent dehydration and stroke, and every jarring motion was an obnoxious little stab. Dad jumped out and locked the chain-link gate behind us.

With a sinking feeling, I realized this was my new neighborhood. At home, I lived along a row of picture-perfect houses with colorful doors. Now I was stuck in a weedy lot between a seafood restaurant on stilts and a kayak store.

"Is this your property?" I asked, trying to think of something nice to say about it.

I love what you did with that rack of moldy life vests. . . .

"No, it belongs to a buddy of mine. But he lets me dock and park here."

Patches of mean-looking brush dotted the gravel lot. I counted six boats in various states of disrepair. One had a huge wasp nest covering the spinny fan part at the bottom of the engine. Wasps circled it lazily, fat red pain-bombs. Two sheds, three canoes, a bunch of wooden pallets, a few dozen tires, and one doorless refrigerator rounded out the array of junk in what amounted to my new driveway.

"Really atmospheric," I said. "Rustic."

We parked next to the pallets.

"Do you get seasick?" Dad asked, hefting my suitcase out of the Jeep.

I put my backpack on and checked for snakes and fire ants before I put my feet down. "Little late to ask that, isn't it?"

"I'm kidding. You won't feel much motion where we're anchored." He shot a bright grin over his shoulder and led the way onto a narrow dock that didn't match the rest of the junky lot. The artificial wood gleamed with bits of plastic, and pretty lights rose from every piling.

"Why is this dock so fancy?" I pointed at the wires and plugs, and a plastic table with a hose attached to it.

"This lot was supposed to be a new development, but the owner went under. All they finished was one marina slip."

A little boat bobbed alongside the dock. It wasn't much— white and flat with a seat and dashboard in the middle. The engine on the back said *150* in big numbers.

My entire intestinal system shriveled up. "You *live* on this?"

Dad glanced at the boat and back at me with his mouth quirked to one side. "No. This is a jon boat."

"Oh." I had no idea what that meant, and my face prickled with embarrassment. Of course he didn't live on a glorified raft.

He held out his hand and this time I took it, knowing it was the only thing between me and the dark water. The last time I'd touched his hand like this I'd been a little girl clinging to her dad as he left again—for good. Now I wasn't sure I wanted that connection.

But I also didn't want to fall, hit my head, and drown.

I hopped onto the front of the boat and flailed my arms for balance when it wiggled under my feet. The threat of toppling into the water briefly distracted me from hating everything.

"Get the bowline?" Dad asked.

"What?" I crouched, lowering my center of gravity. It put me face-to-face with a bunch of ugly growths on the piling, right at the surface of the water. A square black crab scuttled away, waving two tiny pinchers like angry fists. I suppressed a shriek.

Dad's calm voice cut through my silent scream. "The bowline."

"I don't know what you're talking about!" I shouted, my eyes getting hot. Jon boats. Lines. Bows.

I want to go home.

"The bow is the front of the boat. The stern is the back of the boat." Dad kicked a metal thing on the dock. He spoke with infuriating gentleness. "This is a cleat. The rope is a line. Untie the line at the bow of the boat, and I'll tell you when to push off. Got it?"

I didn't get it, but having something to do kept me from curling up into a ball and crying about horrible tiny crabs and murderous sunshine and my dad telling me what to do. I tucked my backpack against the center dashboard and held the edge of the dock for balance as I unwound the line from the cleat. What looked like a secure knot was a series of intricate loops that tightened with tension. I'd have to figure out how to do it if I didn't want to look like an idiot in front of my dad every time we tried to go anywhere.

If we went anywhere at all. Maybe we'd sit on the stupid boat for three months.

The engine sputtered to life, vibrating under my feet. Exhaust and sweet-sour gasoline filled the air, my chest swelling in response. It was the smell of hot ATVs across a cornfield and lawnmowers signaling the end of winter. Small motor vehicles freaked me out—because they were super dangerous murder-machines—but I loved the sounds and smells of people having fun anyway.

Dad met my eye and smiled from his chair. He looked so comfortable there, at total ease on the water in a way he'd never been at ease at home with us. No wonder he'd stayed so far away.

I tried to smile back at him, but my lips formed a shaky grimace instead.

"All right, sweetie. Push as hard as you can."

I shoved, letting out a deep, satisfying growl. The boat cut through the water in slow-motion, the front—the bow—drifting away from the dock and leaving a swirl on the surface.

It was beyond anticlimactic. So much for Hulking out.

There wasn't anything to sit on but a white plank. I gripped the edge of it, my shoulders knotting up with tension at the unsteadiness of the little boat.

"It's all idle speed back here," Dad said. "You want to go out and run full board? Shake off those air travel germs?"

"None of those were words. I want to see the house."
Why prolong the inevitable?

"You're the boss." He turned the boat. The gravel lot, his Jeep, and the kayak store next door shrank away. Down the shoreline, I spotted a much bigger marina with lots of boats—little boats like Dad's and big ones with pointy bows and huge towers. They were all parked in front of a waterfront restaurant with string lights and palm trees.

"What's that?"

"The Oasis. It's a meat market. The food's not bad, though. We'll go early on a weekend sometime before it gets crazy."

It took me a minute to realize Dad meant *meat market* in the dating way, not the actual butcher way. Did Dad go on dates? Did he look at girls? That had never occurred to me. He was *Dad*—a source of hugs I could barely remember and the splinter in my mom's happiness.

We pushed through the water slowly, following street signs—boat street signs that stuck out on big pilings. I turned back to ask, "How do you read them?"

"The channel markers?"

"Yeah, the signs."

"The green squares go on the right when you're leaving port, and the red triangles go on the right when you're coming back. Remember: red right returning," he said. "We don't draw much water, but you need to stay in the channels at low tide so you don't end up on an oyster bed."

Dad's nonsense rattled around in my head, but I nodded, pretending like he was making sense. We passed a green square. A skinny black bird with sleek feathers stood at the top of the pole with its wings out to the side. I waved at it. It tilted its narrow head at me.

"Cormorant," my dad said. "They dive under the water and swim. It's drying off so it can fly."

"Florida doesn't make sense," I grumbled.

The bird was really cute, though.

We headed toward green islands, full of short trees with hundreds of skinny trunks like fingers gripping the water. Thin, long seed pods hung from the branches like ugly Christmas tree tinsel. Mangroves. I knew that much from trying to familiarize myself with Florida's hellish ecosystem. They grew in salt water somehow.

The water around the mangroves was shallow, dotted with dark patches under the surface. It didn't have the pretty, open-sea look of the big bay. This was swampy and alien. We circled one of the mangrove islands, leaving the dark trail of the channel.

My hand itched with the urge to grab my phone and take a panorama to text to Jordan. I clenched the edge of the bench and a nauseating ball of sadness exploded in my belly. How was I supposed to do this alone? Without my best friend. Without editing photos until the shadows deepened and the light sharpened.

With no one to talk to.

I scooted toward the side and looked down at the water. We skimmed over thatches of seagrass and bumpy patches of brown sand. Bullet-shaped fish darted away. A bunch of fatter, lazy fish circled and then rushed off in unison. My eyes followed their trail until they disappeared into the glare on the water.

"That was a school of mullet," my dad said. "They're not as thick this time of year. You'll see them jumping."

"Mullet, like the haircut?"

"Same spelling. Different thing." Dad slowed, and the boat began to drift forward aimlessly like a car slipping on ice.

A flash of yellow darted between the mangroves in the distance. "What's that?"

Dad looked where I pointed. "What's what?"

"I saw something in the trees there."

"Maybe some flotsam? All kinds of things wash up in the mangroves," he said quietly, his voice taking on an edge I couldn't place.

I squinted, but I didn't see the yellow again. It was probably another weird Florida bird.

"There she is," Dad said.

I followed his gaze to a squat, rectangular boat in the distance, anchored in one of the open spaces between the mangrove islands. It didn't look like a floating house. It looked like a floating Styrofoam cooler. We continued our steady approach. The closer we got, the bigger the knot of dread in my chest grew. I'd imagined a houseboat parked on a busy dock full of other houseboats and people to talk to. A boat neighborhood.

No such luck. Mom had doomed me to become Rapunzel in an isolated, floating prison.

CHAPTER TWO

UP CLOSE, THE WHITE houseboat was dingy, yellowing, and stained where water trickled from a drain near the waterline.

Unease swam through my guts. I deflated with a gusty sigh.

The boat looked like something cobbled together from off-brand LEGO bricks: angular windows along one side; a deck upstairs with a railing and a big metal thing that might have been an air-conditioning unit; a metal, spiral staircase flecked with rust and blue paint; an open platform in the front that held two big surfboards; a slide from the roof into the water in the back; one potted palm tree with frazzled fronds. And attached alongside the boat was a huge floating dock covered in Astroturf, which didn't look remotely safe or seaworthy.

"Great. You live on Mad Max's boat," I muttered. Except *that* would be cool and not terrible. This was terrible.

Dad whistled, and a big yellow Labrador jumped down a narrow ramp and dashed from one end of the little yard to the next, barking out a frantic, happy sound.

"That's Leia," Dad said, confirming that the Star Wars shirt wasn't just for my benefit. "She's very friendly, and she loves kids."

I didn't correct him. At some point he was going to figure out that I was almost old enough to drive—and definitely old enough to pass as an adult to a dog.

"Grab the bow for me."

This time, I knew he meant I needed to do something at the front of the boat. The resulting twinge of pride might as well have been elation next to my crushing disappointment over everything else.

"Hey, I'm learning boat stuff!"

Chuckling, Dad turned the boat at the last moment and we drifted gently into the squishy white bumpers that lined the floating dock. I grabbed the metal thing—the cleat—and hung on with a white-knuckled grip, hoping I wasn't screwing it up.

Leia licked my face.

"Ugh. Dog. Dog!" I liked dogs, but I wasn't into going straight to first base with a Lab.

Dad shooed her away with a gentle nudge and took the rope. "Here, watch." He looped it three times, gave it a quick tug, and it didn't budge. "Think you can do that?"

It didn't look any worse than tying shoelaces. In my cautious grip, the rope was well worn and soft as fur. "Yeah. I can manage."

My knot didn't look as nice as Dad's, but it held. Another little flicker of pride warmed me. I curled my shoulders in, shielding it from all the other things that made me feel stupid.

He helped me out of the boat and onto the floating dock, and I greeted Leia while he hauled my pink suitcase and backpack up the small ramp to the boat. She pranced around me, snuffling and soft and not stinky. When she stopped trying to jump, I sank and gave her a big hug. She rested her heavy head on my shoulder.

"Trapped here together," I whispered. "You're my only hope."

"Welcome to *Sea-renity*." Dad gestured grandly, and sure enough, there it was, painted in fancy script along the side of the boat. Not a mispronunciation, but a horrible boat name.

Mortification tickled in my throat. "Were you responsible for that?"

Dad guided me up the ramp from the floating dock onto the boat. Thankfully, it didn't wobble or sway. "No. This is a 1989 Boatel. Only two owners before me. I left the name."

"Boatel. Any more bad puns while we're at it?"

"I think that's it for now. Ready for a tour?"

The boat only looked about forty or fifty feet long, so it wasn't going to be a very extensive tour. Or an interesting one—unless I discovered a secret tunnel back to the world of Wi-Fi.

Back to my friends. The group chats and servers full of people who understood me.

My best friend, Jordan, didn't live near me in Cincinnati. Jordan was my oldest friend. My *Internet* friend, according to my mom, who was careful to emphasize their status like they weren't real. Like they were made of ones and zeros.

(She didn't seem to understand that I was one of them, one of the Internet people.)

At first, my mom had asked why Jordan couldn't pick being a boy or being a girl, telling me that Jordan's pronouns gave her *grammar pains*. I showed her a bunch of posts and articles by doctors and nonbinary folks. After that, she apologized and thanked me for educating her. But that first reaction stuck with me like a paper cut—stinging when I least expected it. I didn't tell Jordan about it, because they got enough crap from their own family.

The Internet was our space. Jordan was my person.

They didn't go to my school. They didn't call me awful slurs because they caught me checking out the girls on the soccer team. They didn't erase the fact that I liked all genders. They didn't care that I was soft and short. I could log off and hide when I didn't want them to know how badly I was doing.

And now I couldn't text Jordan about spotted death rays or shitty crabs because my mom read too many articles about social media permanently scarring kids during their fragile teenage years.

And because of my last post.

"Brynn?"

Dad was watching me.

I wondered what he saw. The thick eyeliner that made me feel like a witchy badass? The ballpoint doodles on the rubbery toes of my Chucks? My pale skin going pink under the scorching afternoon sun?

It would have been easier if he'd taken one look at me and decided I was too awkward for life on a boat. That's what Mom would have done as soon as she saw me in action.

I had plenty of classmates who wouldn't know how to code a custom Tumblr theme or edit a vid, but they did team sports and theater and made friends easily, and my mom pointed them out like paragons of adolescence. Mom probably thought those kids would love spending a summer outdoors learning new skills and making new friends. Sure, I wanted to tell her. They'd probably love it, and they'd go viral for making TikToks about it, because their parents didn't suck.

If Dad cared about me not being the right kind of kid, he didn't show it. He waited for me to respond. Patient. Concerned. Calm.

My eyes began to sting. Why did he have to be so nice? Why was it so easy for him to close a five-year gap?

I didn't want it to be that easy for him. I didn't want to look at Dad's ugly boat. I wanted to voice chat with Jordan in our server and stay up late and sleep in and wake up to check my dashboard first thing in the morning. Jordan understood me, and I missed our routine—the near-constant communication. Mom had carved out my insides when she'd taken all that away from me.

"Would you rather poke around by yourself for now?" Dad adjusted my hot-pink backpack.

I scrubbed my eyes with my hands and shook my head, but I didn't say any of the mean things I wanted to say, the barbs Mom and I played catch with. It'd be like yelling at a bearded kitten.

"All right." He gave a slow spin. "This is the back deck. I picked up a used paddleboard for you. It's the blue one. The paddles are there, and the gear's in the dry box there. A PFD and a whistle—that's the bare minimum by law. And I want you taking water with you every time you go out."

"Go out?" I asked, squinting. "What, like, to the floating movie theater?"

"Go out on the water," Dad said slowly, miming paddling a watercraft.

"Sure."

Unlikely.

None of his terrifying instructions made any sense, but I nodded and tried to look enthusiastic in the face of his bright-eyed earnestness. He showed me the grill and Leia's food and toy box, and how to get to the top deck. When he opened the sliding glass door into the cabin, cold air tickled against my sweaty body. I would have stripped down naked to enjoy it if Dad hadn't been there.

The inside was almost cool in a vintage sort of way, with walls paneled in dark wood. A restaurant booth with teal vinyl upholstery took up most of the kitchen. A huge silver steering wheel stuck out from a console by the sliding door, totally out of place in what was otherwise something out of a quirky diner.

"The stove uses gas," Dad said. "If you don't know how to use it, let me know and I'll show you. It's easier, and a lot quicker to cook on than electricity." He spoke a little faster now and wringed his big hands.

"Are you freaked out?" I blurted, startled by the familiarity of the uncomfortable energy skittering through his body.

He cleared his throat. "What? No."

I recognized that unconvincing tone. But it didn't make me feel better—or at home. The houseboat smelled vaguely musty and dude-like. Mom was big on vanilla soy candles and surface disinfectant made of vinegar and lemon essential oil. I hated those smells, but they were my smells—our smells.

We'd been a thing for five years. A single unit. Buddies. Partners. Toughing out shitty stuff and making our way through our new Dad-less normal.

It's you and me against the world, my mom would say. Before she got rid of me.

Homesickness crept under my skin, reminding me that I was trapped here. Literally trapped. Floating in the middle of nowhere.

I cleared my throat against the gunky threat of a sob. "Cool kitchen."

"It's a galley. Because we're on a boat."

"Galley," I echoed, sounding like an asshole robot. "Got it."

If Dad noticed my attitude, he did a great job ignoring it. He pushed a small door open to reveal a cramped bedroom, carried the suitcase inside, and popped back out. "This is yours. You can put your stuff on the top bunk and sleep on the bottom. Whatever works. I'll sleep on the futon in the living room while you're here."

"This is your bedroom?" Dad was going to spend the whole summer on a thin mattress for me, and I was standing here acting like a brat. No wonder it had been so easy for Mom to send me away.

"Not while my guest of honor is here. Not that you're a guest." Dad frowned and quickly masked it. "This is your home. I want you to feel at home. I hope you'll feel at home."

I glanced at Leia's wet nose smearing the sliding glass door. I wanted to be excited and comfortable and chill, like my dad hoped I'd be. But this wasn't my home.

"Absolutely." Faking enthusiasm was a little easier now that I felt properly miserable for kicking him out of his own room. "It's great." Lanced by a sneaky spike of fear, I added, "But what if it sinks?"

"It won't sink."

I narrowed my eyes. "Humor me."

"We're in six feet of water at high tide. And *Sea-renity* is a big girl. We'd have plenty of time to get out. You could practically walk back to shore."

He wasn't getting off that easily. I placed my hands on my hips in the Wonder Woman pose, which the Internet claimed infused you with confidence. "Gators?"

"Not in the salt water."

"Snakes?"

"Not on the *boat*."

I ran out of menacing animals and moved on to my quieter fear of not being able to sleep. "Where's the TV?"

Dad cringed. "Don't have one."

Great. So much for white noise.

Mom had already warned me that Dad was living off the grid with nothing but an ancient flip phone, like the one she'd ordered for me from a senior citizen cellular service. But I asked anyway, my voice thin with hope. "Computer?"

He gave me a look that succinctly communicated *nice try, kid.* "Nope."

Dad wasn't on my side. He was on Mom's. Ruining my summer was probably the only thing they'd ever agreed on.

I swallowed against a dry knot of disappointment, left with no lifeline at all. "Where do you get fresh water?"

"We'll head in to the marina once a week to fill the tank. And we'll go back to land if there's a big storm."

My bones felt heavy. Unless I wanted to go down a fiber-glass slide into scary brown water over and over for ninety days, there'd be nothing to do here. The potential for mind-numbing boredom stretched out endlessly. My head started to pound. Mom's plan wasn't rehabilitation; it was torture. One of the last responsibility-free summers of my life gone to waste.

"I'm going to unpack," I said, hoarse. What I meant was that I was going to go pee. And maybe cry in the bathroom.

Dad gave me an unhappy little nod that made me want to immediately apologize. He sat on the futon and pulled out a cardboard box full of books from underneath. After I spent several seconds frantically eyeing a tiny door, he cleared his throat. "The head is there—that's the bathroom."

"I thought it was a pantry," I babbled, tucking myself inside and fumbling for the light switch. The inside reminded me of the bathroom in a motor home we took from Cincinnati to Chicago when I was six. Back when we'd done things together. *As a family*, my mom would say.

Even then, I'd heard the punctuation of gritted teeth between every word.

I barely fit on the tiny metal toilet full of brackish water. While I peed, after briefly blacking out from relief, I studied Dad's stuff. A leather bag gaped, exposing a razor, Old Spice deodorant, and a prescription bottle with a drug name I didn't recognize. I washed my hands with bright-orange liquid soap that smelled like the disinfectant in the girls' bathroom at school. The narrow stand-up shower—a beige fiberglass coffin—had dark-green mold around the drain.

For someone's sake, I hoped Dad was single.

I pushed through the curtained door to my bedroom. It was the size of Mom's walk-in closet, with two skinny bunks built into the wall.

Left with nothing to do but breathe through the growing pressure of unshed tears, I unpacked. It took a pathetically short amount of time. I had a couple pairs of sneakers and one pair of flip-flops, and a bathing suit from the old-lady section of JCPenney. My T-shirts, shorts, and sweatpants didn't take up much space on the bunk. Mom had given me a new journal and some skinny Japanese pens in a bunch of different colors. I arranged them to make a rainbow. I dug out my makeup bag and my contacts solution and decided against sticking all that in Dad's cramped bathroom. Then I climbed onto the creaky bottom bunk and peered out the tiny window at the mangroves in the distance.

A shiver of longing brushed across me like a sigh. My breath sucked in, and I rubbed my arms where goose bumps prickled my sun-pinkened skin. This wasn't homesickness; it was something else I couldn't place. I found myself looking for the yellow smear I'd seen from the little jon boat. Other than cartoon canaries, I couldn't think of any birds that yellow.

Something out there didn't fit in. Something, like me, was out of place. I wanted to know what it was. My curiosity was an itch, more demanding the longer I thought about it.

My backpack began to buzz. I jumped like I'd gotten caught doing something I wasn't supposed to do. I pawed around until my fingers reached plastic, and I stared at my vibrating flip phone like it was alien technology until I remembered I had to open it to answer it.

"Hey, Mom."

She exhaled, a disappointed bug in my ear. "Brynn. You didn't call me when you landed."

"Um. Dad was there, and I forgot."

Silence accused me, and I could picture her face—brow pinched, thin lips pressed together tightly. Mom only looked relaxed when she was asleep. Sometimes on the weekends she nodded off in front of the TV, and I turned the volume down, sat on the coffee table, and watched her, trying to imagine how she'd act and sound if she was always relaxed, gentle, and free of all her furrows and creases. Obviously one afternoon without me hadn't been enough to unravel her vibrating tendrils of stress.

"We made a deal," she finally said. "You need to check in every day."

It hadn't been a deal; it had been an order. "I know."

"How's Florida?"

"Okay. Dad does, in fact, live on a boat. I'm on it right now."

"Are you all right?"

A loaded question. My insides cramped up with the reminder that I was certain to be anything but all right sometime soon, because that was how I rolled. Fine one moment, contemplating my inevitable violent death and subsequent decay the next. For a few minutes, wrapped up in regular disappointment, I'd forgotten that I was incapable of being a normal human being.

"Yes," I said, grumpy. Aching. "Dad has a dog."

"A dog? He can't even—" Mom cut herself off. The blank was pretty easy to fill in. She was outspoken in her belief that all men had the emotional maturity of toddlers, and that alone had saved me from forced quality time with my father until now.

My irritation grew, curdling. If Mom thought Dad was too immature for a dog, why was he allowed to supervise the care and feeding of a teenager in a bayou full of baby sharks? She'd explained the theory to me, of course. She had to get me away from the bad influence of the Internet. And she'd even gotten my doctor's sign-off, insisting that her ex-husband was caring and responsible *in his own way*. But I didn't think she believed it.

She didn't want to try anymore. Just like the divorce.

I sighed sharply, sick to my stomach. Sick of her. Sick of him.

Homesick.

"Will you call me tomorrow?" Mom asked. I tried not to hear the ache in her voice, but it wrapped around my lungs anyway. My sadness echoed back, until it felt like drowning.

No matter how mad I was, I missed her. I wanted to hug her, because hugging always made both of us feel better, no matter how hard we tried to hurt each other.

I waited until I could speak without my voice breaking. "I guess. I won't have anything else to do." The words were daggers flying north at the speed of light. I couldn't take them back.

Mom and I were experts at this.

"I'll keep my phone by me," she said, carefully kind. Like a recording. "You can call anytime."

My wall of anger crumbled, because I knew she meant it. She'd probably sleep with her phone right by her pillow, right where I bellied up into her bed like a seal when my mind wouldn't quiet.

Every time my anxiety got bad at night, I still went to her. She'd bolt up, eyes big and confused as she fumbled for her glasses on the nightstand. And we'd watch cooking shows together, sharing a bowl of salt and vinegar chips until our tongues went pruney.

I began to cry. "I love you."

She answered with a raw breath and a sniffle. "You too, baby. I'll talk to you soon."

I flipped the phone shut and threw it onto the bed, where it bounced three times. The sheets were orange and plaid and awful, and the pillowcase was floral and equally awful.

The bed smelled like mildew when I pressed my face into the mattress. I cried until my throat hurt, too wiped out to care that Dad could hear me hating everything about his perfect Florida life.

It turned out the board wasn't for surfing. It was for standing on and paddling around like someone who got lost while surfing. I'd been kayaking before at camp in middle school, but I'd never seen anything like the long, teal board my dad cheerfully assigned to me after I woke up from my rage nap. Once I'd eaten a heaping bowl of restorative mac and cheese, Dad had evidently decided it was time to jettison me.

It didn't make a whole lot of sense to stand on something inherently wobbly. But I wasn't scared thanks to all the middle school kayaking. My therapist liked to point out how easily I tackled some *scary* things. It didn't help.

If I could kayak over weeds likely to tug me under and drown me if I capsized, why couldn't I think about getting my learner's permit without feeling like I was going to shit my pants? Anxiety didn't make any sense. Her advice only made me feel stupid.

Dad carried the board down to the floating yard and eased it onto the Astroturf. The plastic fin dangled off the edge in the water. I struggled to memorize every safety guideline, which he rattled off too quickly.

"Slow down!" I shouted. "This is a matter of life and death!"

Dad's eyes widened, but he explained more carefully after my outburst. A belt turned into a personal floatation device. A leash strapped to my ankle kept the board from drifting away. Bungee cords held down supplies and water.

He pointed to the opening of the bayou, where fast boat traffic hummed in the distance.

"That's the main channel. With people coming in and out of the restaurant tanked, it isn't safe to cross," he said. "Stick to the shallows back here. The mangrove tunnels are fine, but if the tide changes you can get stranded."

He wasn't saying something. I narrowed my eyes. "Is that it?"

"Well, and snakes. Crabs that drop onto you. Actually. Stay out of the mangrove tunnels."

I heaved a sigh where I sat cross-legged on the sticky, fake grass. Snakes. Of course.

Leia draped across my lap like a pudgy blanket. Her warm dog-breath huffed against my knee. Even confronted with the thought of deadly water snakes, my bad mood struggled to maintain its hold in the face of a pup with a wet nose.

Maybe it was too pretty outside to fully commit to helpless rage. The sun set late this time of year, and in the forgiving evening light, everything glowed. The surface of the water winked and glittered at me, and the dark-brown, spindly legs of the mangroves gleamed.

"Ready?" Dad asked.

I blinked at him, and my gut folded up like a wad of paper. So much for being confident about small watercrafts. "Wait. You were serious?"

"I wasn't giving you a paddling lesson for fun. Get up and try it. The worst that can happen is falling in, and the water's warm."

"Warm water carries parasites."

Dad looked me up and down. "Are you actively bleeding anywhere?"

I crossed my arms.

He scrubbed his hand across his face and blushed. "From a *wound*, Brynn."

"No. But brain-eating amoebas can enter your nose and eat your brain. And flesh-eating bacteria only need a hang-nail, not an open wound."

"We've never had a case in these waters."

"Still," I mumbled, looking around for another way to plead my case.

"Did you forget how to swim?"

It was the oldest trick in the entire book, but I bristled anyway. Dad had taught me to swim when I could barely walk. I'd seen pictures of him pushing my stroller to the campus aquatic complex, where he'd been a star swimmer in college. I wasn't fast, but I could swim better than any of my friends, and I loved being in the water—as long as I didn't have to lounge around pretending to be comfortable in glorified underwear that jammed up every nook and cranny on my body and failed to subdue my personal flotation devices.

"I know how to swim," I bit out.

He thrust the paddle toward me, and Leia ambled away, sniffing at the plastic grass. I pushed up to stand and took the slender grip. I'd expected the heft of a wooden oar, but this was feather-light and smooth, with only one curved part, which looked like a spoon, and a small handle on one end.

"You scoop with it." Dad mimed the gesture. "Don't forget to fasten the strap to your ankle so you don't lose the board if you bail."

My lips quirked into a smile as I pictured myself surfing. "Hang ten."

He pushed the board into the water and steadied it with both hands. The floating dock was only a few inches from the surface, and all I had to do was take a step to be on the rubber mat at the middle of the board. I didn't really want to, but I knew I had to make peace with the board if I wanted a shred of independence. Even if independence only meant floating in circles where no one could try painfully hard to cheer me up.

I hated this part. The tug-of-war. Reason losing ground under the onslaught of unreasonable fear.

But it was get on the paddleboard or never go anywhere at all.

The Velcro strap made a satisfying *scritch* when I wrapped it in a tight hug around my ankle.

Holding on to Dad's arm, I took a step that felt like leaping into the Grand Canyon.

The board splashed and wobbled, but it didn't tip over, and I didn't fall. In an instant, I became aware of the bayou breathing beneath me. Sighing.

Soft longing struck me again, as if the water around me was terribly sad.

Dad broke the spell, his voice confident and gentle. "Put the paddle in the water for balance, like a walking stick." He gave me a little push and I drifted away, alone on the water.

I let out a low, worried moan and dipped the paddle. It sliced through the water and propelled me forward and slightly to the side, a drunken dance across the surface. A shaky smile broke out across my face. I looked back at Dad and saw it mirrored there.

Freedom.

My favorite part about kayaking at summer camp had been getting away from the buzz and exhaustion of other people. On the lake, I'd been alone with my head. The good parts of my head. The stories I told myself. The ones that were my fanvids now—all my favorite scenes from my favorite shows mashed together to music. Like a smoothie made of feelings.

Jordan loved the things I created. They wrote shards of glittering poetry that paired perfectly with my edits.

A sharp ache struck me. I focused on my bare toes gripping the rubber on the board and breathed through the bubble in my chest that wanted to be a sob.

"The sun goes down in an hour," Dad called out. "Don't go too far."

Sunset. It'd probably be gorgeous, and I wouldn't have my phone to film it. I wouldn't be able to tell Jordan about it. Jordan didn't even know where I was for sure, or if I was okay at all.

I wasn't okay. But I didn't know if I'd tell anyone that. Even Jordan. Especially after Jordan had become an unexpected ally to my mother.

"Got it," I managed, choked up. I blinked back tears and sucked in a snotty breath. The water made the same sound beneath my board, as if in sympathy.

I'd never had the balance for skateboarding, but the paddleboard was almost twelve feet long. It didn't try to leap away from me. After a few awkward strokes, I found an easy rhythm: twice on one side, and twice on the other. I glided forward through the water toward the mangroves and forgot that I'd been crying.

The board had more grace than the tangle of anger and fear inside me. Every easy stroke unknotted me, leaving sore spots along my ribs. But at least I could breathe.

Below me, the marbled bottom moved. I slowed and watched fish dart away. The nubby surface under my feet was weird but secure. Not too slippery. I lifted one foot and then the other carefully, testing how much the board could rock without toppling me. A quick glance confirmed that Dad wasn't creepily watching my every move, but I angled for one of the small islands anyway, trying to distance myself from the ugly houseboat with the dumb name and his oppressive patience. Nothing made me feel more like a child than being consciously parented.

Pink birds stood in the low branches of the mangroves, and tall cranes held completely still in the shallows, beady little eyes and sharp-pointed beaks fixed on something beneath the surface. I sucked in a slow, long breath, my chest filling with humid air. The heat wasn't so bad out here, with the sun sinking and a gentle breeze tickling along the water.

A jet soared far overhead, the deep, reverberating sound the only reminder of modern life. Everything around me was prehistoric. Spidery trees and dashing crabs and stalking birds. Lumbering rays and packs of fish in formation.

I held the paddle like a spear, imagining prehistoric people hunting alligators or sharks. Cavewoman life wouldn't have been for me—not with my poor eyesight and stubby height and tendency to freak out at the worst moments.

Usually thinking about freaking out triggered an instant freak-out, but no aftershock of fear followed. My breathing matched the fluid motion of my arms without hitching, and my belly only gave a few half-hearted burbles of tension.

It was too early to concede that my mom had sent me here out of wisdom and not desperation, but the whole paddleboarding thing wasn't the *actual* worst.

Without warning, the water broke beside me, and I jumped, startled right out of my damn skin and yelping. The last things I saw before I tumbled off the board were jewel-blue eyes above a jagged smile. And sopping-wet hair plastered to a face that made my heart stutter.

CHAPTER THREE

I KICKED USELESSLY IN the water, helpless as a newborn dropped in a bathtub. My feet touched the squishy bottom, and I screamed. The sound gurgled in my ears, and bubbles gushed out of my mouth and nose. Seagrass brushed at my knees, threatening to tangle me up and hold me under. My toe grazed something sharp and went bright-hot with pain as the ankle strap tugged, an animal grabbing me and thrashing me around. A vise of panic gripped my throat.

Florida was going to kill me. Dead on arrival.

Maybe it was meant to be.

My lungs throbbed.

I stopped thrashing. What if I inhaled? How fast would it be?

Furious blue eyes appeared in front of me in the water. I'd never seen anyone look so angry. A spike of terror pummeled through me as I realized how close I'd come to breathing in. My feet touched the grassy bottom again, and I bent my knees and propelled myself up. When I broke the surface and swallowed down hot gulps of air, she was laughing. The sound was unmistakable—musical and lovely and infuriating. Had I imagined her rage?

When I'd opened my eyes in the water, my contacts had floated right off my face. Now I was wet and angry and blind.

"Grab the board," the girl said. "It's right in front of you."

I flailed and my hand struck the solid fiberglass. My knuckles stung, but I held on, chin pressed to the rubber mat. I wasn't crying, but I was pretty close, breath hiccupping and water streaming out of my nose disgustingly. Panic and shame made a nauseating cocktail. I hoped that if I threw it up, it would be in her perfect face.

"First time paddleboarding?"

The girl held on to the other side of the board. She wore a blurry smirk, and even with my eyeballs no longer working, the startling blue of her eyes stood out like neon lights.

"It was going fine until you scared the shit out of me!" I shouted.

She kicked me underwater, and I jerked my knee away from the cold touch. Then she slithered up onto the board, all freckles and a vivid yellow bikini. I sank deeper until only my chin rested on the board, the startled heat of my body concealed by the murky water.

It wasn't like I'd never seen a girl in a bathing suit before. But I hadn't seen one like this, water glittering on her body, hair a mermaid snarl down her back. She pushed onto her hands and knees and sat back on her heels, her round parts squishing together.

My face got prickly and hot. "You can't commandeer my board."

She hummed. "Are you sure about that?"

Great. She was one of those girls with sharp words that chased my tongue down my throat and made my brain go haywire. They weren't mean girls. Not exactly. Just smart, confident girls who could see right through my eyeliner armor and the defiant bounce of my curls. They weren't Internet people, like me. They weren't scared of anything.

"It's not even mine; it's my dad's." My voice wavered, treacherously close to tears. Distracting hot girl or not, I was still treading water in a cesspool of shady sea life.

And what I'd nearly done lingered on me like pond scum.

She offered me her hand, and I grabbed it before I could think things through. Getting back onto the board wasn't going to be pretty. She tugged me hard, her grip strong and ice-cold, and I only made a slight spectacle of myself as I scrambled up on the board. We rocked, and the board splashed hollow sounds against the surface, but we didn't tip. I tucked my legs beneath myself and faced her, our knees bumping together.

An oddly familiar sadness struck me, and I recalled staring out the window from Dad's bedroom, longing.

Heart skipping around like it was the first day of school, I mumbled, "I'm Brynn."

"Your paddle's gone."

Horrified, I swung my head around so fast I almost toppled back into the water. The long, blue paddle was supposed to float, but I couldn't see it anywhere. It had been so light and futuristic—there was no way it was cheap. Dad had probably spent a bunch of money on it for me, and I'd already lost it.

I pressed my wrinkled fingers against my eyes and bit back hoarse despair. "Florida is terrible."

"I agree." She shifted, the board wiggling. I grabbed the edges for balance and watched her stand. Towering above me, she was leggy and pale, with sunburned arms and freckles all over her body.

With a jolt, I recognized the shade of her bikini.

She laughed. "You look like you saw a ghost."

Yellow, flitting through the ugly trees in the distance. "You were in the woods."

"The mangroves?"

I rolled my eyes. "Whatever."

"Sure you weren't seeing things?"

The urge to push her itched at my palms. I was stuck in the middle of a bayou with no paddle, the sun was going down, and tiny bugs were starting to buzz around my head. To top it all off, a weird girl with no reason to be out in the middle of the water was messing with me. Frustration usually drove me directly to tears, but right now I was a lot closer to committing murder than crying.

"No, I'm *not* sure I wasn't seeing things." I pointed to my eyes, nearly poking them in the process. "And now I lost my contacts and I can't see *any* things. What are you doing out here?"

"I was swimming." She stretched. Her bathing-suit bottom made a perfect, rounded *V* at my eyeline. I tore my gaze away and crossed my arms tightly, hating the simmering heat that tickled my belly button.

"You need to keep swimming wherever you're going so I can get this stupid board back to my dad's boat." I felt a little guilty ordering her to leave. Swimming didn't sound safe. It was getting dark, and the mangroves sang, bugs clattering and whining. Some of the haircut fish swirled and jumped around us, and I couldn't imagine swimming a long way without a raft. She was tall, though. Maybe she could walk.

Barefoot.

In the awful, squishy sand.

I shuddered.

"You're bleeding." She pointed at my foot, where it peeked out from under my butt and my sopping-wet jean shorts.

All I saw was red streaking across my skin and turning pink against the blue board. I wasn't flexible enough to shove my own toe three inches from my face to compensate for my blurry vision. For all I knew, my entire toe had been severed off.

Excellent. I was going to bleed to death. Or attract every mama shark in a ten-mile radius. I scanned the surface of the water frantically, looking for fins. Dad had asked me about open wounds. That meant the danger was real.

She sank into a crouch like a leggy gymnast. "You're fine," she said. It sounded like *you're useless.* "Stop flipping out."

"I'm not flipping out."

"Oh yeah? You're breathing hard, and you're shaking like you're about to meet Justin Bieber."

"What? Ew. He's not even—"

"You stepped on a little oyster shell. Calm down."

I sputtered. "Telling someone to calm down is the worst thing you can say to someone who needs to calm down!"

"Really? Can you cite your sources?"

"Why are you giving me shit on my own paddleboard?" The sound of my yell bounced around us, playing on the water.

She put her hands on her hips. "It's not your paddleboard. It's your dad's."

A low, guttural sound tore out of my throat. I wanted to stomp away from her, but I was stuck with nowhere to go and an eyeful of leggy jerk. "Fine, Ariel. Swim back to wherever you came from so I can go home."

"My name is Skylar." She leaned close. Her nose was pink with sunburn, but her lips were pale. Blue eyes gleamed at me, defiant and cold. "And that's not your home, is it?"

Before I could react, she sprung off the board and into the black water. I squinted, waiting for her to surface. Everything was dark and shapeless now—except for the gash of violent pink where the sun set over the mangroves.

"Come back and visit," Skylar finally called out, her voice farther than I expected. "Unless you're too scared of the water."

I couldn't see her. I didn't want to see her again. But her challenge struck me like a spear. A spear I wanted to throw back at her smug face. "I don't even know where you live, you dick!"

Her laughter carried like slapping waves as she cut through the water, away from me. "Calm down. Find the beach."

Those last words were softer, laced with sadness like the tension at the surface of the water. Still kneeling, I found myself wiping silent tears from my damp cheeks. No one had ever made me feel so many things in such a short time. Fine tremors ran through my fingers.

Without the oppressive sun overhead, my soaked clothes were icy concrete against my skin. I dropped onto my belly for lack of a better way to navigate and began flopping my hands into the water like stumpy T. rex arms.

Without Dad's nice paddle, I didn't make much progress. The water moved beneath me, rushing away from where the houseboat was anchored. I hoped the tide was carrying Skylar in the direction she needed to go. A low wind picked up, pushing my damp curls into my face and nudging the board toward the dark tangle of mangroves nearby. I could hear the branches—soft popping sounds and crackles and whistles. And occasionally, a heavy rustle and snap. Goose bumps lit up my arms and legs.

Snakes.

What if I got stuck in the tangled trees? I couldn't see. No one would know where I was. What kinds of crabs and bugs lived in the labyrinth of branches?

I paddled my arms harder and only managed to keep the board in one place. It was like crawling on a treadmill.

A low hum sounded, and I peered into the blurry darkness hopefully. It grew louder. Familiar. *Dad.*

His little white boat rushed toward me and angled to a sharp stop, pushing waves that rushed over the surface of the board.

"Brynn!" He didn't sound angry, but he didn't sound happy either. I dropped my face to the rubber mat, relieved and humiliated. When I pushed up onto my hands and knees, shaking, my arms burned all over from paddling. Dad reached over the side of his boat and caught hold of me, pulling me on board with a grunt. His hands warmed my wet skin.

"I lost my contacts." I sat heavily and lowered my chin, watching the blur of him yank the blob of the giant board out of the water. It was nearly as long as the whole boat, and it made a terrible squeaking noise as he dragged fiberglass against fiberglass. I started to cry. "And I lost your paddle."

"Hey, hey. The paddle will turn up. The mangroves catch everything that gets dropped overboard around here." He wrapped a scratchy towel around me and scrubbed it at my arms and hair like I was three again. He wasn't doing a good job hiding how rattled he was. "I hoped you were having an adventure, but I should have looked for you sooner."

"I was doing fine until this girl popped out of the water. She scared me so badly, I fell."

Dad's hands stilled at my shoulders. He looked at me closely, a smear of concern, voice taut. "A girl in the water?"

It sounded nuts now that Skylar wasn't right there beside me, drippy and cold and pretty. Embarrassed, I decided it'd be easier to skip right over the truth. I laughed girlishly in anticipation of the lie, a skittering sound my mom would have side-eyed in a millisecond. "Maybe it was a dolphin or one of those sea monster rays." Another weak laugh. "Whatever it was scared me."

I'd keep her to myself—keep the fever-hot crush and stubborn anger tucked deep inside to be meditated upon later. When I was alone.

Dad smiled, the tension in his shoulders easing. He wiped my tears and left me swaddled in his towel for the slow ride back to the houseboat. I held on to the board so the wind wouldn't catch it. Icy drops of water trailed from the tangled ends of my hair onto my neck and cheek.

When we pulled up to the floating yard, the sky had gone dark gray. Leia barked a few times in greeting and sidled up against me, her huge wagging tail thumping my leg. Dad helped me onto the houseboat, giving me his arm when I tripped on the ramp and tripped again on the rail, kicking an empty soda can across the deck. My bleeding toe throbbed and the can rattled, too loud—the final insult in a night full of clumsiness and misfortune.

Forgetting that I'd never be able to publish it, I formulated a text post in my head. The board. The water. Skylar. My friends would be riveted to my ridiculous misadventure.

With a soggy, deflated feeling, I remembered it didn't matter. No one would hear how I'd spent my afternoon.

By the time we stepped into the air-conditioning, my teeth chattered and my eyes spilled over with tears, and I wanted nothing more than the comfort of my upstairs bedroom in my house, in my home. I wanted my phone and my computer.

I wanted my family to be normal.

Divorce had gouged away everything I'd known for the first nine years of my life. In fourth grade, I'd been big enough to know, rationally, that Mom and Dad had split up for their own adult relationship reasons. But I couldn't help feeling abandoned, and my fears had started growing that year, monster-big and growling to me that Mom would leave too.

So Mom had spoiled me.

I had a canopy on my bed thanks to six months I'd spent obsessed with princess bedrooms. A nice laptop, even though I'd killed the first one spilling a milkshake into it. One wall in my room was covered in chalkboard paint and doodles. I maintained a huge corkboard with collages of space photography and anime posters and sexy couture gowns and men with buns. Every year I was obsessed with something new.

I never stuck with anything, and Mom didn't complain. Two weeks of piano lessons. Six weeks of soccer. A month of tennis. One entire day of horseback riding before a horse leaned into me the wrong way and, hyperaware of the muscle and density of the huge animal, I refused to go anywhere near it ever again. Dozens of journals, each with a pretty cover and neglected pages.

Going to therapy wasn't spoiling me—not exactly. But the therapists fueled the spoiling, assuring Mom that all I needed was positive reinforcement from peers and extra physical activity and something to feel successful about.

So she let me drift from one magic bullet to the next, and she let me quit every time something got scary. It pissed me off a little. If she hadn't let me quit, I might have become a tennis pro or a concert pianist—something people admired more than *person who makes cool fanvids and sometimes writes fanfiction about anime characters doing it.*

Now Mom was halfway across the country, and I wanted to quit Florida—to retreat to my bed and the glowing green beacon of Jordan ready to chat with me about stories we made up about our favorite characters. But I couldn't. Because . . . houseboat.

In the room that wasn't really my bedroom, I pawed around the bunk until I found my glasses and shoved them onto my face, relishing the tilted-nauseating rush of clarity. The soft edges and watercolors of the houseboat sharpened back into focus.

Dad bustled outside on the deck, lashing down the paddleboard, and I crammed myself into the bathroom, leaving my wet clothes on the slippery shower floor. Cold water blasted down at me with a stale smell, making me tremble even harder.

The pipes groaned and rattled once the water ran scalding hot. I endured it, eager to get the salt and grime off my skin. But I had the good sense to take the shortest hot shower of my life. Who knew what would happen if I used up all the water? Probably some awful alarm.

The cut on my toe wasn't as bad as it had looked when water splashed the blood all around. It gaped—gross and pink—but it wasn't deep. I found a dusty box of Band-Aids under the bathroom sink and patched it up.

My useless flip phone said it was 9 p.m. when I finally pulled on sweatpants and a baggy T-shirt. It felt like midnight. My arms ached and my eyes were gummy, and a livid sunburn lit up my thighs and forearms. I wanted to call my mom again, just to hear her voice, but I didn't have a good reason to. We'd volley awkward statements back and forth, and I'd avoid telling her about Skylar just like I'd avoided telling Dad. My parents didn't need to know I'd gotten a hate-crush mere hours after arriving in Florida. They didn't need to tell me I was being too emotional, too irrational.

I wasn't going to tell them that I planned on paddling out into the middle of nowhere to show a mean girl I could get my shit together. And maybe, just a little, because I wanted to see her annoyingly perfect face again. With my contacts in this time.

The most horrible thing of all wasn't the desire that had already taken root in me. It was the stray thought that it might be fun to see her again. It wasn't like she'd want to be my friend. But the only alternative to hanging out with her would be talking to the leggy birds that gave me equally judgmental looks.

Nothing belonged to me here, so I'd keep Skylar, the bitchy, hot mermaid of a girl, all to myself.

And tomorrow I'd find Dad's missing paddle and Skylar's secret beach. It's not like I had anything better to do.

CHAPTER FOUR

WITHIN MINUTES OF CURLING up in my bunk bed, I felt the boat rock a little. It should have been soothing, like swaying in a hammock. But I didn't know how to be soothed, apparently. Because as soon as I rolled gently from side to side, I became certain the boat would roll over and trap me under the water. I'd drown in a bunk bed.

The thought grew like a crack spreading across a windshield, getting more detailed, more intricate. I could taste the salt water. My heart thudded painfully. I imagined trying to call out for my dad. I thought about the poor dog not knowing how to escape, and I forgot how to breathe. Springing out of bed, I stumbled into the living room and barreled into the futon where my dad was reading a paperback with a little book light.

He sat up, owlish in reading glasses. "Brynn, whoa. Kiddo. What's up?"

"We're gonna tip," I wheezed, grabbing his bedspread and shaking it for emphasis. "We are going to tip over. I don't know the way out!"

"We're not gonna tip, honey. It would take a literal hurricane to roll this big girl over."

"You don't know that." I looked around for windows and doors. There weren't enough of them. And the water might pour in through them anyway, making it even harder to escape. I'd seen enough movies to know you couldn't swim your way out of a sinking ship. "You don't know anything," I hiccupped, feeling like all the air had already been sucked from the cabin, or galley, or whatever this death trap was.

"Okay. How about this?" Dad spoke to me like he was trying to tame a rabid tiger. "Let's find the sleeping bags and sleep on the deck. I have a mosquito net. It'll be fun."

"Fun?" I echoed, disbelieving. It was so hard to breathe.

"If the boat capsizes, we'll tip over into the water and wake up and it'll be fine."

Numb, I made my way back to my bedroom, gathered my pillow and sheets, and returned to watch Dad blearily assemble more bedding just outside the sliding glass door.

Embarrassed and relieved, I curled up into a ball on top of a sleeping bag, my back to my dad. The mosquito net fluttered gently in the breeze above us, and my heart slowly recalibrated itself to the fact that I might not be in immediate danger of drowning in my sleep.

I thought I heard laughter on the gentle night wind.

"What is that?" I mumbled.

Dad yawned. "Nothing. Try to sleep."

Sunlight knifed at my eyelids. I froze, cocooned in ugly colors on a rustling sleeping bag, and pawed around for my glasses. Everything sharpened into focus. The houseboat. Dad. The wrong side of the sliding glass door. Purgatory.

I wobbled inside, creaky with too much sleep. Dad sat at the kitchen booth, smiling like I hadn't forced him to sleep in his own backyard the night before.

"Lucky Charms?" he offered.

Mom had clearly given him a list of my favorite foods. She probably started with cereal and gummy candy and went on to my long list of defects, starting with my generalized anxiety disorder. OCD—but not the kind in TV shows. The intrusive-thought kind that wasn't as familiar to folks as touching doorknobs or washing hands over and over. ADHD. Seasonal affective disorder. A persistent sense of impending doom.

I knew it was terrible to think of my diagnoses as defects. They weren't. And I'd never let anyone else call their own diagnoses that. But the ugly voice in my head had a way of winning out, whispering shitty things to me until I felt whittled down to a misshapen ball of unhappiness. It made me feel even worse to give in to my own ableist lizard brain.

"Sorry," I murmured, mortified that I'd had two full-ass meltdowns in less than twelve hours of Dad time.

I'd never been a carefree kid, and I knew my mom hated that. Kids were supposed to be happy-go-lucky, careening through life getting broken bones and split lips while parents did all the worrying. But I wasn't built that way. I calculated risks and measured the likelihood of injury and dismember-ment while other kids sped by on scooters and plastic roller skates.

"Don't sweat it. I sleep out there a lot."

"Why?"

"On a clear night, the stargazing is decent. And in the wintertime, it's pretty romantic."

Interesting. I filed away the concept of my dad doing romantic things to consider later.

"Any big plans today?" Dad asked over his bowl of plain brown adult cereal. He spoke with his mouth full of food and wiped milk out of his beard.

I made a face at him, relieved to think about anything other than how I'd acted the night before. "I'll have to check my busy agenda. What day is it?"

"Sunday. I need to go to work soon. Do you want to come hang out on the golf course or stay here?"

I picked out the marshmallows, popping them into my mouth one at a time and snapping my teeth down to feel them explode. The crunch reminded me of exactly why I didn't want to go to work with Dad. "Um. I saw a picture of a gator eating a giant python on a golf course."

"We don't have pythons on our golf courses. That's in South Florida."

"So that's a yes on gators big enough to eat pythons, were pythons to exist there?"

He grimaced and nodded. "Sometimes. Wallace is the only big one on the course that I'm aware of. And he's a good boy. I can usually chase him out of the sixth hole water hazard when he gets feisty."

My butt clenched and I shook my head hurriedly, trying to signal Dad to stop talking casually about fondly named deadly creatures. "Cool. Cool, I'll stay here."

"All right. Stay really close to the boat and take all your gear if you go out on the board. You can use my paddle. I'll bring takeout home tonight," he said. "Do you like lo mein?"

"Pork, no veggies."

"Veggies on the side?"

"No veggies." I faked a shudder. "Zero veggies."

He gave me a sad, long look, spoon poised in the air, covered in a heap of dingy squares. "Are you a meat-atarian?"

"It's called a carnivore, Dad. And no. I don't like limp vegetables drowning in sauce."

"But limp noodles drowning in sauce are okay?" he asked, wrinkling his nose.

I let out a sigh, playing along. "That's the entire point of noodles."

The tension in my chest let up as we grinned at each other with our mouths full. The next three months weren't going to erase the last five years, but sweet cereal and the gleam of happiness in his black eyes helped. More than I wanted to admit.

When Dad went to work, his little boat leaving a frothy path behind him, I stood on the deck barefoot and let the weight of solitude settle. Boat traffic purred in the distance, out of sight. The tide wasn't as high as the night before. The water gave everything a greenish-brown tinge, but it was clearer than I expected in the late morning light. I could see every weird thing on the bottom. A shovel-shaped crab thing moved slowly, leaving a trail in the sand. Its spike of a tail dug a furrow that went on and on, as far as I could see.

I tried to find something to do, putting off what I *really* wanted to do. My nerves were buzzing around like horseflies in my gut, warning me away from the desire to prove Skylar wrong.

Dad's book collection was mostly adventure paperbacks with boats and Maya ruins on the covers, and a few biographies about old white dudes. It took me about ten minutes of sifting through the pile under his futon to determine that I really, really needed to find a library.

I didn't mind relying on real books during my banishment from all things electronic. I kept all my books and manga—even the ones from when I was a kid—each of them worn ragged and stained with spills and finger smudges from reading at the dinner table. Stories of dragons and sword-wielding girls. Shelves full of crushes. I couldn't find anything crush-worthy in Dad's pile.

Leia kept me company when I gave up on reading and sprawled out in the "yard." It bobbed gently, making a sucking sound against the water. She panted in the heat and felt heavy and boneless against me. Being flat made it even hotter. I rolled onto my back and let the sun make my eyelids hot pink. My sunburn flared up. Yesterday's shorts had dried to a crinkly consistency, but I hadn't asked Dad yet how we were supposed to do laundry. I'd shoved myself back into the dirty shorts for lack of a better option.

It only took a few minutes for the heat to become unbearable. I sat up, my head spinning. *How do people survive this?*

I scanned the uneven mangrove shoreline. The scrubby trees formed a wide, loose circle around our little bayou, concealing the opening that led out to the main channel and the marina. Nothing yellow flickered back at me.

I wanted to be brave enough to do reckless things. To chase reckless girls. I didn't want to look closely at the quieter need, the part of me that didn't want to be alone out here.

The part of me that was afraid of where my thoughts might go.

The part that wanted a friend.

And I knew better than to have a crush. I swore off them in seventh grade. Joey Pruitt—puppy-dog smile and big brown eyes—had pretended to ask me out and I'd fallen for it, so wildly happy I went right to my favorite teacher to tell her. She gave me a sad, quiet look.

At lunchtime, he laughed at me and told me my head looked like a mushroom. Thirteen had been decidedly mushroom-shaped in general.

Joey wasn't the worst of it. He was an asshole, and assholes were easy to write off. The true annihilation of my middle school love life happened right before Christmas break, when I drew a holiday card for Gabrielle Diaz. She wasn't the prettiest girl in the school, but she was the only girl who made my heart get jumpy and my chest get hot. She had a brilliant smile, and she sang in the choir, her voice big and brave. When I gave her the card she read it and frowned at me, sweetly puzzled.

"Why did you do this?" she asked. She laughed, then—a quick huff of a sound. "We're not even friends."

That day after PE, the girl with the locker beside me covered her flat chest with her gym towel, squealing, "Don't look at my boobs."

Voices carried over the rushing sound of water, curling steam carrying the cruel whispers to me. "Brynn gave Gaby a love letter. She's a dyke."

The word hit me like a slap. I left the locker room splotchy and hoarse from crying in the shower.

I spent that Christmas break insisting that I'd never go back to school, weeping my way through the last of the Advent calendar chocolate until my mom said she'd email Gabrielle's parents. That snapped me right out of my misery. The only thing worse than being outed to the whole school was having your mom fight your battles for you.

"Brynn." Mom made me popcorn that night, and she handed me the bowl while we watched a show about tree houses in Alaska. "Are you gay?"

I spoke around a mouthful. "Half?"

She smiled, the skin around her eyes wrinkling up like tissue paper. "*Bisexual* is the appropriate term. I think. Unless the kids have a new word for it these days. Sorry, I don't mean that flippantly. Tell me the words you want me to use."

"Yeah, bisexual. I guess. Are you mad?" I asked.

"No, baby. But if those kids give you any more shit, I'll tear them apart."

I believed her. She'd have lost her mind the way she did online when people challenged her political posts on Facebook. Mom went all in, and the last thing she needed was more reasons to stress about my failure to thrive as a normal teenager.

So I didn't tell her anything anymore. That worked out fine. For a while.

But now I was banished.

Leia snuffled in her sleep, pulling my attention away from aimlessly scanning the waterline for signs of Skylar. Disappointment swam behind my eyes. I knew what I had to do to find Skylar. But she'd been right—I was scared of the water.

Sucking in a breath that sounded more wheezy than ferocious, I puffed myself up and plotted out exactly what needed to happen. This way, at the very least, I could follow my thoughts down every worst-case scenario and choose my own misadventure.

I had to find the beach, whatever that meant. I should have asked Dad about nearby beaches before he took off to groom putting greens and repair sprinklers.

So far, the only beaches I'd seen were near the bridge on the way back from the airport. Those were too far to swim or paddleboard to. And they'd been packed with people and tents and cars. Even if Skylar was at one of those beaches, I'd never find her.

I eyed the boards, feeling sick at the thought of standing on one again.

"Get it together," I whispered.

As long as I remembered to take the floatation stuff, the safety whistle, and some water, it'd be fine. I'd look for my lost paddle, I'd keep a tight grip on Dad's paddle, and maybe I'd find Skylar.

No more procrastinating.

I'd never know if I hated her or liked her if I stayed here, safe and bored. I'd never get the satisfaction of seeing her see me pushing myself, despite her cruelly accurate assumptions.

Preparing to do battle with myself and the water, I emptied my backpack and made three peanut butter sandwiches, then wrapped them up in paper towels and aluminum foil. Dad had a lot of reusable water bottles lying around, so I filled four of them and tucked them into the backpack beside the sandwiches. I grabbed one of Dad's baseball hats and crammed it over my curls. A quick survey of the cabinet by the bedroom revealed some musty towels, so I shoved one of those into the backpack too. This time, I wasn't going to ditch into the water.

After a moment of indecision, I left my phone on the bed. Shitty flip phone or not, I couldn't risk tanking it. It was my only lifeline to Mom—even if I didn't want to pick it up and use it.

Leia followed me around the deck as I made my preparations.

"You can't come, tubby. You'll sink my ship," I said, scratching the rolls at the back of her neck.

After digging around on the deck, I found a ten-gallon plastic bucket full of half-empty sunscreen bottles and bug spray. I applied both liberally until my skin gleamed and I smelled like the inside of a well-scrubbed toilet bowl.

Dad had made lifting the board look easy. When I hefted it up by the grippy handle in the middle, I overcompensated, expecting it to weigh a ton. It wasn't that heavy, but it teetered like a seesaw, banging the deck and the rail and the ramp as I dragged it down onto the floating yard. Sweat dripped down my face and the backs of my legs. A stray curl broke free of the hat and stuck to my face.

My belly gurgled. Quiet warning bells sang out.

This was a bad idea.

I wiped the sweat out of my eyes and exchanged a long look with Leia. Her dumb-dog grin prompted a smile from me that chased away some of the bubbles of anxiety. I'd already survived falling in without a life jacket. Rationally speaking—which wasn't my forte—an afternoon paddleboarding wouldn't get any worse than that.

My therapist often reminded me to consider that, more often than not, I accomplished things semi-successfully. I didn't break down crying. I didn't break my bones. I didn't shit my pants or scream or die. My fears were simply a funhouse-mirror version of reality—a sticky ball of chaos and worst-case scenarios.

Knowing my fears were manufactured by my dysfunctional brain didn't make me feel any better, though. Instead, I felt stupid for losing it over my mind playing tricks on me. But once in a while, remembering that I'd achieved doing plenty of pleasant activities without experiencing violent death or embarrassing, terror-related bodily functions helped. I'd screamed with joy on a zip line with Mom after nearly chickening out. I'd joined swim team, despite having stress dreams about going to meets. I'd slept in a flimsy tent at summer camp in sixth grade, and I'd woken up proud of myself.

Right now, remembering that helped.

I needed it to help.

I grabbed Dad's paddle. It was way too long for me, but it would have to do.

After I attached the ankle strap to my two-day-stubbly leg, I fastened the backpack down with bungee cords and wrestled the heavy board into the water. Without Dad's help, I couldn't step onto it delicately. I crawled onto it, bracing myself against the light wobble, and pushed up on my knees. The board drifted away from the dock immediately, caught in the soft swell of water moving in from the bay.

I held completely still, getting used to the feel of the board beneath me. When I shifted my weight, it didn't tilt much one way or another. Falling had been purely my own flailing, not the result of the board tipping over. I pressed my knuckles to the rubber mat—paddle clenched in my hands—and unfolded into an unsteady stance.

"It's you and me, bayou," I whispered.

Leia's bark rang out, low and encouraging. I dipped the paddle in the familiar scoop and started off with the push of the tide toward the narrow lagoon where I'd found Skylar. Irrationally, I wanted her to be right there again, for her to see me standing proud and tall on the board.

Well, not quite tall.

Clouds towered on the distant horizon, mountains of fluff with brilliant white caps. We didn't have clouds like that in Ohio. These were impossibly high, fantasy mountains. As I stared they moved, expanding like ink in water. Beautiful.

The sun baked my shoulders, satisfyingly hot. I imagined it changing me, hardening the parts that needed to be tougher, like a limp piece of clay fired in a kiln. With every pull of the paddle, the strokes evened out. I was strong. Pride simmered under my skin—a feeling I wasn't used to. I smiled and licked my dry lips, basking in the moment before I inevitably did something stupid.

The bayou had a sleepy feel, with the bright sun directly overhead and no wind to sing in the trees. Dragonflies skimmed over the water and small gnats clouded around me, but no fish jumped. Without the splashes, the silence became the empty sound before a longing sigh. My eyes burned from stray sunscreen, and I paused to wipe away the tears. Water couldn't be sad. I wasn't sad.

"I'm not sad," I said, nearly startling myself off the board with the sound of my own stubborn voice. "This is awesome."

When I paddled closer to the mangroves, the life beneath the surface swelled up, some big, unseen thing pushing the water. Whatever it was, I'd scared it away.

That's right. Fear my paddle.

My paddle. That's what I really needed to find. Now that my need to prove Skylar wrong and show her that I wasn't a coward had gotten me out on the board, I could get Dad's paddle back. If I followed the winding paths between the mangrove islands, there had to be a dead end eventually, like the drain in a bathtub. The final resting place of lost rafts and paddles and floating beer cans.

I cut through the water slowly, taking my time, satisfied with my new purpose. The pace became meditative. My toes curled against the mat, and I shifted my weight from side to side gently with each stroke. Left. Right, right. Left, left. Right. Water cascaded off the smooth black paddle each time I moved it over the board. My muscles warmed.

The bayou was mine alone. The mangroves cradled me and the water whispered, and my mind went silent. I was only rhythm. Push, pull. Breathe in. Breathe out.

My pace quickened until I became a water bug skimming along the surface, silent and graceful. I got so caught up in the startling sureness of it that I glided right past a patch of beige sand, where the mangroves rose up around a small mound of earth—a pathetic Floridian excuse for a hill.

"A beach!"

Turning the big board around crumbled all my illusions of grace. I couldn't figure out how to reverse or turn tightly, so I churned back and forth in a twenty-six-point turn until the nose of the board pointed at the beach. Breath heaving with frustration, I looked up to gain my bearings.

Skylar stood on the sand, a tall superhero of a girl, hands on her hips. Yellow bikini bright as a signal flare. "Hurry up!" she called out, exasperated, laughing at me.

I narrowed my eyes and jabbed my paddle into the water. The board launched at her like an arrow.

CHAPTER FIVE

"DON'T YOU HAVE ANY other clothes?" I asked Skylar. She looked exactly the same. The same freckles on her sunburned shoulders. The same pale tint to her lips. Her hair even looked the same, wet and knotted.

She surveyed my jean shorts. "Don't you?"

Coasting toward her in the shallow water and disarmed by her arched brow, I picked at the fraying edge of one pocket. "I pack light. What's your excuse?"

The board bumped against the sand, whispering with friction. It jerked to a stop a whole lot faster than I expected it to and I pitched forward, tripping over my backpack and hurtling right into Skylar.

She caught me with a grunt, and we both fell on the sand. Tiny shells scratched my bare knees and elbows.

Our faces were very close. "Ow," I managed.

Skylar held very still while I untangled myself from her cold body. My inner thigh scraped against hers and my breath sucked in sharply. I felt like fire everywhere we touched, despite the chill of her skin. My heart beat faster than it had on the paddleboard. Ducking my chin to hide my face, I tried to pull myself together so I could look at her without feeling like I was staring directly at a supernova.

She scuttled like a crab away from me and drew her knees up to hug them. For a moment, she looked small, like I'd scared her. I felt an overwhelming urge to reach for her, as if she were sinking into quicksand and needed me to pull her out. Sadness wrapped like barbed wire around my heart. Before I could figure out what to say, some clumsy joke to chase that sadness off, she rolled her shoulders back and broke into an empty, newscaster sort of smile. "So. Where are you from?"

"Cincinnati," I said, grateful for the simple question. I wasn't sure I could spell my own name, between the sadness and the heat and the disorienting sight of Skylar's long legs.

"What's it like in Cincinnati?"

"Shitty." I actually liked Cincinnati just fine, but that wasn't something you said to a cool girl.

She pushed a smear of wet hair off her cheek. "Don't you think Florida is shitty too?"

I tugged the board up a little farther so it wouldn't float away, and I gently tossed the paddle into a patch of grass and sharp weeds. "I'm currently evaluating Florida. This bayou isn't bad. I'm not sold on the heat or the bugs or the killer animals, though."

Skylar gave a sun-bleached, brittle laugh. "What killer animals?"

"Sharks. Snakes. All of them."

She rolled her eyes. "You're more likely to die in a car accident. Or even from a lightning bolt. It's not like this is the Australian outback."

A little ripple of shame ran through me. It had only taken me a conversation and a half for Skylar to notice my anxiety and mock my fears. She wasn't impressed that I'd made it out here. She still thought I was a baby.

Throat tight, I forced myself to sit down beside her instead of scrambling back onto the board and paddling away from her judgmental face. Whether she thought it was impressive or not, I'd found her beach, and now I was going to make it worthwhile. Or at least rest until my arms stopped shaking from all the paddling.

"Are you from here?" I asked, struggling not to snap at her. I shifted my weight. The sand, which had looked soft, was really a gross mix of rocks and mashed-up shells, and they poked my butt through my shorts.

"Yes. I was born here in St. Pete. A Florida native." She stretched out her long legs. Dark-blue polish covered her toenails in chipped patches.

"And you've never heard of anyone getting killed by Florida?"

Skylar made a sound like a broken bell. She didn't answer.

A boat hummed in the distance, somewhere out of sight. The mangroves rattled in a light breeze. Silence seeped in between us, growing until it felt like a wet cloth pressed over my face. I sighed, flattened by the sadness I couldn't shake.

We both looked out over the small lagoon in front of the beach. I couldn't see anything but spindly green. No buildings. No towers or power lines. A few mangrove seed pods floated by like lost snorkels.

Don't be weird, Brynn. Talk to her.

Finding my voice was like breathing underwater. "Are they shaped like that so they can stick in the sand and grow baby mangroves?" I asked, pointing at one.

"How am I supposed to know?"

I picked a broken shell out of a pile of dried sea grass. "You're from here."

Her breath huffed out. "Therefore I'm a phlebotomist?"

A snorting, bark-laugh tore from my throat before I could stop myself.

She whirled on me, her hair slapping against her back like a wet rope. "What?"

"I think it's *botanist*." I wheezed. "Or herbologist. Or herpetologist or something."

"Herpes?" She stared, eyes different—wary but warmer. "Are you on drugs?"

I couldn't stop laughing. Big, breathless honks that made my belly ache. "A phlebotomist draws blood."

"I know that. Everyone knows that." Skylar's gaze became distant again, and I didn't care one bit that her hurt feelings were practically oozing out of her body. She'd tried to tell me that Florida wasn't dangerous. She'd baited me into entering the mangrove maze on my second day out here. She had sharp, mean edges. Served her right.

I felt smug for less than a minute before my mirth evaporated. I wiped a stray tear of laughter from my eye and sniffed.

"How do *you* know what a phlebotomist is?" she asked, too softly to have any bite.

"I'm on a few medications for my mood and ADHD." I had never told anyone my age but Jordan about this. But who was Skylar going to tell? "I have to get blood drawn a couple of times a year to make sure my liver is behaving. Which is actually overkill, because my doses are really low. I guess doctors get paranoid about kids."

"You're not a kid."

"I'm fifteen. So, like, legally. Yeah."

"Yeah, legally. But people still expect you to act like an adult. And be perfect and never mess up or have feelings," she spat. "It's impossible."

It got quiet again. Her defeat was a prickly thing; it was almost like I could feel it on the surface of my skin. I wanted the sensation to go away. I thought about Jordan and how they asked me how my appointments went, but always knew when to change the subject to Kristen Stewart or our latest main ship. For some reason, I couldn't imagine telling Jordan about this—my journey to the beach, the way Skylar made me angry and turned on and worried at the same time.

I couldn't figure out how to change the subject.

Skylar bumped a sandy toe against my foot. "Anyway. You're crazy?" she asked.

"That's the word on the street. Also, that's a super ableist way of putting it, and you should seriously consider not using that word that way."

"What does that mean?"

"Ableist? Ableism? Like sexism except toward disabilities." This is where I would have sent her a helpful infographic. I had, like, ten saved on my camera roll. My fingers tucked against my palm until they cramped. I wanted my phone so badly. If nothing else, to throw it at her.

"I've never heard of that," Skylar said. "But okay."

"Now you have. So you can stop calling people crazy, like an asshole."

"I think I'm allowed to say it if I want to."

"I disagree."

She hummed. "You're running away because you're crazy?"

Anger crackled beneath my skin. "I'm not *running away*," I bit out.

Skylar stretched her leg and pointed her narrow foot at the lump of my backpack on the board. "Then why'd you pack so much stuff?"

My stomach gave a lurch of recognition. "Lunch!" Once I remembered it was there, the gooey peanut butter was all I could think about. I crawled to my backpack, tore it open, and started with the lukewarm water, gulping down long pulls of it. I was thirstier than I'd realized, and it quickly cleared some of the dizziness I hadn't really noticed until I scrambled around.

Hopefully it would chase the empty feeling away too.

Sugar always cheered me up, at least in the short term. Skylar seemed like she could use some. I held out one of the sandwiches. "Peanut butter sandwich?"

She stared at it like she'd never seen a sandwich before and then looked away, shaking her head. "No thanks."

"Whatever." I spoke with my mouth full of the most blissful bite of sandwich I'd ever had. "Your loss." Peanut butter stuck to my teeth and the roof of my mouth, and I closed my eyes and savored every sticky moment. Paddleboarding didn't mess around. I was starving.

The breeze picked up, tickling the back of my neck and making the hair on my arms stand up. I took my hat off and let it cool my sweat-soaked curls. "Is it safe to swim here?"

Skylar eyed me. "Am I really the right person to ask?"

"That's right." I laughed. She was a weirdo who traveled by water. Without a boat. "Are you training for a triathlon or something?"

"No. I play volleyball."

"I'm not good at volleyball. I still wore glasses in middle school, and I was always getting hit in the face."

Skylar snorted in an adorably undignified way, and I laughed with her, remembering the look on my mom's face the fourth time I broke my glasses in seventh grade.

I drank more water and tucked the trash into my bag. Rolling onto my back, I shielded my eyes with my arm. Now that I had food in my belly, the uneasy tension wrapped around my ribs released just a little. The sun pressed me into the earth. The mangrove leaves rattled, and the grass whispered. "It's not that bad here."

"It gets old after a while," Skylar said.

"This is only my second day." I curled my toes in the sand, uprooting flat shells and rocks. The water nearby made a *whoosh-plop-whoosh-plop* sound I recognized as the aborted flight of a mullet. It jumped twice, as if it needed one more attempt to confirm that it couldn't fly.

Skylar groaned. I pictured her stretching and forced myself not to look. "Why are you here?" she asked.

"My mom thinks I need the fresh air. And crushing boredom."

"Because you're crazy?"

I bristled.

One time a girl from school came over to study for geometry. We weren't friends, but my mom was so thrilled I had a classmate over that she went totally overboard, baking fresh cookies and fluttering around the kitchen, distracting us from our practice test. She went to the bathroom, and the girl laughed and said, "Your mom's weird."

My mom *was* weird, but I was the only person allowed to say that. I finished the practice test in a hurry, stiff-backed and sharp and eager to send her away so she'd never look at my mom and think shitty things about her again.

And that's how I felt when Skylar called me crazy.

Every smart argument I'd heard on TikTok tripped and got stuck in my teeth. I didn't know how else to tell her not to shit on mental health issues when she hadn't listened to me the first time. "You really are an asshole."

Skylar laughed. "You're finally figuring that out?"

"Seriously. Stop saying I'm crazy."

"Jeez. Okay."

I rolled over to glare at her or fight her or check her out, and she was right there, inches from my face, perched like a cat ready to pounce. I yelped, and she laughed harder and sprang back, unnaturally quick.

My heartbeat kicked up, anxious-startled-skittering in my chest.

The heat must be getting to me.

A rumble of thunder sounded, and I scrambled to my hands and knees. The gentle breeze that had tickled my damp skin wasn't gentle anymore. The mangroves began to thrash and rattle. Rambunctious wind kicked up little waves with tight ripples and whitecaps. At the horizon, what had been towering cloud-mountains was now a black smear. It pushed toward us like a gaping mouth.

A bolt of lightning forked from the clouds, vivid blue-white.

"Oh." My heart went from racing to thudding. "Shit."

"Fun fact," Skylar said. Thunder cracked so hard my bones hurt with it. "It's almost impossible to paddleboard in the wind. Your body acts like a sail."

"Wouldn't that make me faster?" The wind whipped my voice away.

"Not when it's blowing toward us."

I hugged my middle. The sun went behind the raging cloud, and the air cooled in an instant, a gusting breath of fear. "I'm screwed."

"Pretty much. At least it's not a hurricane."

She sat in the sand and watched me, bored. Even her hair hung limp and wet like it couldn't be bothered to get caught in the excitement of the wind. Growling with frustration, I dragged the board higher into the grass. Weeds and sand spurs stung my feet. Tiny, one-clawed crabs waved at me like angry old men and dove into little holes in the hard-packed sand.

Lightning flashed so close, my scalp prickled. Thunder cracked before I could flatten myself. A scream tore out of me. With nothing left to do, fear took over. Everything was too loud. The wind screamed and blasted sand, stinging my cheeks. "Oh shit. Shit!"

"Stop panicking." Skylar was there, right in my face. "Stay close to the ground and out of the water. The lightning has a lot more stuff to hit than you."

"You literally just said lightning would kill me before snakes did!" Trembling and sick with terror, I hunched over my knees. I dug my fingers into the sharp blades of grass and gritty sand and closed my eyes and wished I had a relationship with God beyond praying for no cavities at the dentist once a year.

"That isn't exactly what I said." Somehow, Skylar's voice carried over storm sounds.

Rain pelted my back, bullets of ice. Each drop stung and sang out against the leaves. The drumbeats quickly gave way to a rush of water like a freezing shower. Everything got wet all at once. My hair. My clothes. The ground beneath me soaked with standing water. I shook violently.

I'm going to die here.

I waited for the white-hot flash that came to me in nightmares—that moment before the plane crumpled into the ground or a flaming beam fell from the ceiling. The end.

Skylar tucked her arm around me and pressed her body close. "You'll be fine," she said, her voice carrying like quiet music over the rain. She didn't warm me at all, but I knew I'd survive as long as she didn't leave me alone.

"I'm scared." I'd never heard this much lightning in my life. It crackled over and over, awful static in the air. And a horrible crash followed each one, hollow and earsplitting. At home we had occasional tornadoes, but I was never outside for them. Or anywhere near them. Did Florida have tornadoes? Would the wind whirl and twist and carry me up and drop my broken body into the bayou?

"Good. If you weren't scared, there'd really be something wrong with you," Skylar said.

I startled and whined with every bolt striking around us, no braver than a dog on the Fourth of July. "What are you, some kind of ninja?"

"What?"

"You're not even flinching."

"This happens every single day in the summer." Her shoulder nudged me when she shrugged.

"It's not like you get stuck out in it every single day." My words strangled off into a yelp when lightning hit so close the flash of light and bolt of thunder came at the same time.

A small fraction of my rational brain recognized that I was full-on cuddling with Skylar, but I was too terrified to feel anything except for a very real concern that I might shit myself. Every time I breathed, I made a little whimpering sound.

Damn it.

I lost track of time and my thoughts flattened to nothing but wordless fear and cold. I don't know how long the storm lasted, but it seemed like forever before the violent rumbles of thunder softened to rolling, distant sounds.

The rain didn't let up, but my fear of being barbecued on the beach passed. I straightened, aching, and looked around. Though giddy with relief, I still shivered like a wet poodle. My underwear squelched and I grimaced, wishing I'd worn a bathing suit. Skylar would dry much faster once the rain let up.

She watched me. "Are you cold?"

"Yes. Obviously." I resembled a dead chicken, pink and soggy and covered in goose bumps. My teeth chattered with staccato clicks.

Skylar gleamed in the rain with the effortless grace of a swimsuit model. She watched me, blue eyes calm. Studying.

"Okay, Miss Expert Meteorologist. How long is this storm going to last?" I asked.

She turned her face to the stormy sky and closed her eyes. The rain fell like tears down her cheeks. "This is a big one," she said, shrugging and looking back at me. "A few hours. Probably until it's dark."

I sighed at her dramatics. She didn't have to act as if being a Floridian gave her a psychic connection to the weather.

"Great," I muttered. Two nights in a row freaking Dad out. Next, I'd be banished to my floating jail cell of a room every time he went to work.

I couldn't find the sun. Dark-gray clouds blanketed the sky, so thick and solid I couldn't tell if they were moving at all. The wind didn't gust the way it had at the storm front—it blasted us steadily, angling the rain in sheets. I'd never been this uncomfortable and cold in my life.

"This is terrible. I ate all my sandwiches already."

Her long eyelashes fluttered with an eye-roll. "You're not going to starve in three hours. And you have water."

"I bet you could catch a fish with your bare hands if we needed to eat, mermaid girl."

Her lips quirked with a fleeting smile. "And then what? Sushi? This isn't campfire weather."

I laughed, picturing us attempting to cut some fat-bellied fish into colorful designs. "How did anyone live out here before technology?"

"They didn't have electricity or toilets or bug spray. The options were, *be alive or don't be alive.*"

"Yeah, I guess being alive beats the alternative," I said.

She shrugged.

"Are your parents going to be worried about you?" I asked.

"I don't think so."

"How old are you?"

Skylar squinted like she had to do math to figure it out. "Seventeen."

That explained her body. I had massive boobs, but the rest of me was still in an awkward, lumpy stage—somewhere between my elementary-school baby shape and what I hoped would become some kind of uniform curving. She looked like a woman—muscular in places and soft in places. Even with the rain freezing me inside and out, a flicker of heat danced through me when I looked at her.

"I guess you're pretty independent then." I cleared my throat, trying to stop thinking about her tan belly. "Did you drive over here?"

"I did," she said. "I left my truck over where they're building those fancy condos."

"My dad said the owners went under, and they're not building them anymore."

Her mouth opened and closed. "Right. Over there, though."

Skylar was hiding something, but I didn't want to press her. Sadness lingered like salt on her skin, as much as I tried to pretend it wasn't there, and I had a feeling she'd tell me something terrible if I asked her why she was avoiding her family and acting shady.

Jordan would have called me a coward for that, and they would have been right. But they'd always been braver than anyone I'd ever known.

"It must be nice having a car." I didn't know what I'd do with that kind of freedom. Probably listen to my own music instead of Mom's boring podcasts. Not that it mattered when I couldn't stand the idea of actually driving a car.

"It is nice. Unless you get grounded over your report card." A shadow crossed her face, and she looked down at her lap.

Maybe the rain was finally getting to her.

"Sometimes I think about what people had to do in the past," I said. "Like, be freezing cold in a boat crossing the Atlantic to move overseas. Or walk really far to get to school. Or pee in an outhouse in the winter. I don't think I could do any of those things."

"You'd be fine. People do what they have to do. I mean, what would you do otherwise?"

"Sit in a corner and die." I laughed.

Her mouth quirked into a small frown.

"Seriously." I tried to catch her eye so she'd know I wasn't joking around. "I don't even go to pep rallies at school because it's loud and I'll have to yell inane cheers. I'm really good at not doing things."

"But you found me," Skylar said. Our eyes met, sending another jolt right down to my tailbone. "You found my beach."

I instantly forgave her for teasing me and being an asshole. The soft pride in her voice wrapped around me like a blanket. I'd given up on getting her approval, and now that I had it, it felt better than I could have imagined. Jordan would have told me it was unhealthy to care so much about what someone thought of me, but knowing that didn't make it any different.

I wanted her to like me, to see me.

And more than that, I wanted her to be happy.

"Why do you come here?" Her beach wasn't much to look at, especially compared to the powdery Florida beaches I'd seen on travel shows. She'd probably be happier right off the bat if she picked somewhere better to hang out and get a tan.

"It has—" She dragged her lower lip between her teeth. "It had a fort over there. I built it when I was little, and I added to it every year. My parents let me take a little dinghy on my own. I had a lockbox with books and snacks. Old plywood and stuff."

"Forts are cool," I said encouragingly. Her voice had lost its sharp edge and had become wistful and soft. She hunched in on herself, and I didn't like it. I knew that look. The weight of sadness that made your bones hurt and your muscles weaken. I rambled the way Mom did in the car when I didn't want to talk to her. "At home we have real forests and trails and rivers. It's pretty cool for exploring if you don't mind getting tick bites and putting yourself at risk of Lyme disease."

"Mosquitoes down here carry Zika." A smile hooked one corner of Skylar's pale lips. "And probably other things."

"Zika's not really a thing anymore."

"Since when?"

"I don't know. Like four years or something?" I shook my head. "You really need to pay more attention to the news."

She huffed. "All I'm saying is you're not any better off down here."

"I agree! This place is deadly. I want to live in a world without bugs."

"A world without bugs would be a world without human life. We need bugs to pollinate plants and feed animals that we eat. That's how life works." Her voice tightened, not yelling but louder somehow, heavier in my ears. "You can't remove something and expect the rest of the world to keep on going exactly the same way."

I flushed, chastised and not knowing what I'd done wrong. Hot, embarrassing tears prickled. I hated the way she made everything feel bigger and loud. "It's just bugs," I mumbled.

A stronger gust of wind caught me and I braced myself against the muddy ground, scowling. My hat whipped away into the branches.

I hadn't seen a snake out here yet, but several venomous varieties lived around salt water. Waiting to strike anyone clueless enough to enter heavy brush or go digging through mangroves for a ratty old ball cap.

Goodbye forever, hat.

"These storms seriously happen every day?" I asked, wiping my eyes. Without the hat, the water dripped and splashed into my face relentlessly. Skylar had a will of iron, apparently. Still as a statue, she never dried her face.

"In the summer. It gets drier in the winter, if you can call it a winter. It's not like we really get cold weather."

"I can't imagine not having snow and seasons," I said.

She smiled. "I don't mind. I hate being cold."

"Could have fooled me. You're not even shivering."

Her expression shifted, darkened.

"Hey, I don't mean it in a bad way." I watched her warily, imagining her darting into the woods like a spooked cat. "I wish I could be as badass as you are."

"No, you don't. You don't know anything about me. I'm not a badass."

The way she said it was pretty final, and I bit back the urge to ask her what her deal was. She was so smart—so sure of herself. I'd sound like a little girl with a silly crush if I pressed her for more when she obviously didn't want to talk to me.

But I wanted to know. I wondered if she had an Instagram, and if her photos mirrored the sadness under her skin or if she took carefully curated selfies. Did she write poetry? Songs? What kind of friends did she have? Did they hang out on beaches too?

What was she hiding from me?

Insides squirmy, I turned my attention to the choppy little waves lapping at my board.

"How high is the water going to come?"

"Another foot or so," she said. "You'll have to drag the board up a little more so it doesn't drift off."

I scooted forward, hunched over to keep my face out of the downpour. The board slipped in my fingers. Even my dirty look didn't prompt Skylar to help, so I struggled with it for five minutes, scraping my knees and knuckles against the razor-sharp shells buried in the sand. By the time I got the board high enough, my breath heaved, and the cold didn't feel so miserable.

Wait.

My words spit out like shots from a pellet gun. "If it storms every day, why didn't you warn me?"

She blinked and a little wrinkle formed between her eyebrows. "I lose track of time."

"If I were your parents, I wouldn't let you go wandering out in the mangrove woods or whatever if you can't even keep track of time." I rose on my knees like a cobra, bloated with self-righteousness.

"You're right, they shouldn't have," she said.

She looked away, eyes bright. In the rain, I couldn't tell if she was crying. Her mouth twisted, lips pressed tight like she was trying to force the sadness to stay inside.

I deflated.

My instincts had been right. She had her own shit going on. She'd gone to her secret beach to get away from all that, and I was yelling at her instead of having the kind of compassion my therapist reminded me to give myself.

"You should come over later." I lobbed the words at her gently. "We have a boxful of crappy books and no TV or Internet. Oh! But we have a waterslide. I haven't tried it yet."

A tiny grin formed a dimple on one of her cheeks. "You have a waterslide on your houseboat?"

I nodded, and her grin widened. Encouraged, I scooted closer, trying to close the gap my angry words had formed.

The rain wasn't letting up. My stomach growled and I shifted, drawing my knees up. "Think I can make it back in this?"

Skylar shook her head. "Don't try it. You'll tire out too fast, and if you fell in, it wouldn't be safe."

I sighed. "I'm tired right now. This sucks." It was getting dark. The water pooled on the soaked ground, dark and pocked with raindrops. I pictured gators and crocodiles rising from the waterline, hungry for an easy target—an exhausted, shivering Midwesterner with no common sense.

Desperate for a way to get comfortable, I opened the backpack and pulled out my now-soaked beach towel. It squished and dripped in my fingers and stuck to the board when I tried to spread it out.

Skylar laughed. "What are you doing?"

"I'm making a bed."

"You're going to sleep in the rain? On your paddle-board?"

I slipped on the board, landed hard on my knee, and cried out, angry all over again. On a good day I was pretty moody, but so far Florida had me swinging back and forth like a sickening fair ride. "Do you have a better idea?"

"Yes. Lie on the mat part and put the towel over your body. Even in the rain, the mosquitoes are going to pick up with the sun going down. You're better off covering your body than trying to use a towel as a mattress." She came close, hands waving around like a conductor's.

Compelled by the calm of her voice, I did exactly what she told me to do. The cold, wet towel wasn't any better or worse than my cold, wet skin. But I liked the idea of avoiding potentially disease-riddled mosquitoes.

"There you go." Skylar crouched, nimble on the balls of her feet, and watched me.

I wondered what she saw, if my bare legs had given her the same soft thrill that I got from hers. Every once in a while after a shower, the naked girl in the foggy mirror looked exhilaratingly grown up. I could picture the blur of my reflection sharpening into confident, sexy lines.

Now, shivering under a soaked towel, I wasn't exactly a thirst trap in the making. But I wanted to know if I had a chance. "Do you like girls?"

"Like in a lesbian way?" she asked.

I wrinkled my nose. "Yeah, like that way."

"No." She scratched her chin. "I don't think so, anyway. I've never thought about it."

"You'd probably know if you did. Without thinking about it," I said. Disappointment twinged at my throat, but she hadn't been cruel about my question—and that helped. "I mean, you know you like boys, right?"

Skylar snorted. "Yes. I liked boys in kindergarten. I've always liked boys."

"It's like that."

"You do?" She tilted her head, examining me as if she expected my queer parts to leap out from under the towel.

I pressed my cheek against the nubby paddleboard mat like a dying caterpillar in a soaked cocoon. "I like boys and girls both. And everybody. All genders."

"That must suck."

A scowl twisted my mouth. "Why is that?"

"Crushes on everybody? I'd never get any schoolwork done," she said.

I watched her for signs of messing with me, but nothing gave away sarcasm or an edge of teasing. "It's not like I like every single person ever," I said. "I mean, you don't like every single boy you meet, do you?"

She huffed a laugh. "Pretty much the opposite of that."

I smiled—and a yawn broke out of me, slow and satisfying. "Exactly."

Skylar scooted closer as the sky darkened. "Have you had sex with girls?"

"I haven't had sex with anybody. I'm going to be a sophomore next near." My mom had been teaching me about sex since I was ten, and I had a pretty good idea how to do it without getting pregnant. But I'd never had a boyfriend or girlfriend, and the idea of letting someone else touch me where I touched myself made me feel more nauseated than excited. "I don't really want to."

I didn't understand why kids were so casual about sex, as if it couldn't literally cause you to die if you did it with the wrong person. When I confessed that to Mom, she totally failed to hide her happiness. A teenager worried about sex was a teenager less likely to get pregnant or infected with an STI, I guess.

"Have you kissed a girl?" Skylar asked.

I wanted to pull the towel up over my face. "I kissed a boy at church camp in sixth grade, but that's it. For kissing."

She closed her mouth tightly, eyes bugging out, and then erupted with laughter. "I'm pretty sure that's not what church camp is for."

"Church camp was not for me at all." It had been one of those ongoing attempts to carve out a circle of friends and a support system for an awkward, shy child of divorce. I'd liked all the nice guitar music, but not the part where all the songs were about Jesus.

Skylar grinned, bright again. When she wasn't sad, she glowed, skin and eyes lit with something I wanted to hold. Something electric and warm. "Not a churchy girl?"

"Not really. It's boring and smells weird. I mean, more power to people who like it. Jesus is pretty popular up in Ohio." Maybe I'd offended her. "It's cool if you are. Obviously."

"I don't know what I believe anymore," Skylar said. It was the kind of statement people made on a bad day, falling into bed and cursing life. But she was serious, gaze sober and calm. Older.

It struck me, with absolute certainty, that she'd lost something.

CHAPTER SIX

I WOKE UP WITH a blade of grass in my mouth and my face cemented to my paddleboard. Every part of my body hurt but especially my hips, where they'd spent all night pressed against unforgiving fiberglass.

All night.

"Oh shit."

I sat up, and the damp beach towel puddled around me. The sun was starting to rise, the sky at the horizon all pink and gray. It would have been lovely if I wasn't definitely grounded for all eternity. My poor dad.

"Skylar." My voice croaked. Maybe it was true what they said about getting rained on and catching colds. I looked around and didn't see her anywhere. "Damn it, Skylar. Skylar!"

Maybe she was off peeing in the bushes. I definitely had to pee in a major way—so much that I stumbled a few feet behind a scrubby fallen branch and peeled my shorts down to squat perilously close to unknown danger. The only thing worse than dying by a snakebite would be dying by a snake-bite to my labia.

As I crouched, trying not to pee on my bare feet, I spotted rotting plywood and planks farther in the brush. Had Skylar gone to her rickety fort?

"Skylar!" I called out. "Your fort sucks. I guarantee you there are a thousand spiders in there."

Despite my best efforts, warm liquid splashed on my toes. In a germ-fueled panic, I waded into the water to wash. My jean shorts were still unbuttoned when Dad's boat churned into the lagoon in front of me at full speed, the bow raised and the water behind it all frothy. Before my heart rate had a chance to catch up to what I was seeing, he pulled right up beside me, beaching the boat on the sand and jumping out as the engine cut off.

"Brynn!" he shouted, grabbing me. He held my face and looked me over. His eyes were bloodshot, and his fear cut through me. I'd never seen an adult so wrecked. My legs turned to jelly. "Brynn. God. Are you all right?"

"I'm—" I shoved my face into Dad's chest and started bawling instead of telling him I was fine. Huge, gasping, snotty, ugly crying. The night had been fun in a weird way, like a sleepover. An adventure. But I could have died or gotten eaten by something, and Dad had been scared—really scared. I'd been scared too.

I must have stockpiled all my terror for this moment.

Dad ushered me into the boat, pulling out his phone as he tucked blankets around me and handed me a bottled water.

"She's fine. I have her. Yes. Yes, you can call off the search. Thank you. I'll call her mother now."

A search. My mom. Shame ripped at my gut with sharp teeth.

I buried my face in the blankets and fought the monsoon of tears, but they kept coming. Hiccupping and loud, relentless cries. When Skylar showed up, she was going to get a kick out of the spectacle.

Dad's phone call with Mom went quickly, all terse and no-nonsense. Dad was defensive, most likely over losing me on my second day in Florida. It wasn't his fault. I'd call her and tell her later.

This is all my fault.

When Dad finished loading my board, my backpack, and his paddle onto the boat, he started the engine.

"Dad, wait!"

"What, sweetie? We need to get you home."

"My friend. She's still out here. Probably hiding in her fort."

He stared into the mangroves and looked back at me. "What friend? What fort?"

"Skylar. I don't know her last name. She was out here with me all night. We got caught in the storm."

Something strange happened to Dad's face. It went red and bloodless all at once. He looked splotchy—like a horrible tie-dyed shirt. "That's not funny, Brynn."

I recoiled like he'd slapped me, confusion curdling to nausea. Of course it wasn't funny. I knew I'd really screwed up by getting lost. Like, beyond screwed up.

Before I could defend myself, the engine roared to life and he gunned it, pulling us off the sand and into a lurching reverse arc. I scanned the beach desperately for Skylar, but she didn't come out. Maybe she'd gone home, swimming whatever path she took to her beach.

But if she'd really done that, what a dick move. How could she leave me out there alone?

Anger mingled with the sickness of guilt.

We flew across the bayou. It was already hot, the surface a mirror. I turned my face into the wind, letting it dry my hair. The tears kept coming, coughing out of my chest and cold on my cheeks.

The houseboat came into view and relief made me feel weak and tingly. A shower. A real bed. Food. Water. Leia. One night sleeping with bugs and rain, and suddenly my prison was a five-star hotel.

Dad didn't ask me to help him catch the dock this time. He stalled the engine and scrambled forward to brace our gentle impact. I ducked my chin and clutched the blankets closer. All I'd proven to be was a complete screwup, incapable of exploring without endangering my life and frightening my parents.

He tied up and gave me his hand. I hesitated, scanning the water one last time.

"What?" he asked, gentle but sharp. I tried to tell myself it was fear, but the sickening sensation of being in trouble—of deserving to be in trouble—overwhelmed me.

"Do you think she got home all right?" A slow, careful question.

"Who, Brynn?"

"Skylar."

Dad's eyes lost all their kindness, the skin beneath them bruised with lack of sleep. "I don't know how you've been getting online, but this has gone far enough. It isn't a joke."

A low sob tore from my throat. "What isn't a joke?"

"Stop it, Brynn!" His voice boomed, a thunderclap that stole my breath.

I lowered my chin again and pressed my lips together against another shuddering cry.

He scrubbed his hand over his eyes. "I know it's normal for kids your age to be fascinated with death. Normal for—for you. But this isn't the time. Don't do this."

Rage formed a tight, burning knot in my chest. I wanted to scream at him. Wildly. Violently. My anxiety wasn't fascination. And Dad's condescending tone fueled my unhinged anger. I wasn't acting out for attention. Not now. Not ever. I thought about death when all I wanted to do was live normally, free of its shadow and the awful finality of it. The forever of it. The decay. My mom and dad and me and everyone we'd ever meet burned to ash or rotting in the ground forever and ever and ever.

None of that had anything to do with Skylar.

Dad wasn't making any sense.

Nothing made sense. And just as quickly as my anger had risen, it fell—driven away by a tidal wave of anxiety.

Tears streamed down my face. I couldn't breathe, and I didn't even want to try anymore. I wanted to pass out and wake up at home in Ohio, where my mom at least tried to understand what I couldn't help.

Dad's expression softened. "Brynn. It's disrespectful, that's all. Time doesn't make it any better."

High-pitched static buzzed in my ears, drowning out the sound of his voice.

I sucked in a shallow breath. The floating dock swayed beneath me.

"Losing a bright girl like that," he was saying, his mouth tight and concerned, his voice fake. Had to be fake. A hallucination.

He wasn't talking about Skylar. Not *my* Skylar.

Cold hands.

Cold in the water.

Always in the water.

"St-stop," I stuttered. He was wrong.

But she'd touched me. She'd been there. She wasn't lost.

"Our community went through a lot—her parents went through a lot."

My face twisted, making the sunburned parts sting as I hiccupped, "What?"

Dad closed his eyes. The pain was clearer then, carved deep around his eyes, knotted in his fingers as he wrung one of my sandy, wet towels. "I was the one who found her."

I can't breathe.

"I shouldn't have blown up at you like this, but I think about it every day. I saw her yellow bathing suit in the water—I thought it was a plastic bag."

The flash in the mangroves. The thin fabric hugging her hips.

His voice broke. "Then I hoped she was faking—the way kids do at the pool. Waiting to get rescued. But I turned her over and her eyes were . . ."

Her eyes were so blue.

And they were so, so sad.

"Stop it," I choked. To him, to the rush of images— bloated skin, rotting skin.

Dead, dead, dead.

"Please don't joke about it anymore, Brynn. Please."

A thousand bees hummed in my skull, growing louder and louder. Louder than my horror, my disbelief.

I was going to pass out.

Dad caught me when my knees buckled. "I was so scared I'd find you like that too. When the board was gone, and the storm rolled in so quickly. I can't lose you, baby girl."

A low, keening sound rolled out of my chest. The horizon swayed and my heart rattled and buzzed. On bad days I knew I was unwell, and on the worst days I called myself crazy. But for the first time I wondered if I'd truly lost it.

I'd spent the night with a *dead girl*.

Was anything real? Was I even in Florida at all? I had a private, sneaky fear that my entire life was a hallucination— that I was really in a coma or sedated, staring at a blank wall and filling it with the hopes and dreams and hurts of a teenage girl.

I'd always been able to squash that fear. *Unreasonable.* *Unlikely.*

But Skylar was dead? Drowned. Bloated blue eyes staring my dad down. Skylar burned up or buried somewhere. Or worse, worse, worse—Skylar existing only in my head.

Dad was in my face, hands on my cheeks, mouth moving soundlessly. All I heard was the angry roar of my own thoughts, fluttering wings making my vision go gray.

This was more than panic. I couldn't catch my breath. Couldn't speak. Couldn't see.

Couldn't.

Skylar.

It turned out Dad *did* have a girlfriend: Paula—a registered nurse with a Jet Ski and scrubs covered in teddy bears.

Paula sat on the edge of the futon and finished taking my blood pressure. The cuff squeezed me, reassuring, and then let go. I wanted it to stay there, grasping my bicep in a hug.

Dad stood a few feet away, shoulders rigid and arms crossed tightly at his chest.

"It's still a little high—not alarmingly so. But, Hunter . . . if you're really worried, you should go to the emergency room. I'm not experienced with—"

She met my eye and tripped on the words.

I filled them in for her. "Mental illness?"

"That's not what she said." Dad shot me a warning look.

I wanted to hate Paula on principle. It was kind of my job as a child of divorce. Hate every lady in my dad's life forever while siding with my perpetually single custodial parent. But Paula's hands were very soft, and her hazel eyes were kind. She had a faint accent and dark-brown hair that fell down her back in a long, thick braid.

And she was beautiful—rich, brown skin, long lashes, and a flawless complexion without even wearing makeup.

She also fluttered with something I recognized. Raw nerves greeted me in her cold fingers and the tremble of her hands, in the darting looks she gave my dad. I couldn't blame her for being anxious. They'd probably never planned on introducing her to me, but here I was, recovering on a futon on a houseboat after passing out cold. *From feelings.* And maybe a little dehydration and exposure.

The rest of it—*dead bloated rotting*—seeped into the edge of my awareness, but I couldn't go there. Not right now when I needed to seem normal to this nice lady.

I couldn't have been passed out that long, but she'd made it here quickly—scooting across the bayou in a life jacket and her work clothes. Her white shoes dried outside and her scrubs were still damp. She offered me apple juice from a straw.

"Are you feeling shaky?" she asked.

Skylar.

As hard as I tried, I couldn't get her out of my head. My gaze shot to the glass door and the deck beyond. For all I knew she'd be standing there, a dripping figment of my imagination, walking all jerky and twisted like a vengeful spirit in a horror movie.

Except even now, I wasn't frightened of *her*. I couldn't be. She was sad.

She was alone.

I couldn't talk about her. I wouldn't. For the good of everyone involved, this had to be my secret. Dad didn't need to know that I was really, really sick. I'd figure out how to get better without help from him or his cute girlfriend. Or worse, without either of them telling my mom her big plan to fix me didn't work. At all.

"Only a little bit shaky," I said. "It was really cold out there in the rain."

Paula smiled. She had one crooked tooth that snaggled at me adorably. "And I thought the air-conditioning at work was bad."

"Where do you work?" I asked, surprised that I actually wanted to know. Or at the very least, wanted to think of anything but blond hair floating like seaweed.

"At a pediatrician's office down the street. Well, not down the street from the boat." She laughed, breathy and soft. "Nearby, though."

"It's a good thing she's nearby," Dad said. "I was about to call the coast guard. Again."

A boatload of coast guard boys in snazzy uniforms sounded like a decent distraction. But meeting them barefoot and stinky and damp all over sounded like the worst.

In typical Brynn fashion, the quick flare of excitement in my belly at the idea of cute boys searching for me piggy-backed right into embarrassment, which hurtled right into despair.

I was on a roller coaster with no lap bar.

I choked, coughed, and started crying. "I'm sorry, Dad." He'd been out there looking for me all night. And coast guard guys had too. All of them thinking I'd fallen into the water and drowned.

Like Skylar.

"It's okay." He crouched beside me, close enough to brush against Paula's leg. She stiffened and scooted away from him.

They hadn't officially told me they were dating, but I saw it in every hesitant glance—and the fact that she'd left work to help me.

I wiped my nose. "Now I know to stay away from the thunderstorms."

Once a day. I knew because Skylar told me. Because she knew everything about the bayou. She knew things I didn't know—couldn't know.

So how could she be a hallucination?

"Yeah, the afternoon storms are pretty bad," Paula said.

A shiver ran through me. I was already losing the thread of what we were talking about. "Got it."

If Skylar was real, I had to find her again and ask her why she chose *my* life to ruin.

But that was a lie.

I had to find her again because I already missed her, and I had to know if I was missing something real—dead or alive—or if I'd made her up. Invented a friend. I didn't know which possibility was worse.

My eyes welled up. They were dry from the sun and the salt, and I winced at the sting.

"What is it?" Dad asked.

"Nothing. I'm just really glad I'm back." I scrubbed at my tears over and over, too raw to contain them. But a tiny flame of hope lit up in me, the kind of stubborn flare that got me through days and weeks when I felt useless, felt like a burden, felt like I couldn't go on.

I had to prove to myself that she'd been real.

That I'd really talked to a dead girl all night.

That it wasn't all in my head. I already had enough in my head. No vacancy.

A sick laugh tried to fizz out of me, but I swallowed it back. I wouldn't be able to explain what was so funny—that I'd spent my whole life hating everything about death only to end up with a crush on a dead person.

"Do you want to try to take a shower?" Paula asked. "I'll stick around until you get to sleep if you want. Mostly for your dad. He's going to have a stroke if you sneeze."

I forced myself to nod, wishing they'd go away and leave me to untangle my thoughts. They both helped me up, and I looked down at the wet spot I'd left on the futon—on Dad's bed. Guilt grabbed my throat.

I bet he's sorry he let me come here.

Paula rummaged through my suitcase and found soft clothes while I showered and finally warmed up.

My breath hiccupped. Anger and deep sadness warred, so big in my chest that it felt like my ribs would crack. Paula and Dad were just outside the door worrying about me—judging me. I wanted to be left alone, but there was no escaping them. No way to get away from Dad thinking I'd made a horrific joke about a dead girl. No retreat from Paula's niceness. Niceness I didn't want or deserve right now.

I wanted to scream.

The water beat down on me until my skin went spongy and pink. I rinsed my mouth with the stale, clean water and spit it out over and over again, swishing it around my teeth. They needed a good brushing, but I didn't have the energy for it.

When I turned the shower off, Paula opened the door a crack and handed me a towel. She helped me to my room and turned her back while I got dressed, wobbly and disgusted by the texture of the carpet under my feet.

I'd never been this tired in my life. After marinating in my own thoughts in the shower, exhaustion dampened my mind. I tucked away the image of Skylar and my guilt-stained curiosity over Paula and Dad's relationship.

A violent yawn split the dry skin at the corner of my mouth. I licked the sore spot. Paula was watching me.

"Have you guys been together for a while?" I tugged my wide-tooth comb through my wet curls, wincing at every snarl.

She gaped at me until shock became a shy flicker of a smile. "A year and a half. It sounds like a long time when I say it out loud. Hunter—your dad—wanted you to get settled in before he said anything."

"You don't have to explain." My voice came out dull and unkind. I didn't try to fix it. I didn't have the energy to make her feel good when I felt so empty. "I barely know him. He doesn't have to tell me all his private stuff."

"I don't want to be private stuff," Paula said, recovering from a flinch with a gentle smile. "But I don't want to push you either. You're almost an adult."

Mom loved to remind me that I was still a child. She never referred to me as a young adult or almost an adult.

I found myself drawn to the way Paula stayed close even though I was being a bitch. "If I ask you something, will you promise not to tell my dad?"

Paula frowned. "No, I can't promise you that. But I can promise I won't tell him unless I'm worried about your health and safety."

I debated for a long moment as I folded myself onto the bunk, my limbs weak. My muscles ached from shivering for so long. I had to know. It was worth risking getting Dad riled up all over again.

"How long ago did Dad find that girl in the water?"

"Skylar McKenzie?" Paula sighed. "Her school's doing a memorial run on their cross-country course later this month. I keep seeing signs. It says fifth annual. So it must be around five years now. Poor girl."

She didn't look distressed—only sad. Dad probably hadn't told her anything about me claiming to have hung out with Skylar. That was good.

I made my voice as casual as I could, but it was still hoarse from the night out in the rain. "A memorial run?"

"She loved to run. And she was a volleyball star." Paula massaged her palm with her thumb, gaze distant. "She was supposed to go to college that fall. With a full ride." She met my eye and swallowed, and then her soft smile came back— watery now. "You never know. You really never know."

"I think about that all the time."

"Think about what?" she asked sharply, going back into nurse mode like she was assessing symptoms.

"Death. I mean, not really death. But how life can end so quickly, I guess. It really freaks me out." I offered a tiny olive branch of honesty. If she and Dad really liked each other that much, she was probably here to stay. And I wanted her to know about my anxiety. From me. Not from my dad. "Sometimes I have a hard time not thinking about it. Like the thoughts invade."

She sat down on the bed beside me, a solid twelve inches between our thighs. "It's good that you can talk about that, Brynn. Some kids don't share what they're going through."

"You said I was almost an adult." I tried to smile so she'd know I wasn't really mad, but my muscles couldn't quite make it. I probably looked like one of those emojis with a flat mouth.

"Ah." Paula's snaggletooth smile came more easily, like sun breaking through the clouds. No wonder Dad liked her.

"I mean, some young women don't share what they're going through."

I squeezed the ends of my hair dry with a scratchy towel. It brushed my shoulders and left my T-shirt wet. If I scrubbed too hard to dry it, the curls would fall apart into a frizz-bomb. The simple routine helped me focus on something other than wondering if death was like sleeping, or like nothing, or what nothing felt like, and how I'd die, and how Dad would die, and how Paula would die.

And how Skylar *had* died.

"I have a day off later this week," Paula said. "Maybe I can show you around town?"

The question startled me so much I dropped the towel. "Like, just us?"

She handed it to me slowly, as if she expected me to bite her. "If that wouldn't be weird."

I'd never hung out with any adults other than my mom and my doctors and my teachers. Mom's parents were ultra-old, and she didn't have any other family in town.

It would be weird.

"It wouldn't be weird."

And maybe I'd be able to learn more about Skylar. About what had happened to her.

Dad peeked his head in. "Are you girls okay in here?"

A wild yawn twisted out of me. I covered my mouth and nodded, dizzy with exhaustion. I took the towel, spread it across my pillow, and curled up against it.

"Gonna try to sleep, sweetie?" Dad asked.

I nodded, burrowing into the thin mattress, which squeaked in protest. After the paddleboard, though, it was a feather bed. I watched Paula stand up and hover next to Dad in an awkward near-hug, and I snorted. They were ridiculous.

Just like that, everything became too much. Not in the way that made me panic or cry, but in the wonderful way that turned my mind off like a flipped switch. Too much to process. Too much to feel. Too many hours out in the cold rain. Too many aches and pains. A smile too sharp to be real.

I closed my eyes.

The houseboat rocked me to sleep.

CHAPTER SEVEN

WHEN I WOKE UP, everything was fine. I stretched in the squeaky bed for a full minute, fuzzily wondering why I was looking at incredibly ugly decor. A knock sounded at the door, and I remembered several things in rapid succession.

I'm on a boat.

In Florida.

Because, Mom.

Also, dead girl.

"I'm up," I yelped, pulling my blanket up to my armpits in case my boobs were trying to escape the threadbare sports bra I slept in.

I didn't even have time to manage a decent stomach cramp about everything that had happened, before Dad poked his head in and started talking in a three-cups-of-coffee manic way. "We're going fishing!"

I couldn't go fishing like everything was normal. I had to go find Skylar. "But you have a job," I said weakly. It's not like I could tell him I had important plans to locate Skylar, demand to know what her whole dead deal was, and then yell at her for tricking me into thinking she was alive.

"The golf course will survive without me for one day."

I pictured alligators roaming putting greens and rogue weeds climbing up the little flags that marked golf holes, or whatever they were called. But he didn't seem concerned about that.

I knew what he was really concerned about. I could see it in his weak smile and the circles under his eyes. Even his beard looked sad.

It was my fault. I'd disappeared for an entire night. I'd hurt him. Badly. And I was already planning to go off on my own again and talk to the girl who he'd—I couldn't think about that part. I couldn't.

Dad was scared to go to work. He was scared to leave me alone. And he was never going to take his eyes off me unless I acted happy and not at all obsessed with a dead girl. I had to pretend to be normal if I ever wanted to see Skylar again.

I didn't know if I knew how to act normal. But I had to try.

"Cool. Fishing." My smile felt like Silly Putty. "Let's do it!"

I got dressed in a daze, peering out the small window at the water, looking for her. Needing to see her. Needing to know I hadn't lost my mind.

Breakfast tasted like mud as I forced myself to listen to Dad talking about different fish species. I'd never been fishing before. But I'd never been paddleboarding before either, and that hadn't stopped me from learning how to do it quickly enough to get marooned on a ghost beach. Fishing with my dad couldn't go any worse than that.

At least, I thought so, until he showed me the bucket full of frantic, reddish-brown crabs he'd picked up at the marina. And the other bucket full of adorable shrimp with heads and tails and cute antenna and dozens of tiny feet that propelled them in circles as they tried to escape their plastic prison.

"We have to kill them?" I asked, touching the surface water.

Dad looked up from installing some kind of bubble machine in a cooler full of greenish-brown salt water. His mouth twisted to one side. "The bait?"

"Yeah, the crabs and the shrimp." How could he not see how adorable they were?

"That's the point, Brynn." He poured the shrimp into their slightly bigger cage, and they darted to each corner, nudging their horned faces at the side over and over, their pulsing brains too small to recognize the futility.

The crabs scurried around their stinky bucket, saluting me furiously.

They had no idea they'd die soon.

Would it be worse if they knew? I figured it must be. The anticipation. The horror. Shuddering, I made myself smile at Dad. At everything. The doomed shrimp. The angry crabs. The barely there sun on the early morning horizon. The fishing pole Dad rigged up for me, and the tackle box full of hooks and tools and shimmering plastic minnows with more hooks and big, painted-on eyes.

I had to maintain an exterior of delight over all things fishing or Dad would fixate on how I'd nearly gotten myself killed. If he thought about it too hard, he'd probably make me come to work at the golf course with him. And I'd never get back out on the water alone, with Skylar.

It was nuts to want to find a dead girl. I knew that. But I had the sunburn and mosquito bites to prove that I'd really been out there—that it hadn't been a dream. While I had nothing to prove that Skylar had been real, there was no way Dad and Paula had been talking about someone else. Dad had even mentioned her yellow bathing suit.

I'd had no way of knowing that, so I couldn't be making it up.

Right?

The weird thing was, I didn't have *that* hard of a time believing I'd hung out with a dead girl. She hadn't been scary in the way other dead things were. She hadn't made me think about being dead someday, the way bug corpses and packages of raw chicken did.

I was more angry than freaked out, because I hated being lied to. I hated people thinking I couldn't handle things. Being dead didn't give her the right to make a fool out of me.

Dad caught me glaring at the water. I quickly pulled my chapped lips into a grin, which hopefully didn't give him the impression I'd been watching for flashes of yellow and contemplating throwing angry crabs at a pretty girl.

I couldn't stop scanning the mangroves, but I didn't expect to see her. I couldn't feel the cold sadness that surrounded her like an oil spill. Now I knew those strange waves of misery had been her. Just like the wind before the storm, she had her own atmosphere.

Be here, now. That's another thing my therapist recommended all the time. Mindfulness. Which basically meant shutting off thinking about the past or the future, which was pretty fucking difficult. Especially when I couldn't trust my own mind in the first place.

"Brynn," Dad said, putting his hand on my shoulder. The touch dragged me back into myself.

Genuinely relieved, I offered him a weak smile. "Yeah, I'm ready."

We set off under a sky sleepy with cotton-ball puffs of clouds. I wore one of Dad's windbreakers. He wore a shirt with Baby Yoda inexplicably riding an alpaca. As soon as the boat started moving, the engine drowned out the hum of my thoughts. Fabric slapped against my skin and my hair whipped into my face. Vibrations rattled my spine in a soothing sort of way.

Sitting on my bench seat near the bow, I clutched a piece of rope tied to a metal hook. I knew the rope wouldn't help if we struck one of the water street signs or a rock below the surface. I'd fly out of the boat and break my neck and drown. Or I'd pitch over the side and the propeller would dismember me.

Still, the rope was solid in my fingers, and I needed something to hold on to so I wouldn't scatter into a million frightened pieces.

Tampa Bay opened up to us when we rounded a corner of mangroves, and I gasped, tasting salt from the gentle kisses of surf that sprayed from beneath the bow every time we slapped against the water. The bay went on and on and on, flat and beautiful. Far in the distance, another skyline rose like a floating city, gleaming with the light from the rising sun. A pair of massive pelicans glided over the surface of the bay, their wings absolutely still. For a moment, we skimmed the water beside them, matching their speed but none of their eerie grace.

A silent laugh bubbled out of my chest. I couldn't remember the last time I'd laughed like that—like someone had tickled me.

I licked my lips and leaned into the wind. This was flying. The engine screamed behind me, the wind roared in my ears, and I became light.

I reached for the familiar shape of my phone in my back pocket and stiffened, immediately thinking I'd lost it overboard. It wasn't there. It was safe—in Ohio.

My fingers closed into a fist. I couldn't take a picture for Jordan. And even if I could, I'd have no way to send it to them.

I couldn't save the moment. I couldn't prove I existed, here.

Thinking of Jordan made me realize I'd gone a whole day without wanting to talk to them. Yesterday had been a pretty eventful day, but it still felt like a betrayal.

"Sorry," I exhaled into the wind. I was sorry for ignoring Jordan. I was sorry for spending time with my dad only because I needed him to leave me alone. Feeling bad was a sick sort of comfort. It was easier than thinking I had a real chance at being a good friend or a good kid.

Dad steered us along the shape of the coast, sticking to where the water was darker blue. Deeper. When the light shifted, I could see the marks of shallow places. Paler blue water and tinges of brown sand. He dodged effortlessly between them, at home on the water the way Mom was at home on the highway.

My dark mood began to lift when a dolphin broke the surface. A littler one rolled beside it, and then they disappeared.

A whole world existed below us—things I'd never see or understand. I'd watched a documentary about the deep ocean once, and scientists believed it was as much an open frontier as outer space. Sea life was completely alien. An inhospitable, upside-down world we could only visit.

That was pretty cool. An unknown, like death, but not a horrible one. A living one.

The boat slowed as we approached a tower made of metal and wood. It rose nearly forty feet, and the choppier, darker water of the bay slapped against the huge girders that disappeared into the depths. Smelly bird poop slicked every surface. The huge sign at the top hung crooked, metal dented and weathered. I hadn't expected to see weird dystopian stuff out here on the water.

Holding my nose, I asked, "What is it?"

"A marker for the shipping channel," Dad said. "The big tankers line them up from a distance to know they're on course. And . . ." He grinned—brighter and cleaner now—as if the whipping wind had scoured him clean too. "Fish love it."

I stayed out of his way as he opened a storage box and pulled out two anchors. He fastened one line to the front of the boat and one to the back and tossed the anchors overboard. I shuddered and looked away, trying not to imagine the thick metal sinking and nudging against the bottom, utterly alone down there in the dark. What if I got caught in that anchor rope?

"Should I carry a knife or something?"

Dad glanced at me as he fooled with the rope, doing something to make it tighter. "A knife?"

"To get free if I fall overboard and get caught in ropes."

Dad frowned, and I knew I'd said something wrong. "If you want. But I'll keep an eye on you. I want you to relax. Catch some fish. It's meditative for me—maybe it'll help you."

I didn't need help. I needed him to ignore me like he'd done for the past five years.

I needed to ask Skylar why she was haunting Dad's bayou.

"Sure." I had to stop thinking about it or my thoughts would swallow me up. "Sounds good." I gave him my best totally-normal-teenager smile. It felt like a sticker plastered over my mouth. "Show me how to fish."

He got the poles out, handed me one, and showed me how the reel worked. I understood the basics—turn a crank and your hook comes back, possibly with a fish. But when he cast his poor skewered shrimp out into the water and it plopped inches from the channel marker, I assumed he was using actual sorcery.

"You'd better throw mine out there too. I'm not going to be able to replicate those moves."

I watched closely as Dad grabbed one of the shrimp. It wiggled in his hand, curling its tail like a scorpion's barb at his palm. He winced, and I wanted to high-five one of the shrimp's hands. Or feet. Whatever they were. *Stick it to him, little guy.*

Dad held a small hook like a sewing needle and threaded it right through the shrimp's skull, below the bone that formed a horn. It kept wiggling.

My stomach turned. "Does it hurt him?"

He gave me a quick, confused look. "I don't think so? It'll stay alive as long as you don't pierce the brain."

"That sounds like a good rule of thumb in general."

Dad laughed, the sound a little flat. He talked me through the casting process, and I immediately forgot everything he was saying in favor of watching my poor shrimp take its final journey.

"Here you go." Dad handed me the pole. "If you feel a bite, reel in some. Or tug. That'll set the hook."

"If I feel a bite?" I frowned at the pole and the gossamer monofilament that disappeared into the water.

"It'll feel like a tug. You'll know."

"Hmm." I sat down and tested reeling it in. Pretty straightforward. The gears moved in a steady, mesmerizing way, coiling the fishing line back onto the reel. I spun the reel very slowly, picturing my shrimp's slow return to base. Dad was right, it was meditative. Spin. Spin. Spin.

Bite.

"Oh!" I stood and shook my pole, excitement setting off like a flare. "Dad!" The end of my pole bent toward the water with a furious tug, and then all the resistance stopped and I flailed back, stumbling to sit heavily on my bench.

Dad laughed, watching me. "Looks like you got robbed."

"That jerk fish!" My heart raced. I'd made contact with a real fish. It had battled me, and I'd lost. My shrimp was gone. I had to avenge it.

With another shrimp. But still.

"I need more bait," I said, forgiving both of us for all the shrimp murder. I understood now. There literally were bigger fish to fry.

We fell into a routine—each taking turns losing our shrimp to the sniper fish below the surface. Every tug sent a thrill through me. What was down there? What would we find if we managed to reel something in before it spit the hook out?

What if—

"Shit." I gasped, scanning the water. "Do the killer cow-face rays hang out here?"

Dad stifled a laugh. "No, buddy. Only itty-bitty ones."

I shot him a glare. "Are you sure?"

His eyes crinkled with a gentler, warm smile. "I'm sure."

My skin got itchier as the day went on, pink bumps and bright sunburn reminding me that only yesterday I'd scared Dad out of his mind. My in-the-moment bliss shattered. Once I remembered, guilt hung around in my gut like the remains of a bad meal. Guilt for making him worry. Guilt for taking the paddleboard too far from the houseboat. Guilt for only doing this because I wanted him to decide I was safe to leave alone.

And quieter, sneakier thoughts came for me too. Thoughts that bubbled up and burst against my lungs.

I'm crazy.

It'll get worse.

I'll never be normal.

These thoughts were my oldest friends. I let them wrap around me. It was easier than fighting it, easier than trying to be any other way.

The sun came out from behind the clouds, and with it came the nauseating heat of Florida summertime. Dad pressed bottles of water into my hands every fifteen minutes or so, and after a while he introduced me to the grand tradition of peeing in a Home Depot bucket at the back of the boat. I used a towel like a cape at the hair salon to cover my body. Horrified at the thought of Dad looking at my pee, I gripped the bucket carefully, dumped the liquid overboard, and then scooped up some seawater to rinse it out.

I nearly dropped the bucket when it filled rapidly with water. As we'd floated there, secured with our anchors, I'd forgotten how powerful the water below us was. It could grab a bucket out of my hands, turn a boat right over, and pull it down into the dark.

It had taken Skylar.

It could take me.

Dad still had his back to me, so I gave myself a moment— eyes closed, breath shaky. Part of me hated her screwing up my already screwed-up summer. For the first time I could remember, I was doing something sort of fun with my dad. Doing daddy-daughter things. And I was only going along with it so he'd believe I wasn't the kind of person who snuck off to talk to dead girls.

I cleared my throat to let him know it was safe to turn around.

"Your turn to bait your hook," he said.

"If I drop a shrimp, it's your fault for giving me too much responsibility." I shoved my hand into the cooler full of bubbling water and clueless shrimp. Using my hand like a big scoop, I swirled it around until the hard shell of a shrimp brushed against my fingers. I tried to grab it gingerly, the way Dad did, and it flopped right out of my hands.

It took three tries to get one. I held it tightly. The weird, shiny exoskeleton moved a little, but it was harder than flesh. I wasn't going to hurt it by squeezing it.

"Sorry, dude," I murmured. It was like performing surgery. The sharp barb of the hook slid easily through the thin shell. My shrimp kept wiggling and his clear organs kept pulsing.

We were all made of liquid and slippery organs. Life was improbable. Fragile. It was only a matter of time before something ripped us up and ruined us and we died. It didn't take anything for me to kill the shrimp. Soft, terrible.

Abruptly, I dropped the hook and the shrimp and my pole. They clattered to the deck as I choked on bile at the back of my throat.

"I can't. I can't!"

I sat down heavily, closing my eyes and breathing through hot waves of nausea.

Dad rubbed my shoulders and put a cool cloth on the back of my neck. "That's okay. You're okay." With my eyes closed, I listened to the rhythmic slap of waves and the occasional distant hum-whine of an airline engine. Somehow, Dad knew to stop talking and let me be.

It took a long time for me to calm down.

When I opened my eyes, the water blinked back at me.

Dad's hand tightened on my shoulder. "Were you having *any* fun?" he asked, not sounding hopeful. Just tired.

Our eyes met. I didn't have to lie. "I was." It wasn't fishing that was terrible, it was the thing in me that wouldn't let anything be fun for long.

Some of the tension around his mouth faded. He smiled, and I saw the young guy my mom had fallen in love with. A cheerful, earnest dude.

Dad had left his pole in a holder made of white plastic pipe, and it suddenly bent double behind him. I let out a series of unintelligible swear words, gesturing helplessly at the situation. Laughing, he took my hand and guided me to hold the pole. It shook and thrummed with the strength of whatever was tugging the line.

"This is the fun part. You can do it, Brynn. Slow and easy. The hook's set. Now you have to fight it gently or the line will break."

"None of that makes sense!" Still, I laughed a little.

Reeling in the fish seemed to take hours. Sometimes the fish pulled so hard the line went backward, the reel whining in protest. When the line went slack, I pictured it coming toward us like a torpedo. I reeled in as fast as I could, until my arm burned. The butt of the pole dug into my thigh where I braced it to get a better grip.

I saw a blurry flash of silvery white under the water. "Fish! Fish!"

Dad whooped. "It's a baby bonnethead!"

"What is that?"

"A little shark."

"Shark?" I shrieked, nearly throwing the pole into the water. "Why are we inviting a shark onto our boat?"

Dad grabbed it and helped me hang on. "It's a foot-and-a-half long, Brynn. It isn't Shamu."

"You mean Jaws." *Dads.*

I kept reeling in, and Dad grabbed a net on a stick and dangled it into the water. "You're so close now. You're doing great."

The poor dumb baby bonnethead swam right into the net. Dad scooped it up and set it down at our feet, where it flopped and grunted. It had a vaguely sharklike shape, but miniature. White-bellied and gray-backed. It was kind of pretty, in a small-mouthed, chompy way.

"Is it going to be okay?" I asked, starting to feel the familiar creep of sick-panic. I didn't want to hurt anything else today.

Dad crouched beside it and draped a wet towel over it. "It's fine. Help me pick it up," he said.

I set my pole down carefully and put my hands where he showed me. It was strong, pulsing against me like a wet muscle. Dad used a long, thin pair of metal pliers and quickly worked the hook out of its mouth.

"All free. Toss him back in."

I squeezed the towel around the baby shark with both hands. "Will you take a picture and text it to Mom?"

Dad's face did something complicated as he pulled his phone out of his back pocket. "Ready? One, two, three!"

After posing with the tiny predator, I lobbed it over the side of the boat. It hit the water with a plop and disappeared like a dart.

"Wow." I exhaled slowly. "I caught a fish."

Dad scruffed my tangled hair and I didn't shy away from it. I kind of liked the way it made me feel—like he was proud of me.

"You didn't catch a fish," Dad said. "You caught a shark! Not bad for your first time."

We kept fishing until the sun beat down at us from directly overhead and our shadows disappeared in the unforgiving noon heat. We huddled together and ate peanut butter sandwiches and Oreos. It didn't occur to me until later that, for a little while, I hadn't thought about Skylar, or the past, or the future.

CHAPTER EIGHT

DESPITE MY EFFORTS TO act like a normal kid, for the next two days, Dad still didn't trust me enough to leave me alone for longer than it took to take a dump. Which was happening more often than usual.

Anxiety. It's a party.

I spent hours watching the water and willing Skylar to come close. But she either ignored me or had never existed in the first place. Or maybe even ghosts couldn't read minds.

The longer I went without seeing her, the more I worried I'd had a serious mental break. Now I needed to see her not only to talk to her but to confirm that she was just regular dead girl stuff and not a terrible hallucination.

"Do you mind if Paula comes over for family dinner?" Dad asked, jarring me out of a careful study on the patterns the waves made when the wind picked up.

I turned from the window, steeling my features so he wouldn't see how weird it was for him to say "family," as if she had anything to do with our family, or he and I were family—the kind of family that had *family dinner*.

Weird or not, dinner with Paula would break up the monotony of my growing desire to chuck myself into the water to swim in circles until Skylar appeared.

"I don't mind." Maybe *Mom* would mind me having family time with another lady, but she'd abandoned me for the summer anyway. She didn't get any say in this, despite the knot of guilt telling me I shouldn't betray her.

While Dad went to pick Paula up at the dock, I showered and put deodorant on and examined my nose for stray blackheads, as if that would be the first thing she'd check. Fluttering excitement always made me preen, for lack of something more constructive to do. It wasn't until Dad pulled up with her on the bow that it occurred to me he'd left me alone. Trusted me alone.

A different kind of excitement lit up in me. Soon, he'd leave me alone for longer. Soon, I'd find Skylar.

Paula brought empanadas stuffed with cheese and spinach, and Dad made teriyaki chicken and rice in an electric rice cooker. I ate ravenously—finally back in touch with my appetite despite the aftershocks of anxiety in my gut.

Mom called it my *nervous tummy*, which sounded a lot cuter than the actual situation. My gut listened very carefully to my anxiety-brain. Whenever I couldn't shake the hum and crackle of anxiety, my body made sure to empty my bowels in case I had to run from a saber-toothed tiger—or whatever dumb evolutionary trait had led to my defective intestinal tract.

Inevitable bathroom trip or not, I couldn't say no to gooey cheese.

Awkwardness hung out like a fourth person at the table, staring us down. Daring us to try to fill the silence.

We didn't.

While Dad cleaned up, Paula opened the tote she'd brought along and handed me a pile of books—a few vintage romance novels, some science fiction books, and a field guide about Florida fish.

"Hunter said you don't have much to do over here. These are mine. I'd love it if you borrowed them," she said, as if she was asking me a favor and not doing something startlingly sweet for me.

I took the books and shuffled through them carefully, scanning each cover. "Thank you."

None of them were really my style, but they were better than Dad's books, which I'd decided were romance novels for dudes. Cars. Boats. Sex. Guns. More cars. Surprisingly detailed descriptions of abs. More guns.

Paula's books were dog-eared and stained in places, as if she was the kind of person who read in the bathtub and at the dinner table. It further endeared her to me, and I inexplicably wished I could tell her about the constant ache of *Skylar* at the back of my mind.

She motioned to hug me that night when Dad and I took her back to the dock on the jon boat. I shied away like an awkward cat, and her mouth opened in a silent laugh. We both mumbled apologies at the same time.

I slept better that night, full-bellied and still catching up on the hours I'd lost on the beach. Dad watched me at breakfast. The hair stood up on my arms as I felt him examining me, taking stock of the circles under my eyes, maybe. The flaking burn on my shoulders.

"Do I look awful?"

He straightened. "What?"

"You're doing a laser eye thing." I motioned with my fingers. "Scanning."

"No, no. I was just—"

"Worried, I know."

His mouth softened, making his beard ripple. "Actually, I was thinking you look fine, and I was worrying too much, and I should get back to work and make sure Wallace hasn't eaten anyone."

For a moment, I pictured a cannibal golfer. Then I remembered Wallace was a gator. Neither made the sport sound appealing. "I have lots of stuff to read from Paula," I said, trying not to sound too eager for the chance to finally escape his stifling concern.

Except being left alone would mean I could make choices. Like hiding under the covers until he returned.

Or looking for Skylar.

My hands got as cold as hers. It was one thing to imagine looking for her. It was another thing entirely to actually do it. I wasn't sure if I could. I wasn't even sure if I could handle being alone with my thoughts.

When Dad finally left, he idled the boat as if he was just as reluctant to put distance between us. Feeling nauseated, I waved the book in my hand and settled in a lounge chair in the shade. He watched me until I couldn't make out his beard from the back of his head. And then I gave reading a solid effort. I told myself it was because I needed to make sure he was really gone, but the truth was I was putting off learning if I was haunted or having a nervous breakdown. Or both.

I stubbornly learned about a zebra-striped fish—inexplicably called a sheepshead—and a snub-nosed, bullet-shaped fish called a snook. Dogfish looked nothing like dogs, and catfish only resembled their namesake with a pair of wiggly whiskers.

Between every page, I glanced at a dusty outdoor clock on the wall, justifying it as a natural reflex to check the passing time. But the truth bubbled under my skin: I was stalling. I was a coward.

One fish blurred into the next, and I turned each page after skimming a few words. Fin. Scales. Gills. Teeth.

Enough.

Dad wouldn't be gone forever. I was running out of time.

Hands trembling, I set the fish book down and scrambled into my bathing suit. The tight spandex stung against the sunburn on my thighs when I wormed the suit up my legs and fitted it around my body. I hated wearing a bathing suit. It squeezed my middle and pushed my boobs in every direction. I'd be happier naked, with all my parts free to roam as the universe intended.

But that didn't matter. I had terrifying things to do, and I had to do them in a hurry.

The water seemed especially dark. I looked for storms, but the clouds in the distance were still white. I reminded myself that I knew how to swim. I did. I had to.

"All right, Brynn," I muttered.

Without a paddle, I had no choice but to flop onto my belly on the board and use my hands. Instead of giving myself time to consider what I was doing, I kicked off from the dock. Leia drooled at me worriedly. I glided forward, toward the mangroves, and then the tide caught the board and I did a slow-motion, aimless slide.

I couldn't control the board without a paddle.

All this waiting and churning anticipation and tricking my dad, and my plan to look for Skylar wasn't even going to work. I was stuck.

Boiling over with frustration, I planted my forehead against the board and snarled out an incoherent cry. Shame washed over me. Another meltdown. More weakness. Every time things got hard, I lost it like a damn toddler. Too many nights in a row plagued with insomnia and I cried in homeroom. My yearly flu shot made me weep. An assembly at school left me weak-kneed and sick over the thought of all of us being slaughtered, crammed together on the bleachers with nowhere to go if the building caught fire or someone started shooting us.

All those moments of weakness flooded me now, where I was flopped on the paddleboard, at the mercy of the tide. My brain filtered normal shit into terrible shit, and a screaming current of frustration followed. I was broken. I'd always be broken.

Sneaky thought spiral, catastrophe. Doom.

Worst.

"Stop judging me, Leia!" I called out, desperate for something to take my rage out on that wasn't my bruised sense of worth.

It took me ten minutes to get back to the dock.

I paddled my hands like frantic duck's feet, splashing water all over my sides and legs. Tears burned my eyes, and my face heated. The only person who could see me was the big, doofus dog, but humiliation soaked through my body anyway.

The bayou held a secret—a secret only for me. A secret—a wicked smile—I longed for. And I couldn't get away from house arrest on my dad's shitty floating trailer long enough to discover what it meant.

I put the board back on the rack and dried it carefully with a beach towel so Dad would never know I'd taken it out. Sniffling and sore, I sat on the edge of the dock and dangled my feet in the water. My skin grew progressively darker in the depths—toes orange and wiggling, nearly out of sight.

She had been brave. Confident.

"You're an athlete," I said. "You're strong. How did the water take you?"

Skylar didn't answer.

I paced around the houseboat, caged by the water.

The boat contained exactly nothing interesting.

Dad kept his stuff in a cabinet in my room, and I didn't feel right going through it. Beyond his pile of books and his fishing equipment, the boat was sparse. I guess that prevented everything from being taken over by clutter. This was basically a floating tiny house.

But at least it had a second story. I took the narrow spiral staircase to the top, where the wide sky gave me space to breathe. From up there, the roofs of the marina buildings and the low skyline of downtown St. Pete peeked from behind the smear of green. I'd almost forgotten about the rest of civilization. Close but just out of reach. Unless I wanted to get run over by a big speedboat on my way to land.

A big airplane descended in the distance, sinking below the low line of mangroves. It was all black—some kind of military plane. A silver passenger jet echoed its path farther away, over at the airport where I'd landed. The real world still existed. Ohio was still out there.

Mom.

I hadn't called her back in two days. My throat locked up every time I considered it. She called Dad instead—every few hours—and he stepped out onto the deck to speak to her, too quietly for me to hear.

After the night on the beach, I knew she'd ask me lots of frantic questions about my health and well-being. I didn't want to talk about it. Not with Mom; not with Dad. Not with Paula. I didn't even like thinking about it. The memory of being out on the beach, of Skylar, gnawed at my shoulders.

Sadness struck me so violently I had to grab the rail to stay on my feet. I gripped the hot metal and sucked a breath in through my nose.

It wasn't just my sadness.

"I know that's you," I whispered. Saying it any louder felt like too much. Too absurd. Too unreal. Maybe, like this, I was just talking to myself, and not to the dead girl radiating helpless despair.

"I hope you're enjoying yourself!" I shouted, emboldened by what was probably budding heatstroke.

Or maybe I was desperate for her to pay attention to me.

I scratched the peeling skin at my arm until my heart rate evened out. Then I noticed the waterslide right beside me.

The surface was dry and powdery to my exploring touch. In my limited experience with waterslides, it helped if they were wet.

Water shimmered at the base of the slide. My mouth itched with an echo of whimsy—the opposite of the heaviness still sour and syrupy at the base of my tongue. I wanted to do something fun and stupid and childish that Skylar couldn't ignore. Something that might make her laugh, or at least wash her sadness off my skin.

I did some calculations based on how deep the bayou was and came to the vague conclusion that I probably wouldn't hit the bottom if I flapped my arms and kicked. And if I hurried, I wouldn't be in the water long. The ladder on the floating dock would make it easy to get back onto the boat. My odds of a violent, slide-related death were pretty low.

Even if a shark happened to be circling, my big-ass splash would probably frighten it off.

This wasn't my style. I'd never been a thrill seeker. I avoided roller coasters over concerns of vomiting and dismemberment. As a kid, I'd climbed up playground slides and then carefully scrambled back down to escape the swooping sensation of falling.

Possessed by the need to shake off the longing and loneliness that clung to me like an infection, I picked my way back down the stairs and grabbed the pee bucket from the deck. I filled it carefully with water and hefted it up with a grunt. The water sloshed, sending me off-balance. It weighed a lot more than I expected it to. Sweating and panting, I carried it back upstairs. Tiny tidal waves echoed against the plastic.

I set the bucket down and tipped the salt water down the curved slide. The surface still didn't look all that slippery, but I plopped down and pushed off without giving myself time to change my mind.

A surprised *whoop* bubbled out of me, and I grasped at the air helplessly, trying to slow down. The water smacked my whole body at once and rocketed up my nose. I surfaced sputtering and laughing. As I treaded water, a wicked sneeze shot salt and snot out of my face.

"Ew." Skylar bobbed in the rippling waves, inches from my face. Her blue eyes sparkled with silent laughter. "That's disgusting."

I nearly drowned right there. There was nothing to grab on to when my limbs went rigid. Numb with shock, I made myself flail and doggy paddle to the ladder, where I hurried up the aluminum steps. My arms and legs shook so hard, the water sprayed from my skin in shiny flecks. I collapsed onto the deck.

I hadn't thought I was scared of Skylar—even knowing she was dead.

Now I wasn't so sure.

Leia barked relentlessly beside me, and I hesitated to turn around to look back at the water. Since I knew what Skylar really was, would she reveal her true self to me? Would she be rotting, teeth and sinew gaping from her cheeks? Dead. Dead. She was dead.

"I'm sorry," I whispered, loathing my imagination, the way it betrayed her and made her something ugly and frightening when I'd told myself she'd never scare me.

"Brynn."

I buried my face in my arms, flat on my stomach like a baby having a tantrum. The sun hammered down at me, so hot I imagined I could feel every pulse of a solar flare.

"Brynn, please."

A low, weak sob escaped me. Foolishness prickled through me, a sick, hurt sensation. I hated that she'd tricked me. Hated that I thought we could be real friends.

That part was worse than being ashamed for worrying she'd turn into a zombie before my eyes.

"You lied to me," I said.

She didn't answer.

Leia's barking subsided.

I turned in a panic and scanned the surface. In my weakness, I'd lost her. I'd lost my chance. Nothing disturbed the water but the ripples I'd left getting to the ladder.

"Skylar, I'm sorry." My voice sounded small, lost in the wide-open space around us, the water and the birdsong and the distant jet engines. Anger ricocheted back at me. My emotions were Ping-Pong balls scattering and bouncing, and I wished I could grab one. And maybe throw it at her. "I mean, I'm also pissed that you let me believe you were alive."

She burst from the surface a few feet away from me, gaze stormy. "It's not my fault you didn't think any of it was weird. Who lives in the mangroves? In a bathing suit?"

"Why would I think you were dead?" I shouted. "Ghosts aren't real!"

Leia growled, but when I hushed her she sank beside me, panting and whuffing.

Skylar treaded water effortlessly. In fact, her arms and legs weren't even moving. She hovered there, the water lapping at her long neck. I tried not to stare at the eeriness of it as she pressed her lips together and cocked her head. "Yeah?"

I was arguing with a dead girl, and I cared more about being right than her being dead. Maybe the most unreal thing about Skylar was her ability to piss me off and turn me on at the same time.

"Fine. Ghosts are real," I said. "Or—or! I've lost my mind."

"You lost your mind way before you came to Florida, and you didn't see ghosts back then."

"That's exactly what a hallucination would tell me." I sat on the edge of the dock with my feet perched on the ladder. She floated closer, expression careful, like she expected me to kick her in the face. I considered it.

"Do you really think I'm a hallucination?" she asked. The waves lapping at my toes were sad, sad, sad.

I sighed. "No." Leia seemed to see her too, and I didn't know much about dogs, but it seemed unlikely we'd share a hallucination.

The wrinkles at Skylar's brow softened. She offered me a weak smile. "Cool houseboat."

"It has a slide." I wiped away lingering tears. Now that we weren't fighting, relief washed through me, cutting down the hot barrier of anger—and leaving me raw.

And hopeful. But I didn't know what I was hoping for.

Skylar's smile widened. "I saw. Nice moves."

"By *moves*, I assume you mean nice face-plant."

"No one goes down a waterslide gracefully." Skylar bit her lip. "I went down this huge slide at Adventure Island, and my top came all the way off at the bottom. I stood up before I noticed. At least your clothes stayed on."

"That's because this is an industrial strength one-piece." I plucked at one of the stupid ruffles at the hips and tried not to think about Skylar with no top on. Her breasts were little and firm looking, and mine were big and bouncy.

Dead or not, she was still hot. And funny. And magnetic in a way I couldn't place.

And she didn't *look* dead, beyond the faint paleness to her lips I'd chalked up to the chill of the water.

It didn't make sense to treat her differently. Not to me, anyway. I didn't want people to tiptoe around me because I'd had a panic attack in the locker room during PE in seventh grade. It wasn't the same thing—but I got the need to be treated like everyone else. At least in the nice, mostly-being-ignored way.

Although, wanting to have a healthy relationship with a dead friend probably wasn't the best step toward faking being normal.

Skylar was watching me adjust the hem of my bathing suit when I looked back at her.

"You look great," she said.

I snorted. "So you're a nearsighted ghost?"

She rolled her eyes. "Shut up."

"You mean I look great despite not looking like . . ." I gestured at her slender body.

"I meant you look great." She looked me up and down, and then looked away. "You shouldn't shit on yourself like that."

Damn it. She was right.

Other kids called me fat sometimes, and I hated the way they said it. They made it an insult. They meant the shape of my body was my only defining characteristic. I didn't always love my body. But I was strong and my body was healthy, even though my brain tried to derail that as often as possible.

"Do you ever feel crappy about your body even though you know you shouldn't?"

Skylar let out a soft, sad sort of laugh. "Yeah. I mean. Who doesn't?"

"You look perfect to me."

Her expression darkened. "I'm not."

The sun went behind the clouds, and I shivered as cold drops of water ran down my back from my wet hair. "You don't control the weather, do you?"

Skylar's lips quirked. "No, Brynn. I do not control the weather."

I needed her to smile. "Dare me to go down the water-slide again?"

The corner of her mouth twitched into something close enough to a grin. "I sure do."

If she'd been a friend—if she'd been alive—I would have grabbed her hand and dragged her with me. But she stayed in the water, floating there with spooky stillness while I made my way around the deck and up the stairs to the slide. I didn't expect to see her when I looked down—I still expected a moment of clarity, the realization that I was having a mental break.

But there she was, waving at me, yellow bikini dingy under the water.

My journey down the curved slide wasn't any more graceful the second time around. I hit the surface hard, got water up my nose, and sputtered at the surface. Her laughter rang out like wind chimes. I wanted to listen to it forever.

"Real nice. Make the girl from out of town go down the slide so you can laugh at her," I said, laughing too.

"God, it's not that." She giggle-snorted. "It's your face on the way down. You look like you're jumping out of an airplane."

I shuddered, treading water. "I will never jump out of an airplane. Ten feet high on a waterslide is enough free-falling terror for me."

Skylar swam closer, putting very little effort into it. How hadn't I noticed that before? She floated as if the water carried her. My laughter quieted. "Are you always in the water?"

Tendrils of quiet sadness brushed against me as her dark lashes swept down, shading her eyes from my view. "Or my beach. Always."

I shivered, not even kind of used to rubbing up against a dead person's feelings. "Aren't you cold?"

"No." She didn't say it like it was a good thing.

I squinted at the sky. The clouds on the horizon were still nice and far away. I wasn't going to get stranded in a horrible storm this time. "You can't feel the heat either?"

"I don't know." She sank under the water and surfaced. A tight, agitated breath blasted out of her. "I always felt like that. Like I couldn't feel things all the way. I don't know."

"That's okay." I spoke to her the way my mom spoke to me when I lost it in the car and pressed my face against the window to feel the glassy chill. "You don't have to know."

"Why are you so nice to me?" Skylar asked.

Good question.

"I don't have anything against dead people."

She rolled her eyes. And then scrubbed them once. "That's not what I meant. I mean, I'm not very . . ." Her sharp shoulder rose in a shrug. I recognized a flicker of shame in her eyes when she looked away.

"Did you pick me? Like to haunt or whatever."

"I'm not *haunting* you, asshole."

I fought a wave of disappointment. I wasn't special—I didn't mean anything to Skylar. But the universe had decided to show her to me. There had to be a reason.

A wisp of dread nagged at me, but I couldn't put a name to it. It lingered like an itch.

"How did you drown?" I asked. She'd played sports and lived in a place where people probably learned how to swim when they were babies. Had she hit her head or passed out in the water?

Skylar turned her eyes on me with so much intensity I recoiled in the water, sending big swirls at the surface the way fish did when they darted by unseen. Fear crossed her face, and then her gaze went steely. "I didn't drown. I was murdered."

CHAPTER NINE

SKYLAR'S CONFESSION RANG IN my ears.

Murdered. *Murdered.*

Something that happened on TV. Online. Not to people I knew. Not even to dead people I knew. It was too terrible, too much.

"How?" I asked hoarsely, for the first time in my life unable to conjure the specifics of a horrific death. A heavy, wet blanket dampened my thoughts.

Skylar slowly shook her head, her pale lips pressed in a thin line as if she'd glued them together.

"You can't tell me," I said, certain of the abrupt realization. That's how these things worked. Curses. Magic ghost stuff. "Like Ariel not being able to tell hot Prince Eric she really had a tail."

She narrowed her eyes. "I don't have a tail."

"I know, but, like, you know what I mean."

After a long, cloudy silence, Skylar nodded. "I know what you mean."

"I'll figure it out."

She flinched. "You don—"

"It's okay!" I had a purpose now. A way to help her. A reason to believe she was real and really needed me. A curse, or whatever this was, made more sense than the horrific thought of random people getting sucked into a lonely, wet purgatory. She wasn't a product of a severe mental break. She was a murder victim, trapped and seeking justice, and the universe had plopped me into her bayou, where I could save her. Where I could feel her longing and sadness.

Because I understood it.

"I'll figure out what happened," I whispered again.

She watched me, her gaze distant. She probably didn't believe a girl like me could help her. I didn't blame her. I'd already almost gotten myself killed just paddleboarding. She had no reason to be hopeful.

I waited for her to say something—even make fun of me for deciding to solve her murder—but she looked away, and her chest rose and fell sharply with a silent, empty sigh. Then she swam away, slipping under the surface without leaving a ripple.

"I promise," I whispered. If I discovered who'd killed her, maybe the bayou could let her go. I didn't want to think about *where* she'd go, but anything had to be better than being in the water forever.

I climbed onto the deck and watched a distant fish jump and splash. Whoever had left her in the bayou had made it look like an accident.

Left her floating there.

I shuddered. Thinking about it gave me a headache. I didn't believe in heaven. But I secretly hoped that I was wrong—that the moment I died I'd show up in a lovely place with all the people I'd ever cared about.

I hadn't believed in ghosts either. And it still didn't make much sense to me. Why was she the only one? *Was* she the only one? Maybe Florida was a dumping ground for restless spirits.

But I didn't really believe that. We were connected. Not just because I liked her. I'd felt her heavy longing before I'd seen her or heard the bright-sharp-beautiful sound of her voice.

I showered and changed, numb and at a loss. The afternoon passed in a blur of books I couldn't concentrate on. Where would I start? I'd made a promise and I had no idea how to stick to it. Normally Jordan would have helped me look things up. They weren't into the occult, but they loved research. The chase of it. Jordan would have this solved in a few hours. Maybe I would too if I wasn't stuck with zero Internet to consult.

Suddenly, I missed Jordan so much. And now, on top of that, guilt twisted behind my breastbone. It wasn't like I was friend-cheating on them. This was an extenuating circumstance.

But I still felt like a dick.

"Is it that bad?" Dad asked.

I blinked at him, blank to the passage of time, trying to remember what we were talking about. A glob of mac and cheese slid off my spoon and plopped back into the bowl.

"If it's gross, I can make you something else."

We weren't even talking. I'd been staring off into nowhere with a spoonful of noodles slowly congealing. I shoved a bit into my mouth and made an encouraging sound—even though it tasted like wet cardboard. "Thinking about that fish book from Paula," I said with my mouth full. "Lots of fish."

"We can go out again next weekend." His cheeks and nose were still sunburned, and it made him look like a young Santa Claus. My sunburn was more of the incandescent variety—mostly on my thighs. "If we get a keeper, I'll show you how to clean a fish and we can grill out here."

Mmmm, slimy fish guts. I forced a smile. "Okay."

"Paula's going to take you to do some fun, girlie things tomorrow so I can get some work done here on the boat," he said. "You can come to shore with me, and she'll pick you up at the parking lot."

"What kind of work?" Was he making that up? It didn't look like Dad did things like dust or clean grout.

"Some repairs. A little painting." He glanced aside in a somewhat shady way. I figured it had something to do with personal guy stuff or Paula, so I let it go. Plus, I had bigger fish to fry: "What are *girlie things*?"

I wasn't sure what Dad associated with being a girl. He lived on a sad houseboat and worked on a golf course. Girlfriend or not, it wasn't like he spent a lot of time with young women.

Also, gender norms could suck it.

He cleared his throat. "I meant . . . girls doing things. She's going to take you to the library."

I sat up straight, my anger whisked away. "Perfect!"

Paula and I did not share a taste in books, and I needed a fresh batch. But more important, I'd have the chance to do some research on Skylar the old-fashioned way. I needed to read the news about her death. And maybe a school yearbook would have some information on who her friends were. Someone had wanted her dead—a rival? A boyfriend? A maniac stranger who'd killed others the same year?

My pulse drummed a suspenseful backbeat as I tried to keep my breathing steady. Whoever had killed her, I was going to find out. They hadn't only murdered her, they'd trapped her in the bayou forever, dooming her to swim in the same dark water and watch the same wild storms roll in night after night.

Tonight's regularly expected storm abruptly began to lash at the houseboat. Thunder and lightning crashed all around us, but after facing a storm head on, it didn't scare me at all. Even the creaking shudders of waves were better than waiting for a bolt of lightning to strike me dead.

Dad went out once or twice to make sure his little boat was still safely tied up along the floating dock, and Leia whined pitifully on her dog bed by the sliding glass door, but beyond that the storm was nothing more than a rush of background noise—loud, yet softer than the turmoil in my head.

I had to figure out how to get Skylar out of the bayou.

Paula picked me up at the junk lot dock in a little red Honda with sun-faded graduation tassels hanging from the rearview mirror. She played indie rock and smiled shyly at me at every red light.

"I was thinking we could get pedicures before the library," she suggested hesitantly.

Mom got pedicures twice a year—once at the beginning of the summer and once at the middle of the summer. Each visit had something to do with wearing sandals. Part of me had always wanted to at least sit beside my mom in one of the huge massaging recliners, but she'd never asked me over. I'd figured she needed the time away from me. Even if it was only twenty feet.

Normally, I would have been excited to try it with Paula but stopping to get our nails done would take time away from our library trip, and I needed as much time as possible to investigate Skylar's murder.

I opened my mouth to say no but caught the gleam of painful hope in Paula's eyes. "Sure," I lied. "That sounds good."

I tried to look on the bright side of the delay. If anything, this was giving me a chance to see more of the city where Skylar had lived. Maybe it would help me understand what her life had been like.

We pulled into a strip mall with a dry cleaner, a sports bar, a Thai take-out place, and Salon Nails. Paula held the door open for me, and I walked into the bright smell of chemicals and perfume.

I sneezed.

Paula said "Bless you" absently.

She put our names down on a piece of paper at the front desk and showed me where to pick out my color. At home, I had a basket with about fifteen different nail polishes. I liked glitter and obnoxious pink and deep navy blues and grays. The salon had every color imaginable, and I stared at the glossy rainbow, frozen with indecision. I hadn't brought any polish with me, so whatever I picked now would be on my toes for a month. Maybe even the rest of the summer.

My palms went cold.

Tiny choices mattered. They influenced entire days— entire lives. Red-toenails-Brynn would have a completely different day from blue-toenails-Brynn, and I had no way of knowing which color would keep me safe.

I'd gotten better about making decisions and not obsessing over the consequences of them, but Skylar and Florida and my sunburn and the constant pressure of wanting Dad to think I was happy and normal weren't helping. How long could I keep acting normal before the habits and fears that tried to rule me took over?

I see you, intrusive thought.

"Did you pick a color?" Paula asked.

I made a squeaky sound and shook my head.

She ran her hand along the bottles. Her nails were short and painted a faint, shimmering pink. "How about I pick?"

When her fingers skimmed over a bright, canary yellow, my heart skipped several beats. But she didn't pick it. She picked a deep, stormy blue and held it up in the light from the front window. "Like it?"

I did. It was perfect.

The balloon of indecision burst, and I took a clear breath.

"That's a good one," I said. "What's it called?"

She turned it over and laughed once. "Wet Jeans."

"Ew." I plopped into a big leather chair in the waiting area. "Sounds like a recipe for a yeast infection."

Now that I didn't have to make a decision, my nervous system slowed down. I closed my eyes and soaked in the terrible yet totally soothing spa music. We sat in blissful silence. I knew I should ask her polite things—if she had brothers or sisters or pets or hobbies. But the words wouldn't come.

If I got too close to her, would the rift between me and Mom grow deeper?

At some point it would deepen so much I wouldn't be able to cross it. Not with a stretch or a leap. Not with anything.

My stomach began to ache with anticipation, but a woman with a warm smile and long silver earrings beckoned me over. The bizarre sensation of having a stranger touch my feet overpowered the hurt of thinking about Mom.

Pedicures tickled. Horribly. But they weren't the worst—despite the embarrassment of needing the tech to avoid the cut on my toe. The only bad part was watching two women with iPads and unrestricted access to the entirety of Beyoncé's Internet. I wanted to leap out of my chair, splash across the slick tile floor, and rip the tablets right out of their hands. Maybe I could squeeze off a message to Jordan before someone had me arrested.

I sighed.

Paula glanced up from a woodworking magazine. "You okay?"

"I was missing my friend."

"I bet it's really hard being away from home all summer." She spoke like she meant it, so instead of telling her it was fine, I nodded, letting the truth hang between us.

"They're really cool. We do a bunch of things together even though they don't live in my state."

"A lot of my friends from nursing school are travel nurses now, so we have Netflix dates when our schedules line up," Paula said. "It's kind of nice being able to do friend things in my pajamas."

I grinned. It sounded like she got it. More than Mom did, anyway.

When we were done, I had gleaming blue nails. I tipped my nail tech, and she thanked me. I hoped her job didn't suck as much as it seemed like it sucked.

I couldn't think of a single job that sounded un-sucky. Jobs sounded worse than school, despite money being involved. From what I could tell, adults complained about work every day and complained about the weekend being too short and hoarded precious time off and tried to pack as much fun and adventure as possible into two days.

I didn't want to work. I guess that made me lazy.

Paula opened my car door for me. Her nails were teal. "So? What did you think?"

My eyes watered from the bright sun after the serene glow of the nail salon. The library was next on our agenda, and after thirty seconds in the parking lot I was already looking forward to more air-conditioning. But more important, I was looking forward to sneaking online.

"I liked the hot water and the hot towels around my feet at the end," I said, angling the air vents toward my face. "Five stars. Would pedicure again."

I wiggled my toes. They gleamed like jewels. Mermaid toes. If mermaids had toes. The nail tech had carefully trimmed every shred of dead skin from around them, and she hadn't chastised me for the extra dead skin at my pinkie toes where I picked them relentlessly while reading books or watching TV.

"I know it's odd," Paula was saying as she started the car, "but I like the cheese grater part the best."

"I didn't let them do that." I shuddered.

No one in the salon had squirmed or cried while having their dead heel skin shaved right off their bodies, but I couldn't help thinking it must hurt. At least a little. What if the technician slipped? Surely feet had important arteries in them. One wrong sweep and I would have bled out into the bright-blue water swirling around my ankles. No thanks.

"You don't need it." Paula pulled out into the main road. "Your skin's still growing, not aging."

"That doesn't sound like an actual thing."

"Maybe not officially. But think about it. We grow and grow until we achieve our target age. And everything after that is downhill."

"Decay," I said.

She glanced at me. "Yes, exactly."

The radio filled the silence that unfurled. I couldn't tell if she thought I was strange or if she felt the same, quick bubble of kinship. People who never thought about death and loss troubled me. Paula seemed to recognize that we were all tumbling toward the end. Even someone like me who supposedly still had baby skin.

We pulled into the North Community Library lot and parked under a sprawling oak tree. "I know it doesn't look like much, but it's a great branch."

I agreed with her assessment; North Community Library looked like an old office building. But at least it wasn't in a strip mall. Most of Florida was made up of a Tetris-like tangle of strip malls, from what I could tell.

When we walked in, the library revealed itself like a performer exiting a cake. Surprise! It contained plenty of crowded bookshelves, rich with the scent of dry paper and printer ink and rubber stamps. In middle school, libraries had been prisons. I was forced to visit one after another to complete tedious research papers using some ass-backward version of the Internet. Once I didn't have to use libraries for school, I realized they were the literal best thing ever.

Free.

Books.

What wasn't to like?

But I couldn't let my book excitement distract me from my mission. Middle school research papers had taught me how to use the archives in a public library, and now I had to put those skills to use.

And maybe sneak onto a browser, log into my Gmail account, and tell Jordan that I wasn't dead.

And also maybe beg them to email me recaps of our favorite shows in case I made it back to the library again during the summer.

And probably also ask them to log in and turn off my Tumblr queue so Mom didn't freak out, thinking I was somehow still posting.

But first, I had to lose Paula.

"I'm gonna go find some stuff to read."

"What do you like to read? I need something new!"

So much for a brilliant excuse to go off on my own.

Paula liked reading epic fantasy books, so we spent nearly an hour drifting through the new releases, comparing book covers and reading the jacket copy of one crinkly new library binding after another. She liked intricate magic systems, and I preferred Japanese manga about sports players with secret monster-fighting alter egos. We sat on the thin carpet and amassed two piles of books to check out.

"Wait, can I even check out books?" I asked. "I don't have a Florida permit."

"I'll check out your books with my card. We can fib that we're related."

She said it like it didn't mean a thing and kept skimming through the book she was debating borrowing. A curl of warmth tickled through me. We weren't really family, but she was treating me like that. Sharing parts of herself. Taking me to do fun things. Talking to me like I wasn't a baby.

Guilt followed the warmth. Mom was at home, probably worrying about me, and I was hanging out with my dad's girlfriend. And liking her. A lot.

"I told my grandmother I'd pick up a few biographies for her," Paula said. "You good by yourself while I browse?"

I patted my pile of books. "I think I can keep myself busy." As soon as she rounded the corner, I left my pile behind and hustled toward the newspaper archives. Except I couldn't find any newspaper archives, and I wasn't even sure what I was looking for. If this were a movie, the newspapers would be in a dark room with weird light-up microscope things for reading old papers. Nothing in this library looked like that. It was mostly new shelving units, banks of computers, and overstuffed, bright-orange beanbags.

"You look lost."

I whirled at the sound, startled—even though the voice was soft, like a reed instrument. A skinny boy wearing way too many layers for summer pointed at the information desk sign above him. "I mean . . ." He swallowed audibly, and his lanky neck moved with it. "I work here. If you need help."

My belly did the flitter-flop thing it did when someone fell into the unpredictable Venn diagram of my crush criteria. Big, gentle, brown eyes. Natural hair scattered in every direction, and deep-brown skin. He pushed his glasses up his nose with his palm, and I looked away quickly, feeling a blush crawl across my face. "I was looking for the newspapers."

"Um. Like archives?" I nodded and watched his hands fidget. "They're actually on the computer," he said. "I can show you if you want."

The computer.

Of course.

I tried to act cool while I jogged alongside his long-legged steps as he led me to the computers. The system wasn't that complicated. One of the desktop icons led to a newspaper archive portal. I selected the local paper from the drop-down and halted.

He was still there. Watching me.

Watching me attempt to creep on a dead kid.

"I'm Brynn," I said, hoping to drive him away with my awkwardness. That was usually how it went. Especially if I thought someone was cute.

"Logan." He wore a T-shirt with a cat on it, a cardigan over that, and skinny jeans with purple sneakers. A volunteer badge sticker curled at the edges, like it was trying to jump off his chest. I wanted to grab his hand, pull him behind the shelves, and kiss him. The urge intensified the slow burn at my cheeks.

Once a month my hormones made me extra horny, and apparently I was directing every ounce of that toward this poor librarian who only wanted to do his job. And maybe this time it was even worse because of Skylar.

Humans got extra horny when confronted with death. According to my mom, anyway.

She'd explained that to me once when we'd watched a superhero movie and a guy and a girl had started making out while still bloodied and scratched up—which had been disgusting and unsanitary and a little bit awesome.

"Great, well. I'll be Internetting now," I said, letting my voice take on the dismissive tone girls used with me when I hovered by them in the hallway trying to be a person who talked to people.

Logan adjusted his glasses again, but not quickly enough to hide a puzzling flash of hurt I didn't have time to parse. I had sleuthing to do.

He headed back to the information desk, and I stroked the keyboard absently, the pads of my fingers mapping out the familiar landscape. My chest swelled with so much joy I thought I might cry right there in the library. Mom thought being online was bad for me, but that was hypocritical. She spent as much time online as I did. Updating Facebook, messaging her friends. Didn't she understand how important it was to measure out thoughts and words with control? It was so much better than trying to trust my brain to connect to my mouth without spitting out something idiotic.

The fury I'd packaged up and left somewhere deep in my bowels returned with a crampy vengeance.

Somewhere along the way, I'd stopped thinking of Florida as complete torture. But that didn't mean I had to forgive Mom.

She'd taken everything from me.

When my cursor hovered over the browser, my email and *Jordan* a few clicks away, my hand locked up.

I'd made a promise. A promise even rage couldn't shatter.

Logging into my personal email wouldn't be like sneaking away from the houseboat on the paddleboard. Mom had been sobbing, snot-nosed and wild-eyed, and she'd raised her hand like she'd wanted to hit me. She'd tugged at her own hair instead. The sound she'd made had been ugly and wet. The sound of a frightened animal. I'd promised her then, again and again, that I'd take a break like she wanted me to. That I'd stay offline for the summer.

Mom would never know if I disobeyed her, but I'd know forever. I didn't need another failure weighing me down and making it harder to look her in the eye.

Searching for Skylar on a library archive system didn't count as disobeying Mom. I wasn't sneaking online for whatever unhealthy gratification my mom thought the Internet gave me. I was doing it for Skylar. I was doing it alone.

I started typing. The click-tap of the keyboard was a lullaby, gentling the hurt of being so close to Jordan and still an impossible chasm away.

Her name made everything real. The sharp angles of the letters made me sit up a little straighter.

Skylar McKenzie.

Missing Volleyball Star Found Dead.

My breath sucked in with a hiss. Missing. So she hadn't been out with someone or fallen out of a boat in front of witnesses. At least, not according to what the public knew. I clicked on the next link, this one from a few days before.

Search Continues for Missing Teen.

Three days. It had taken three days from the report of Skylar going missing to the discovery of her body. I recoiled from the screen at the sight of my dad's name in the next article. "'Local groundskeeper Hunter Costa discovered the body of a Caucasian female near Weedon Island Preserve. While a positive identification has not yet been made, authorities believe it is the body of missing teen Skylar McKenzie,'" I read out loud, my voice hoarse.

She smiled at me from the page, her hair dry and curled in big, ironed waves. A spacey school picture background gleamed behind her. This was her yearbook photo. She'd been like me, going to school. Thinking about college and starting her grown-up life.

Grieving Parents Announce Memorial Scholarship. I memorized their names. Jonathan and Patricia McKenzie—a personal injury attorney and a real estate agent—both of them polished and bright in their professional headshots, and drawn and blurry with sadness in the candid shots from a press conference about Skylar.

Nothing explained why she'd been out in the water alone in a bikini. I wanted to grab the computer and shake it. Had everyone been so blinded by grief that they hadn't noticed how strange it was for a girl to be found all alone in the water?

I should have tried to get more information out of Skylar before doing this. I needed to know if she'd been sunning at the beach, hanging out at a bar with older kids, out on a speedboat, or paddling by herself. Had she driven to the shore? Had she walked? What had happened to her clothes?

The next headline caught my eye, and I had to read it four times before it sank in.

Missing Teen's Death Ruled Suicide.

I recoiled from the computer, covering a gasp with clammy fingers. The words were so ugly and stark.

"No," I mumbled. "She wouldn't."

She wouldn't have done that. She wouldn't have lied to me.

Nausea hit me like a shift in atmospheric pressure. I pressed my fingertips against my cheekbones and exhaled slowly, breathing through the waves of prickling heat. There had to be an explanation. I had to calm down. I didn't have time to curl up in a ball on a beanbag and cry until my thoughts stopped racing.

The people who'd investigated and written that awful article didn't know Skylar the way I did. I knew the truth. Because Skylar had told me herself.

Murder.

"Okay," I whispered, willing myself to stop trembling.

I'd seen enough procedural TV shows with my mom to know that crime scene people or coroners or whatever really knew their shit. So there had to have been a pretty good reason for them to make a huge mistake. And that meant . . .

I forgot how to breathe for a second. This wasn't an accident or something that had happened in the heat of the moment. Whoever had killed Skylar had gone out of their way to make it look like she'd died by suicide. No one was trying to solve Skylar's murder because no one knew the truth.

"There you are!" Paula said, causing my soul to briefly leave my body.

I turned and forced a casual *I'm not sneaking* smile. She had my pile of books and hers, and they barely fit in her arms. I stumbled out of the chair to help, so eager to distract her I forgot to close out of what I was looking at. But she didn't glance at my screen suspiciously the way Mom always did. She didn't even seem to notice I'd been on the computer. Maybe she had no idea about Mom's ban and Dad's agreement to keep me offline for the summer.

My heart was beating so hard, it felt like it was going to vibrate right out of my chest like some body-horror anime.

I wanted to crawl under the desk forever, never having to think about how a real murderer had gotten away with killing Skylar.

"Good news!" Paula smiled hugely. "They said you could have your own card. They just need to scan your driver's license."

I fumbled with my bag, fingers numb. "I have my student ID. Will that work?"

"Let's find out!"

At the information desk, Logan spent a long time scrutinizing my floppy high school student ID. It gave me time to catch my breath. "Cincinnati?" he asked in a mumble.

"Usually. I mean, always. I'm only here for the summer."

Paula glanced at me, her grin more crooked than usual. I wasn't sure what that meant, so I frowned back at Logan, hoping my lack of a driver's license wasn't going to result in a lack of things to read on Dad's boat. I really needed distractions, now that I was sure a for-real murderer was on the loose.

Logan handed me a newly laminated library card and a skinny card with a hole in it for sticking on a key chain. His nails were super short, nibbled down to ragged edges.

"I don't need that one," I said, trying to hide how badly my hands were shaking. "I don't have keys with me. I don't even think the boat locks."

Logan gave me a long, owlish look. "You live on a boat?"

"A houseboat. I mean, it's more like a barge. I'm not even sure it moves on its own."

"It moves," Paula said. "Hunter brings it in for water and gas for the generator and propane."

The three of us drifted into awkward silence until I patted my pile of books. "I'll take these. Not *take them*. Borrow them."

"Check them out," Logan said. He scanned each quickly with a handheld scanner, which chirped enthusiastically.

I pictured him branding it like a laser gun and said, "*Pew! Pew!*"

His furrowed gaze slowly rose to my face, and I blushed.

The computer spat out a receipt with the due date, and Logan tucked it into one of the books. "Did you need anything printed from the newspaper archives?"

"Newspaper archives?" Paula asked.

The blush on my face became a livid rash of embarrassment. "I was looking up Dad," I said weakly. Logan's eyes flashed up at me, and I met his gaze with my best attempt to psychically convey that he needed to shut up.

He cleared his throat and nodded. "I look up everyone I know when I'm bored. Turns out my English teacher is also a world-class shuffleboard player. And my super-old next-door neighbor worked for the circus for sixty-five years."

"I don't know my neighbors' last names. I mean, in Cincinnati. My current neighbors are mullet."

I didn't even know most of my neighbors' first names. Did they know me?

Would they look me up if I disappeared?

Would they care?

Logan said nothing, probably thinking I was bizarre for talking about the fish in the bayou like they were real neighbors. A wave of melancholy struck me. I shoved a stray curl behind my ear and studied the ugly laminate counter.

Paula slid her books over to Logan and dropped her library card on top of the pile. "These are mine. Nothing like a summer reading marathon."

Logan began scanning them. "For sure. It's too hot to go outside."

Despite having discovered a horrible clue and nearly being caught creeping on Skylar's news stories, my heart still tripped giddily with recognition of a kindred spirit. I liked Logan—exquisitely cute volunteer librarian with a healthy distrust of Florida heat. If I was living a normal life, I'd be back here tomorrow, checking out more books for the chance to check him out.

"What do you like to read?" Paula asked, confident and casual, like a normal person talking to a normal person.

"Right now? Biographies. I'm taking AP US History next year, and I figured it'll be more interesting if they seem like real people and not a bunch of—"

"White dudes in white wigs?" I asked.

Logan laughed, and the sound reverberated down my spine. "Basically."

"I'll stick to my fantasies." Paula scooped up her pile and cradled it to her chest lovingly. "My brain is still burned out from nursing school."

"I get it," I said. Mom read true crime novels with silhouettes and shadows on the covers. We all had our own fandoms. Although, spending the summer reading boring history sounded terrible to me. I'd figured Logan for someone buried in Tolkien.

Another patron got in line behind us, so Paula thanked Logan, I mumbled something between a goodbye and a thank you that sounded more like a caveman rumbling, and we headed off.

Was my search screen still open, or had a screen saver taken over—preserving Skylar's privacy? I wanted to run back inside, close it out, and sneak one last look at her photo. It felt like walking away from her all over again. In the newspaper archives, she was real. She'd existed. Back on Dad's bayou, she'd be a ghost again—a ghost who wasn't giving me the facts I needed. Not yet, anyway.

A quiet, terrible ripple of fear lapped at me. What if the murderer had some way of knowing that I'd been snooping?

There was no way. Probably.

I shuddered as we stepped into the parking lot. The black asphalt kicked up waves of heat that stung my legs, and I started boob-sweating like it was my job.

Paula's car unlocked with a *bleep-bloop* sound, and she looked at me over the roof of it. "Cute, huh?"

"What?" My ears were ringing. It took me a moment to remember where we were.

"That boy at the library." She gave me a knowing grin, and I realized she'd attributed my shuddering to swooning and not despairing.

I didn't have to try too hard to force a smile, despair and all. "Yeah." A pang of guilt hit me, though. Was it possible to cheat on a ghost?

The ride back was quiet. Paula played the radio softly, and I pretended to read the back covers of each book I'd checked out. The injustice of Skylar's death made me want to scream. Someone had been careful and cruel enough to set her up, to make everyone think she'd done something she hadn't.

No wonder she was stuck in the bayou. She was waiting to be avenged. I had to fix this, no matter what. I had to find the truth—and set her free.

CHAPTER TEN

THE TIDE WAS LOW when we pulled back into the lot. I'd learned to recognize it by the rings of barnacles and oysters around the dock pilings. While Paula tucked her books into a tote bag and reapplied lipstick in her visor mirror, I walked over to the seawall and looked down, half expecting to see something yellow shimmering under the water.

A putrid smell struck me and I stumbled back, but not before I spotted a fat, bloated catfish bobbing on the surface. Its pale-white belly snagged on the sharp oysters, torn open and spilling slimy guts. Milky blue-white eyes stared at me, empty and bulging.

The books tumbled out of my hands and my knees struck the rocky ground hard. I swayed too quickly to catch myself, swimming in nausea. Paula rushed to my side and put her hand on my shoulder, but it was too late. The connections sparked together in my mind, and I couldn't un-see the graphic images my imagination had supplied.

Skylar.

She'd drifted on the tide like that, dead. Dead and rotting. Distended. Full of gases that made her body rise to the surface. And she wasn't beautiful and suntanned and sleek anymore. She was dead. Her body turned to ashes or unrecognizable. Gone. Gone. Gone.

I doubled over onto my hands and knees and retched. A vile mix of breakfast cereal and milk splashed onto the rocks between my hands, narrowly missing the books. Paula made clucking sounds and rubbed my back, but she was a million miles away. I was alone here, twisted up in the vision of Skylar—my friend. Skin gone wrong and shiny. Eyes glassy and unseeing.

She was dead.

"Brynn. Honey. Breathe through it; you're doing great." Paula pounded on my back with her palm like I was choking.

I sat back on my heels, wiped my mouth on my arm, and started to cry. I didn't have the energy to crawl away from the puddle of sick, get up, ask for water, or do anything but moan out unhappy, wet sounds.

She'd been smart and energetic and strong and someone had taken her life and the water had ruined her, reduced her to nothing but an empty, ugly thing floating on the surface. Frightening my dad.

Haunting me.

Trapped.

"It's not fair," I sobbed out.

Paula was stronger than she looked. She got her hands under my armpits and hauled me up to drag me back to the passenger seat of her car. I struggled to focus on her, on the towel she was pushing into my hands. When my watery gaze finally settled on her face, her expression was gently stern. Professional. This was Paula the nurse, and she didn't mess around.

"Are you pregnant?" she asked very quietly.

An ugly snort tore out of me. "Oh God, no. I haven't even had sex. Ever."

Her shoulders softened, and she let out a loud breath. "I figured Hunter would have told me, but then I thought maybe you hadn't told him, and you're so young. Not that I'd judge you. But I wouldn't wish any of that on a girl your age. And I'm babbling now."

I smiled a wobbly smile and wiped my nose. "A little bit." My mouth tasted the way Mom's latte cups smelled when she accidentally left them in the car all day.

Paula crouched in front of me, holding on to my knees for balance. Her gaze drifted to her hands, and she grabbed the car door instead, making a soft, apologetic sound. "Do you want to talk?"

I hadn't thrown up in a long time, it kept repeating in my mind, making me shake—guaranteeing that I'd add this to my list of things to worry about doing in front of people. I scrubbed my mouth with the towel and tried to clear my head.

"It's probably food poisoning, right?" I asked, desperate for her to attribute this to something other than my failure to be normal.

"I'm not ruling out a stomach bug, but you looked freaked out. You can talk to me, you know. Or I can call your dad and get him to hurry and pick us up. Or he can take you to a walk-in clinic. Whatever you want to do."

I wasn't used to having so many options presented to me at once. Mom always had a game plan, and I went along with it because that's what I was supposed to do.

"Um."

None of these options were going to make Skylar not dead. And I couldn't tell Paula or my dad that I was crying over a girl who'd died when I was a kid.

"My vote is talking," she prompted gently. "Unless you think you're going to hurl again. In which case, my vote is going over to the dock to wait for your dad. There's a hose." She spoke softly, a little playfully. A faint sheen of sweat lit her face, though, beading the makeup at her upper lip.

I'd scared her.

"I saw a big, dead fish," I said, willing to mete out a little of the truth so she'd stop asking me to talk. "It bugged me out."

"I thought you went fishing with your dad a few days ago." A suspicious little furrow formed between Paula's brows. "Didn't you see dead fish then?"

"I didn't kill any fish!" Bile rose in my throat and I coughed, willing it back. "I don't like dead things."

"You're not alone in that. We had to work on cadavers at school, and I passed out the first week. Twice. The second time I had to get stitches." She lifted her bangs and showed me a faint scar at her hairline. "Smacked right against the side of the worktable on my way down."

I grimaced. "Not sure that's helping." But it was. Somehow. Her voice carried me out of the fog of what I'd imagined, and now she was close and real, and it was a million miles away.

"No one likes dead things." Paula's voice was serious until a smile twitched at the corner of her mouth. "Except zombies, I guess. And serial killers. You're not either of those, I assume, so it's completely normal to get freaked out. And you didn't grow up around the smell of low tide in the summer."

"You won't tell Dad?" I asked, hating how small my voice sounded.

Paula glanced out at the bayou, troubled. "I'd have to tell him if I was concerned for your health or safety. But I don't think I need to tell him that you got sick over a dead fish. Unless you think I should."

"If I throw up any more, I'll ask him to take me to the doctor," I said. "I promise. I hate throwing up more than anything."

"You sure about that?" Paula's lopsided grin was back. She was already onto my encyclopedic list of hated things, but she wasn't making fun of me.

She didn't care about my flaws, and that made me wonder what hers were. Everyone was like bruised fruit, deep down. Nice to look at, but soft and broken in places.

Another hysterical, quiet laugh erupted from my throat. "I can't believe you asked me if I'm pregnant." Maybe her flaw was a lack of filter.

She slapped my knee playfully. "Shut up! Do you have any idea what teen pregnancy rates are like in this country?"

"They're not as bad as they used to be. Sex education is working. Or people are spending more time online than canoodling." That's what Mom said, anyway, while cheerfully reminding me that kids were starting to figure out exactly how much they had to lose by having intercourse.

Although, I had the entire Internet at my disposal, so it wasn't like I was unaware that even oral would probably give you a cancer-causing virus. Everything about sex sounded like a hot mess to me. Especially right now, with my mouth tasting like steaming garbage and a corpse-fish still out there bobbing against razor-sharp oyster shells.

Except.

Even now, part of me wondered what the good parts of sex were like. The parts where someone like Logan would find the places where I wanted to be touched. The parts where I'd put my hands-mouth-fingers on someone like Skylar.

I wiped my nose. *Not Skylar. Never Skylar.*

"Honey, you're thinking so loud it's making my head hurt."

"Like, in a metaphorical way, or in a my-dad's-dating-a-telepath way?" I was only half kidding. If ghosts were real, how could I rule out superpowers?

Paula laughed. "Your dad told me you were great, but I didn't know what to picture other than a little girl. You're a lady."

I cringed.

"All right, all right. A person? Wow, there's no non-weird way to say that, is there?"

"Not really." When I hazarded a deep breath, it didn't come with any shaky sounds or puke feelings. I gave Paula a weak smile. "We can call Dad to come get me now. I'm sorry I scared you."

"Don't be sorry about that." She offered me her hand and left me leaning against the side of her car while she retrieved the books, sidestepping the horrible puddle of vomit I'd left in the gravel. A seagull swooped down at it the moment she got out of the way, and another followed behind, letting out a joyous *caw*.

"Well. That's the grossest thing I've ever seen," I said. Puke-eating birds. Florida continued to sink to new lows. Maybe I'd been too quick to downgrade it to *not the utter worst*.

"Oh my God. Don't watch." Paula looked away, giggling.

We stood together in the sun, and I turned my face up to it, letting it paint the backs of my eyelids hot pink. I was going to grow a million new freckles on this trip. The sun's radiation was probably planting the seeds of future devastating and disfiguring skin cancer, and I'd end up with gruesome scars on my face or a missing ear, but in this moment I couldn't bring myself to fan the flames of my fears.

I wanted the sun to bleach me clean for a few minutes— to clear my mind of Skylar and cute librarians and scary, sticky sex and murderers and ugly, dead fish and my dad dating a cool chick and my mom at home getting pedicures by herself.

My dad's boat buzzed toward us, and all I could think about was him finding Skylar—and believing what the newspaper said about her.

I had to fix this.

CHAPTER ELEVEN

FOR TWO DAYS, DAD stayed on the houseboat. I muffled the vibrating anxiety in my bones by reading my library haul of manga. I read on the roof of Dad's boat under the shade of a bright-teal umbrella. I read in bed, my thin mattress crinkling below me. I read at the breakfast table and with a peanut butter and jelly sandwich in one hand and over dinner with my dad giving me furtive, bemused looks.

The alternative was exploding with the need to continue my investigation.

Whenever I wasn't reading, Skylar came rushing into my head, whispering to me like gentle rain at the tail end of a summer storm. I pressed my forehead to the window in my bedroom, my breath fogging the glass and the oil from my face leaving a smear. In the distance, the mangroves were green bruises on the skyline.

I could feel her out in the water. It was like the itch of a scab about to fall off. Worry. Waterlogged sadness. I was used to these feelings, but usually they belonged to me. Not someone else.

She was out there. Waiting for me? Avoiding my dad? Avoiding *me*?

I had so much to ask her. I needed to know if she felt the passage of time, if she talked to anyone else. I needed to know if she made me feel things on purpose, or if her sadness bled out of her like a hemorrhage. I needed to know who killed her, but she couldn't tell me the truth—even if she knew. The shadowed look in her eyes had told me everything I needed to know. It was a secret. A secret only I could uncover.

With nothing to pull me away from my spiraling thoughts, I pictured her death. A paddle to the back of her head, a brick weighing her down, strong hands thrusting her below the surface while the water churned with her desperate struggle. My heart beat sick-fast when I thought about her last moments, of her fear and confusion and the awareness of oblivion an empty breath away.

That's what I hated thinking about the most. Oblivion. Nothing. Forever. As unfathomable as the universe around us stretching endlessly, impossibly big, horrible, terrifying. One of my therapists had suggested I recall the time before I was born, and when I'd made a face at her and told her I couldn't remember the time before I was born, she'd reminded me that I hadn't been aware or lonely or frightened. The worst-case scenario was that death was exactly that—a lack of awareness. But I didn't take comfort in that, because it still seemed like nothing. A chasm. An eternity.

Being alive scared the shit out of me most of the time, but being dead would be so much worse.

"But you're not nothing," I whispered to the quiet mangroves. "You're still here."

Dad and Paula asked me to go with them to a matinee at the movies, and I complained of a stomachache to get out of it. Paula took me aside while Dad went to the bathroom, asking me if I was okay in a super-significant tone that probably meant she wanted to make extra sure I wasn't carrying some cute librarian's baby.

So I told her the truth: "I want to be by myself for a little while. Please."

"I get that." The toilet flushed with a loud *pop-whoosh*. I still wasn't used to the violence of a boat toilet. She glanced at the door and looked back at me with a private smile. "I wouldn't mind some alone time with your dad."

"Gross." I pictured them cuddling, or worse—making out in the theater.

She laughed, the sound a warm comfort. Dad gave me a big, lingering hug, and they took off on the little boat, leaving behind a stream of frothy water like a contrail across the dark bayou.

Finally.

My body went hot and cold. I paced on the fake grass, waiting for the right moment—when I was sure they were gone and weren't coming back for a while.

"Skylar McKenzie!" Her name burst out of me like a thunderclap. Leia barked twice, tail wagging. The empty expanse of water around us carried my voice into the distant mangroves. We might as well have been in the void of space. "Skylar! I know you're there."

"You don't know I'm here," she said. "Isn't that the problem?"

I spun on the floating yard and nearly pivoted right off the edge. She bobbed there, smiling brightly, lashes wet, hair tight against her head—cheerful as an otter at the zoo. My legs lit up with goose bumps and my muscles forgot how to function. I sat down hard and the breath rushed out of me with a *whoosh*.

"I looked you up at the library," I gasped out.

Her pale, long arms undulated, but I was pretty sure she didn't need to tread water to stay afloat. "Couldn't you just use your phone?"

"I'm banned from phones. And the Internet. Thus, the library."

Her smile faded like a dimmed light. "What did it say about me?"

"It said you died." I glared at her, angry that someone had killed her—and stuck with no target but her face.

She rolled her eyes. "Spoiler alert."

I hesitated for a moment, not wanting her to know that no one had sought justice for her death. "It didn't say you were murdered. It said you died by suicide."

Her gaze flickered down, and the water lapped at her chin as she sank lower, like a child hiding under the covers. "No one knows the truth."

My breath blew out in a gust. "So why can't you tell me who did it? I can make sure everyone finds out what really happened."

The water covered her mouth.

I resisted the urge to dive in after her and kill her all over again. "Skylar, this is stupid. Just tell me."

"I can't," she said. Water flowed out of her mouth as she spoke. I shivered.

Did she breathe? Was the water part of her? I pictured it flowing through her veins instead of blood. Maybe that's why her lips were always pale.

"Are there ghost rules?"

"What the fuck are ghost rules, Brynn?"

"You tell me! Is there some magic shit going on? Did you get killed by—I don't know—like, a demon?" My voice softened, sympathetic. "Did it curse you?"

Skylar huffed out a wet laugh, breaking the eerie spell. Now she was a girl again, lost in the water. Uncomfortably sexy. "You watch too much TV."

Embarrassment flooded my blood vessels like sparks and my voice got a little shrieky. "Really? Is this TV's fault? Because last time I checked, most dead people didn't stick around. Eternally."

"And when's the last time you checked?"

"People die all over the place! You're the only ghost I've ever seen."

Her shoulders went angular with a sharp little shrug. "Are you sure?"

"You're being obtuse on purpose, and it sucks!" I yelled. "I'm trying to help you, but you won't answer my questions. And you're messing with my head. And I don't even know if you're real—"

"I'M REAL!" she shouted.

I sucked in a big breath, ready to bellow back at her, fired up with the heat of an argument and all the tension that blasted out of me with my anger. But she started to cry, and that ruined everything.

It felt like someone disconnected all the bones in my body. I rocked forward onto my hands and knees. "Skylar . . ."

"I'm real." She closed her eyes, and tears ran down her face. She hiccupped. "I'm real. I'm real."

The water rippled around her. I hated it. It didn't make sense. Dead girls shouldn't displace water. Or cry.

My stomach went echoey and cold. Mom's bloodshot eyes were at the edge of my awareness. The rawness of her voice. Her despair. "Don't cry," I whispered.

I was still wearing a ratty pair of sweatpants and a tank top from the night before. Rolling the soft gray cotton up my legs, I exposed my pale calves and the spiky, dark hair that shadowed my sunburned skin from giving up on shaving in the tiny bathroom. I sat on the edge of the dock, and she swam up to me and put her face against my leg, holding on to it like she'd sink into the depths forever if she let go.

Her skin was ice, but her grip was soft and strong. I pushed my fingers into her tangled, wet hair and stroked her head while she sobbed against me, saying the same thing over and over.

"I'm real."

"I know," I said, bracing myself against her despair. It blanketed me, not mine but so heavy. "I know."

Her breath hitched, and she pressed her marble-smooth forehead against my shin and whispered, "I'm sorry."

I got my bathing suit on in a hurry, trying not to think too hard about how weird it was that I'd asked a dead girl to wait outside—in the water—while I changed clothes. Already peeling from my last burn, I slathered on so much sunscreen I felt like a basted turkey by the time I returned to where she treaded water.

She was watching me like she expected me to disappear. Eager and scared at the same time.

"I'm not the dead one, you know." I stood at the edge of the floating dock, my freshly painted toes wiggling where the fraying fake grass poked at me. "I'm not going anywhere."

"You will. You'll go home." Skylar reached out to pet Leia at the edge of the dock, but Leia shied away with a high whine and sat down out of reach. "You'll leave."

My breath thinned out as anxiety crept along my skin, reminding me that Dad wouldn't want me in the water by myself.

I focused on Skylar. I wouldn't be alone. She'd warn me if there was danger.

She'd dared me to go off on my own. She made me brave.

"I'm not going to leave you here," I vowed.

I did a cannonball and kept my legs tucked tight against my middle so my feet wouldn't accidentally touch the slimy, grassy bottom. When I came up for air and treaded water, she was right in front of me.

A shiny oil-slick of sunscreen pooled around me, filmy on the surface.

"Sure," Skylar said. "You'll never leave. You'll tell your dad you have to stay in Florida so your dead friend won't be sad."

I didn't mean to blurt it out, but the memory was still so strong that it clawed right past my throat before I could swallow. "He found you."

She didn't pale. Not exactly. But something changed in her eyes, like a shudder that ran through her entire soul. "What?"

"My dad was the one who found you. I told him your name, and he freaked out and got super mad because he thought I was messing with him."

"What did he see?" she asked in a hoarse whisper.

"I didn't ask." That was private. And terrible. What I imagined was bad enough.

She swallowed hard, but the tension around her eyes eased. "Maybe that's why I'm not invisible to you. A connection or something."

"I don't want to talk about it anymore if you're not going to help me solve your murder." I tried to cross my arms stubbornly, but that made me sink.

"It's not like I don't *want* to help," Skylar said, shoving me gently under the water.

I laughed at the tickle of her touch, and Skylar grinned, a hairpin turn from her sadness. As much as it exasperated me, I related to her emotional shifts. We could be Ping-Pong balls together, never settling on one feeling for too long—especially not the awful ones.

"I believe you," I told her.

"So what are we going to do?" she asked.

"We're kind of limited to how far I can swim," I said, already out of breath.

"No way, you're strong. Come on." Without waiting for me to agree, she cut through the water, graceful and quick.

Nothing about following her made any sense, but I did it anyway. I wanted to be near her. I wanted to show her I was tough. Focused on the churn and splash of her feet, I breathed through my fear of the unknown right under my soft belly. Feverish worry tickled my skin, muffled by the physical exertion that kept me focused on the present.

I swam surely and quickly, keeping up with her long strokes through the water. My heart beat hard and I breathed raggedly, lit up with the soreness of exercise without any of the mind-numbing boredom of actually exercising.

Then my knee struck something soft and I screamed, swallowing a mouthful of briny water in the process.

I was starting to get used to the tinkling-bright sound of Skylar's laughter. "Jesus, Brynn. It's a sandbar. It's not attacking you."

Squishy, wet sand cupped my knees like a foam mattress. The water came up to my boobs, and it rushed around me. The outgoing tide had been carrying me away from the boat the whole time. No wonder I'd gone so fast.

"This is like an underwater beach?" I asked, rubbing my stomach where anxiety tried to rush me back to the boat.

"Basically. It's a nursery for sea life."

"Baby sharks?" My voice squeaked.

"More like minnows and horseshoe crabs." She snorted. "Weirdo."

"Baby sharks have mom sharks, that's all I'm saying."

Skylar splashed me. "Pick up some of the sand. Feel it."

I did as I was told, all ticklish inside from the way she sounded so confident. It wasn't sifting, soft sand like the kind in a sandbox. This sand was almost furry, the way it clumped together and oozed around my palm. I played with it, smoothing it out, and the friction of my fingers revealed three tiny shells. They rolled across my palm, tiny and dark green.

"They're baby snails. I think." Skylar leaned in, peering at them. Something had changed. She looked from the shells to my face like a kid showing off a straight-A report card. She glowed. I felt her joy mingling with the now-incandescent glow of my crush on her. "Cool, right?"

I tried to watch the snails and not her mouth. "Are they going to come out and slime me?"

"No. They're probably freaked out that you tore them out of their habitat."

I dropped the snails back into the water like they'd burned me. "Dude! You told me to. I didn't mean to destroy their houses."

She laughed, and the sound swept through me, achingly pretty and so alive. When I leaned forward, it wasn't because I meant to—it was because she pulled me into her magnetic field.

Her laughter died off when my lips touched hers.

We both kept our eyes open, blurry-close and blinking, hers big and blue and startled. One chaste peck in middle school hadn't given me enough practice, so I kept my mouth closed, lips pursed against the slight part of her surprised, cold mouth.

She put her hands on my arms and held me there—didn't push me away. I dared a brush of tongue against her lips, and she tasted briny and wet.

"Brynn."

I closed my eyes, but she stopped kissing me. Her forehead pressed to mine, cold and strong as concrete. "I'm not into girls," she said gently.

"You're not alive either.'"

She shook with a quick, silent laugh. "Seriously, though."

Sighing, I pushed my arms around her and dropped my head to her strong shoulder. My boobs squished up against her chest, but now that I knew it didn't mean anything, it was the kind of hug friends gave each other.

Were we friends?

"I thought you said you didn't crush on everyone you meet," Skylar said, voice soft at my ear.

"I don't." I hardly crushed on anyone at all. Not like this. Not this much. "It's you."

The water lapped against my sides, warm and cold at once. Now that we weren't swimming, I shivered. The hot sun overhead baked my shoulders, but Skylar's cold touch and the water sapped the rest of the heat away.

"I'm sorry I didn't ask before I did that." I knew better, and now the emptiness of rejection mingled with shame for not making sure she wanted me to kiss her.

Skylar pulled away so she could look at my face. "It's okay. I mean, if you need to practice, we can."

I splashed her. "I don't accept pity kisses. Especially from—" The joke withered in my mouth as Skylar flinched, like she expected a blow.

"Dead girls?"

"Sorry." I poked her stony knee under the water. "Not funny."

A loud, wet sigh sounded *behind* me and I screamed, startled right out of my damn mind. I ended up in Skylar's lap, arms squeezed tight around her neck. "What the hell is that?" I sputtered out.

She blew my curls out of her mouth and looked over my shoulder. "Manatees. Looks like a mom and a baby."

An enormous shadow moved under the water. "Oh my God!" I wailed. "It's going to get us."

"They're sea cows. Not orca." She wound her arms around me in a firm hug. "Which, by the way, also don't eat humans."

"They do eat cute baby seals," I mumbled. Her strong grip made me feel safe. Curiosity warred with the urge to attempt to walk on water back to the boat.

A gray snout surfaced with a whooshing breath. It looked like a wet football. When it sank into the water again, a perfectly round swirl appeared behind it. "That's the tail," Skylar said. "It's like a big paddle."

Reasonably sure the manatees weren't going to kill us, I pulled out of Skylar's arms and pushed up to stand so I could get a better look. A smaller shadow—about the size of me— followed alongside the huge shadow. Mother and child sea cow plodding across the bayou, eating slimy seagrass. The big one came up for another breath, and its back rose to the surface too. Stark white scars crisscrossed its leathery hide.

I frowned. "What happened?"

"Props. Boats go too fast on the shallows and hit them. She's lucky it didn't kill her. It's tough to be at the bottom of the food chain, I guess."

She stood next to me, taller. Water cascaded from her arms. I slipped my hand into hers and she didn't pull it away.

"Did a boat kill you?"

"Are we going to play Murder Twenty Questions?"

I squeezed her fingers. "Serious question, though."

"No. A boat did not kill me. And I think that would have been classified as an accident."

"I don't know how people murder each other in Florida. For all I know there are boats and alligators and golf clubs involved all the time."

Skylar laughed. "You're funny," she said, in a way that beamed like sunlight through my chest, instead of making me feel ashamed or self-conscious. I felt the same way when Jordan shared my edits in their rec lists. When smart people said nice things about me, all the voices in my head that said otherwise went away for a little while.

"Can you talk to animals?" I asked.

Skylar snorted. "No. I don't think animals have language."

"If those manatees could talk, they'd be complaining about people probably."

"Pretty much all animals would. Except for dogs and cats, because they're lazy."

The manatees entered deeper water, shadows blending until they disappeared. I listened hard for another blast of breath, but I only heard the distant hum of a boat and the rumble of a jet engine in the distance.

I never wanted this afternoon to end. Maybe this was what summer was supposed to feel like. Hot sun on my shoulders, wet fingers tangled with mine. "Do you have any dogs or cats? I mean, you know, did you?"

"I had a cat. Jeffrey. I'm allergic to dogs."

I knew she didn't have any siblings, because her obituary and the articles about her disappearance only mentioned her parents. Her parents. They had to be reachable. They'd had well-established careers here in St. Pete. Maybe they knew something.

I'd have to find out. But I wasn't going to tell Skylar that. She'd already seemed so distressed when I told her I talked to my dad about finding her. Talking to her mom and dad felt worse. Something more intimate. Worse than a parent-teacher conference.

"What?" she asked, squeezing my hand.

"I was thinking about cat names."

"No, you weren't." Skylar didn't press.

"Did you have a boyfriend?"

"Sometimes. Nobody special."

"You're special," I blurted.

She laughed. "Okay. Sure."

"You must have been really popular."

"I didn't really think about it."

"That means you were popular." Pretty, athletic, confident people probably walked through life in a total state of oblivion. Although Skylar being super popular and carefree didn't really mesh with the sadness that covered her like a second skin.

"I wasn't a weirdo, if that's what you mean." The way she said it, fond and smiling, made me feel proud of being exactly that.

"What'd you do for fun?"

"I had volleyball practice all the time. I studied all the time. I kayaked sometimes and took a lot of naps. I don't know. Normal stuff. I was . . . I meant it about the beach. I used to go out there and make forts when I was in middle school. But I didn't really have time for anything fun in high school."

She abruptly let go of my hand and took a few sloshing, jogging strides to the edge of the sandbar. Before I could ask her what she was doing—if she was running away from my questions—she dove into the water where it darkened. I braced myself for her to disappear into the depths that kept her secret, but she surfaced immediately and looked back at me. "Come on, we better get going before this tide rips any harder."

Whatever that meant, it sounded ominous. Muscles tensing, I followed her, flopping more than executing a shallow dive. It was a strategy of sorts. I'd seen lots of shadowy fish dart away from the paddleboard. My goal was to scare every living, potentially dangerous creature for miles.

Skylar was right about the tide.

My anxiety couldn't get ahold of me, because I was too busy trying to stay above the surface. Every time I looked up to see how close we were to Dad's boat, it looked farther away. The tide pushed me like a strong wind, angling me off course and fighting every stroke.

Skylar swam beside me after a while. "Slow down. It's a marathon, not a sprint."

"You sound like an inspirational poster," I wheezed out.

"Those are bullshit."

Her encouragement helped, though. When I stopped racing the current and took gentle, easy strokes, I made more progress. And my lungs stopped screaming like they were going to hurl right out of my chest. Skylar wasn't out of breath, but she watched me closely.

"Would you be allowed to save me if I drowned?" I asked, each word a choppy sound between ragged breaths.

"I don't know." Her concern brushed at me. I liked the way it felt. "I've never tried to do anything like that."

"Have you tried to talk to other people?"

"No." She spoke softly, sad. "Nobody." If we'd been sitting next to each other I would have reached for her, compelled to make some of that sadness go away. But if I stopped cutting through the water, I'd sink. And the irony of drowning beside a dead girl wasn't lost on me.

I put my head down, face in the water, up for a breath, over and over. My hand struck something solid and I gasped in a mouthful of water, only recognizing the dock in front of my face when Leia began licking my forehead frantically and whining. I'd made it.

It took me a long time to catch my breath.

"You want to see something cool?" Skylar asked.

I didn't. I wanted to flop up onto the dock, dry off in the sun, and possibly throw up, and then sleep forever. But she took off swimming, and I couldn't let her go alone.

My body was a weak blob. I followed slowly as she pushed off from the dock and swam toward the back of the houseboat. I gave the boat a wide berth. The dock didn't scare me, but the underside of the boat did. I couldn't explain why, but the thought of brushing my feet against the bottom of it under the water sent spikes of sick fear through me. And I didn't know where the propeller was. It wasn't currently spinning, but I'd seen what it could do to a manatee's hide— and my skin wasn't thick like that.

I was so busy thinking about all the ways the boat could kill me that it took me a while to see what Skylar was trying to show me.

"I knew he was being sneaky," I said, my voice tight with exertion and laughter. This must have been Dad's boat project while Paula and I had gone for pedicures and books.

Bright blue letters in a flowing script covered the back of the boat over the faded, painted-over words that had been there before. A name. The boat's name. The new name my dad had given her.

Brynn's Tide.

CHAPTER TWELVE

"OKAY, I GIVE UP. What's wrong?" Dad asked around a mouthful of fried chicken he'd brought back to the boat after his date with Paula. "You've been quiet all night."

My fingers were coated in delicious grease and salt, and the chicken had almost been tasty enough to distract me from the nausea of Skylar out there in the dark, in the water, always.

I sighed and wiped my hands on a paper towel. "You named your boat after me."

Dad frowned. "You went in the water?"

"I went swimming. Is that all right?"

"Of course," he said in a way that sounded like *absolutely not*. He spooned a heap of baked beans from a Styrofoam bowl onto his plate and looked across the little galley table at me, gaze troubled. "I didn't think you liked the water here."

I ruined a perfectly good mouthful of chicken by starting to cry.

It came out of nowhere, pathetic and quiet. My head ached, and I'd managed to get a sunburn again, and my dad liked me enough to put my name on a boat even though I hardly ever saw him or talked to him. And when I did talk to him, it was only to give him a false sense of security. Everything hurt, and I couldn't explain why. I didn't want to explain or think about it. I only wanted to cry, but not in front of my dad or on top of my dinner.

I was ruining his whole night. Just like I always ruined things for Mom.

"Sweetheart." Dad squeezed into the booth beside me and put his arm around me. He pulled me close. We hadn't hugged since the first hug at the airport. He smelled Dad-like, and his arms were strong, and I gave up on trying to act like an adult and sobbed onto his chest pathetically, getting snot and tears all over the swordfish on his horrible T-shirt.

"Are you okay? Do you want to call your mom? Can I do anything?" He patted my head, and his voice rumbled against my face.

I sniffled out a laugh. "I'm fine. I'm sorry."

Dad craned his head like an owl, forcing me to meet his eye. "You're not fine, and you shouldn't be sorry."

That made the crying worse, but I smiled a little bit too.

And then opportunity hit me like a laser beam. Dad's concern and unwavering love weren't worn down and jaded like my mom's. I felt marginally guilty for taking advantage of him, but that didn't stop me. No matter how tired and sunburned and emotional I was, I had to focus on freeing Skylar.

"It's that . . . I'm almost sixteen," I said carefully, kind of relieved to blame my meltdown on something reasonable. "I'm having fun, and I had fun with Paula too, but I want to explore a little. Like, the town, not just the boat here and the water. I want to do normal summer things."

Despite his frown, Dad was already cracking. I could see it in the lines around his eyes and the tightness of his mouth. My dad was an adventurer at heart—he'd always been the reckless one, at least according to Mom. He'd sympathize with a desire for freedom.

"I won't go online," I added. "I can take the bus around. Just for a few hours? Like, to the store for tampons and stuff."

When in doubt, I always tossed in a few tampons. It worked pretty well on my gym teacher.

"I can drive you to the pharmacy for anything you need. I need to bring the boat into the marina for water and fuel tomorrow anyway. And we need to keep an eye on Alonzo."

"Uh." I blinked. "Who?"

"The storm?" Dad leaned back a little, breaking our awkwardly intense eye contact. "It's a tropical storm right now, but you never know what they'll do over the gulf."

"No Internet or TV or civilization, remember?" I shivered. Afternoon thunderstorms were familiar to me by now. I'd braved them with my bare skin. But seriously scary weather like tornadoes and hurricanes, and other horrible natural events like tidal waves and earthquakes—those terrified me. They were the planet's way of removing parasitic humans, and they didn't take prisoners.

"It's the first storm of the season, and a really early one," Dad said. "That usually means it won't be a big deal."

I narrowed my eyes. "That sounds like a fake weather statistic."

He pushed my hair behind my ear, and the curl sprang right back against my cheek. I blew on it.

"Does your mom let you run around Cincy by yourself?"

"I walk home from school, and I'm allowed to go to the comic book store, the grocery store, and the boba tea place. Dad, I'm going to be driving next year. I'm not in middle school."

Dad hummed. "All those places are right by your house."

A knot snarled up in my chest. It used to be *our* house. I didn't have time for angst, so I pushed past it and brought out the big guns: I pouted.

This never, ever worked on Mom. But she had a much better handle on my crap.

Dad's eyes widened. "Fine. But only for two hours, and if you're not back at the marina when I tell you to be back, you won't have the privilege anymore. And! I'm only saying yes because if we end up in the storm's path, we'll have a few boring days."

None of the storm stuff sounded very good at all. Nor did it sound boring. But my heart kicked around joyfully anyway, because Dad was going to set me free and I'd have two whole hours to try to track down Skylar's parents to see if they knew anything about her murder.

"Thanks, Dad." I launched into an embrace to play the part, but when he put his arms around me and hugged me back, I didn't want to let go. And I felt shitty for lying.

But not shitty enough to tell him the truth.

Nothing about the weather screamed impending tropical doom. It was simply hot. Thickly, horribly hot. I wore jean shorts, and the backs of my knees dripped with sweat that ran down my calves and pooled in the soles of my sandals. Dad was talking to a guy at the marina who kept glancing at me like he thought I was going to run off with one of his fishing poles.

I chewed stale bubble gum I'd found in the junk drawer in the galley and watched a huge tubful of pale-brown shrimp dart around. The marina smelled like fish and gasoline, but not unpleasantly so.

If someone had asked me a month ago if I'd be into those smells, I would have laughed and made gagging noises. But the salty-fresh smell of the bait made me think about Skylar and the sandbar and the manatees and the mangroves. Everything was so alive out here.

My chest tightened.

Almost everything.

Dad and the marina guy—who looked closer to my age than Dad's—hooked some hoses to *Brynn's Tide*. She was completely out of place beside the fishing boats and yachts, an unwieldy cube that had churned painfully slowly across the bayou to the marina. Even getting her ready to go had taken hours. I sympathized with that level of high maintenance.

Right next door, servers in polo shirts and white shorts were setting up outdoor seating at the seafood restaurant. Beach sand formed an artificial shore dotted with huge umbrellas and fire pits. A leathery old man with a gray beard sat on a stool and tuned a guitar hooked up to a lonely amp. I had a feeling he was about to start singing about margaritas any second.

While Leia barked at the marina guy from behind the sliding glass door, I wandered along the dock, checking out the fixtures and bait wells and the big metal cleats that fastened boat after boat alongside the huge gas pumps. I'd never considered the fact that boats needed gas stations.

"Hey. You're the girl from the library."

I attached a name to the soft voice before I spotted him. *Logan.* He sat on a boat a lot fancier than Dad's, still dressed for a wintry library despite the sun beating down on us. He'd traded his skinny jeans for shorts rolled above his knee, but he wore a cardigan over a tight striped shirt.

I wanted to hate his style, to tell myself he was trying too hard. But I found myself grinning immediately. "You're the boy from the library. What are you doing here?"

He looked up and down the boat he sat on. "Boating?"

"It looks like you're sitting."

"My friend and his mom are inside paying for gas."

I don't know why I'd expected him to be with a crew of fishing dudes, but it surprised me to hear that. I was instantly annoyed at my own surprise. Just because I didn't know anything about boats didn't mean boats were inherently dudish.

"What?" he asked, watching me.

I forced the thoughtful frown off my face. "Do city buses run around here?"

"Why? Are you running away?"

I couldn't tell if he was joking or concerned. For a fleeting moment, I considered inviting him to come with me. "I don't have my permit. Or a car. And I want to go shopping."

"There's a stop about a quarter of a mile up the road where the Goodwill is. If you ask inside, they have some bus maps." He shifted to one side to get into the shade.

"Thanks." I fidgeted with my hair, feeling his scrutiny. It was fair. I'd cataloged his entire outfit. But he was stylish, and I was wearing cutoffs and a T-shirt with Sailor Moon on it. Plus, my skin was splotchy pink and peeling from getting nuked by the sun two days in a row.

"Why were you looking up Skylar McKenzie?" Logan asked.

My throat went dry. "Why were you spying on what I was doing?"

His frown deepened. "I wasn't. I saw it open on your screen, and it was weird seeing her name. People don't usually talk about Skylar anymore."

My lie wasn't too far from the truth. "My dad was the one who found her. I wanted to read about it."

He watched me silently, brow knit with a single, dubious crease.

"What's your problem?" I snapped, a million times more harshly than I meant to.

Logan flinched. "I don't have a problem. I guess I stress about copycats, that's all."

My brain shorted out. I saw my mom crying. I saw a wall of angry messages and Jordan refusing to respond to my tantrum after they reached out to my mom. I saw worry in Logan's warm eyes.

"You don't even know me!" I couldn't tell if I was yelling or not. My ears felt stuffy. "You don't have any right to say that I'd . . . to think I'd do that."

"You're right," Logan said quietly, too kindly. "I don't know you."

My breath hitched. I sniffled hard, abruptly aware that I'd sounded fully unhinged. "Look. I don't even believe that Skylar died by suicide. So you can stop stressing or whatever."

Some passing waves rocked the boat where Logan sat staring at me. His chest rose and fell with a sharp, tired sort of sigh. "No offense, but why wouldn't you believe that? You're not even from here."

I felt my face heat. What could I say? That I'd been hanging out with Skylar recently?

"It's just a hunch," I mumbled, wanting to walk off the dock and disappear.

"Kind of a weird hunch."

Now that Logan thought I was a psycho obsessed with a stranger's death, I might as well lean in and see if he had any useful information. "Did you know her?"

"Sort of. My oldest brother dated her. But a few years . . . before."

The hair on my arms stood up. I scratched idly at my elbow, trying to hide the goose bumps. "Sorry for his loss."

Logan's jaw tightened before he replied. "Yeah."

"What was she like? Do you remember?"

"This line of questioning is not reassuring me," he said. Before I could argue, he went on hesitantly. "I was a lot younger, so I didn't really talk to her. She took me on a kayak ride with my brother once, right after we moved. She knew a lot about the area."

"You're not from here?"

"Not originally. Anything else?"

He'd been too little to have any good clues for me. But the more he talked, the more I wanted to know about him—not because of Skylar. Just because. Too bad he already thought I was nuts.

"Just one more question." I decided to take my shot anyway. Maybe it was the heat. "Do you have a Tumblr?"

A faint grin returned to Logan's features. "I have a few."

I'd never swooned before, but I came very close to it right there in the sun thinking about Logan with a stable of side-blogs. Basking in the dazzling glow of the Internet-by-proxy, I spelled my username out for him carefully, twice, until I was pretty sure he'd remember it. And prayed my current blog wasn't a parade of shitposting. "All my posts are from my queue until August," I added. "I got grounded from my phone and going online."

"That sounds challenging."

"For me?"

"For your parents. It's pretty easy to get online."

I pointed to *Brynn's Tide*. "Not from that thing."

A lady in a bathing suit coverup and hot-pink flip-flops walked up to the bow of the boat and untied the line. A boy with matching red hair and approximately six billion freckles followed her at a jog and jumped onto the back of the boat.

"Logan, push off," he said, only then seeming to notice me. Except he didn't notice me the way Logan had. He looked through me the way the kids at school did.

The lady climbed into the boat and scooted Logan off the bench with her hip, starting the engine with a flick of her wrist and pulling a wide-brimmed hat from a cabinet under the steering wheel.

"You a friend of Logan's?" she asked over the sound of the engine.

"No," we both said quickly. Our eyes met. I looked away first, blushing.

The woman pursed her lips and smiled at the same time. "Nice to meet you."

"Oh. I'm Brynn. That's my dad's houseboat. He's getting boat . . . supply stuff."

She nodded with an indulgent expression. Logan pushed the dock hard, and they idled away. Their pretty white boat cut through the water like a swan. Sitting in the bow, Logan gave me a quick, small wave.

My stomach somersaulted, and I nearly jumped out of my sandals when I heard Dad calling my name.

"I think we should ask your mom before you do this," Dad said for the second time. We sat together on a narrow bench in front of a bus stop marked by a sign tagged with graffiti. Traffic whooshed by us on a five-lane road, startlingly quickly, so different from the lazy pace of the bayou.

"She'll say no."

"Exactly." He sighed. "I can drive you around. It isn't that bad hanging out with me, is it?" His tone was weary, not playful—and my heart twisted at the sound. In my hurry to investigate Skylar's death, I hadn't considered that Dad would think I was avoiding him specifically.

"I like hanging out with you," I said. It came more naturally than I expected. "But didn't you want to do things by yourself when you were my age?"

I knew absolutely nothing about Dad at my age. His parents had died within a few months of each other when I was a toddler. No one had ever told me embarrassing stories about him or what he was like in high school or what his weird habits had been. As far as I was concerned, he'd emerged fully formed as a bearded, good-natured guy with inconsistent taste in T-shirts. Today's was a periodic table shirt with a pun about the element of surprise.

"I had a job when I was fifteen. I was a caddy on the golf course near my house."

"You golf?" Despite his golf course job, I couldn't remember ever seeing clubs around the house.

"Actually, no. But I like walking and nature, so that part is nice. I guess that's how I ended up doing almost the same thing as an adult." Dad had grown up outside Boston, and every once in a while, the faintest hint of a cartoonish accent came through. "Turns out you can't do *that* much with a horticulture degree."

"Did you have a girlfriend when you were fifteen?"

"I had two that year." Dad smiled and his hand scrubbed at his thick beard. "Sylvia. We met at church. And Melissa. Captain of the mathlete team."

"You were a mathlete?"

Dad sputtered out a laugh. "No. But they practiced on stage in the cafeteria, where I had running detention for half the school year. She was so smart. I love smart girls."

"Me too." It came out naturally. It wasn't until Dad glanced aside at me, unable to mask a flicker of surprise, that I realized what I'd said.

"Yeah?" he asked, voice a little higher than normal, but still a valiant effort to sound nonchalant. I guess Mom and Dad hadn't covered my sexuality when they chatted about my grades and health.

I nodded, and he nodded, and a bus pulled up, noisy and stinky. Given Dad's awkward nod back and dazed look, I probably should have stuck around and waited for the next one, so we had more time to discuss why my bisexuality wasn't a big deal and wasn't anything he needed to flip out about.

But I had important things to do.

"Bye, Dad." At a loss for what to do, I raised my hand and gestured at my palm until he gave me a robotic high five.

I skipped up the stairs and sat down as the bus pulled away. Out the window, Dad was still sitting on the bus stop bench, waving weakly and looking vaguely ill.

Digging out the map I'd gotten from Goodwill, I plotted the route. First, I had to get to the library again to find the McKenzies' address. Then I had to get to their house and hope that they'd be home on a weekday.

Tapping my sandals rapidly against the rubbery floor, I endured the start-stop pace and the lingering smell of exhaust and disinfectant and acknowledged the growing buzz of anxiety building in my veins.

For a very short time, I'd tried meditating, but the free guided meditations online were hit or miss. One had suggested pretending the anxiety was bonus energy, and then shoving that ball of energy into my hips for powerful orgasms. Having only recently discovered the wonder of orgasms, I found them to be more than powerful enough. The only result of that particular meditation was that I thought of it every time I did what my latest therapist said to do—which was to acknowledge the anxiety.

"Hi," I mumbled. "I know you're there. So, apparently you're coming with me to do some detective work."

A woman reading a book with angels on the cover glanced at me and hurriedly looked away when our eyes met. I shrugged. We were on public transportation. If a sunburned girl talking to herself was the weirdest thing the lady saw today, she'd be winning.

Thinking about energy-orgasms amused me enough to push away the sharpest edge of the anxiety. It swirled around in my lower intestines, cramping up but not quite violently. At least I wouldn't be confronting anything dangerous or deadly.

Unless the McKenzies had killed their daughter. Though that seemed unlikely. I had a hard time imagining them faking the raw grief in the photos I'd seen—the etched lines of despair that grew deeper with each passing day and became stony masks of devastation once Skylar's body had been found.

They had to know more than anyone else, though. Skylar had been their kid. They'd know who she'd been dating, what her hobbies were, who her enemies had been, if she'd been threatened or stalked, or if she'd frequented dangerous places.

My phone buzzed in my bag, and I scrambled to answer it. Only one person had the number to the horrible, ancient flip phone, and if I let it go to voicemail Mom would start catastrophizing immediately. "Mom! Hey."

"Hi, baby. What's that noise?"

"It's a bus going by. Me and Dad walked to the Goodwill outlet. They have tons of cool stuff." It was only partially a lie. We'd perused plastic lawn ornaments and an inexplicable aisle full of Halloween decorations, after picking up the bus map and schedule.

"Are you having fun?"

"I have a pretty bad sunburn, but I'm having fun."

"I wish you'd be more careful, Brynn. You don't know anything about the area." Her voice tightened, and I could feel her trying not to lecture me about all the ways I could get killed. She'd gone to several of my therapy sessions this year, and we'd worked out together that sometimes her paranoid mama-bear instincts made my fears a lot worse. That was obviously difficult for her to swallow, though.

Especially when I'd almost gotten myself killed by lightning already.

"I'm learning about the area. I saw a manatee and a baby manatee yesterday. They look like footballs. Huge ones."

Mom laughed. "I've seen them at the zoo. They're so ugly they're cute."

I smiled easily. She had a loud, happy laugh I didn't hear very often. "I'm being more careful, I promise."

"And your dad's keeping an eye on that storm?"

"I just heard about it last night, but I think so. We brought the boat in for supplies or whatever. He says we'll get a hotel if the storm comes our way."

"You don't sound worried about it," Mom said, surprised.

"Apparently not being able to go online and track the storm helps." *That, and being obsessed with a dead girl who has nothing to do with hurricanes.*

"Well, I'll let you go. Will you call me tomorrow when you're somewhere quiet so we can talk?"

"Yeah. I'll talk to you then. Love you, Mom."

"I love you too, Brynn."

She hung up seconds before the bus gave a prerecorded announcement for the next stop. I skipped down the stairs, thanking the driver on my way out, and stood on the curb catching my bearings and comparing the street signs to the map. One block to the south and I'd be back at the library.

I found the McKenzies' house on a real estate map and glared in dismay at the winding mess of a neighborhood that wasn't anywhere near the library. Despite being a long way on land, it was close to the bayou by water, tucked deep into the mangroves, away from the traffic and the boatyard.

Skylar had lived on a canal.

I scribbled the address down and drew a rudimentary map, my fingers trembling with a thought I didn't want to acknowledge. Had Skylar died in her own backyard? Had the tide carried her lifeless body through the dark waterways out to the bayou, where my dad had found her, days later?

Hurrying out of the library, I glanced at the empty information desk. I knew Logan wouldn't be there—he was on a boat. But my heart stuttered traitorously when I remembered how he'd looked there, confident and concerned at the same time.

Outside, the sun was in full force. Up in Cincinnati, it got hot and muggy, and we had our fair share of biting bugs and sweat. This heat was more than uncomfortable. It sent adrenaline rushing through my body as if I were standing too close to an open oven or a raging bonfire. At the same time, it immediately fatigued me. I wanted to crawl into a shady spot and pant like Leia out on the dock.

But I couldn't do that. I had to keep going.

My skin turned pink as I waited for the bus, checking the time on my flip phone compulsively. I hadn't put sunscreen on, too busy hatching my transportation plot to think about practicalities like food and avoiding more peeling.

By the time the bus finally showed up, my sweat-soaked curls were sticking to my face and my neck. I wobbled up the steps, and the driver arched her brow at me when I swayed and struggled to catch my balance.

"You sick?" she asked.

"Dehydrated. I think." I fed my fare into the machine beside her and collapsed into the very first seat. "Do you know which route I need to take to get to Sand Dune Elementary?" I asked. It was the closest landmark to the McKenzies' neighborhood.

"This route." She snapped gum and tapped bright-purple fingernails against the big steering wheel as we idled at a red light. "Fifteen-minute ride this time of day."

"Okay. That's not too bad." I'd have to hurry once I got there, but it was still doable.

"You not from around here?"

Cold air-conditioning sent shivers through me. My thighs slipped and slid against the plastic seat beneath me every time the bus moved. "I'm from Ohio."

I braced myself for more questions and cobbled together excuses. As we drove by fast-food restaurants and one strip mall after another, I developed my backstory. I was visiting some family. My brother's car had broken down, so I had to take the bus to meet my cousins.

I didn't have a brother or cousins, and I wasn't sure what one would do with a bunch of other kids during the day in the summer. Play outside? Sit around playing video games? Maybe they'd have jobs, and we'd try to get jobs in the same place. My pulse picked up and my hands went cold as I struggled with that last bit of the puzzle. Why was I going there at all? My cousins could pick me up if they had cars and we had plans.

My story didn't make sense.

I was freaking out over nothing. The bus driver had clearly moved on. She watched the road and hummed to herself, and I sank into my seat in relief.

We picked up a few more riders. Safe from further interrogation, I tilted my head against the window and evened out my breathing. We were an exhaust-coughing oasis barreling through post-apocalyptic levels of heat.

Sometimes when I was alone in public, I imagined what would happen if I ended up facing disaster with the people around me. A woman with a pudgy infant and a toddler in shorts with a butterfly on the butt sat at the back of the bus. She stuck one long leg out to try to keep the toddler from running down the aisle.

They'd be no help.

Two boys who looked a few years older than me sat with their legs spread wide and a full seat between them, as if revolted by the idea of accidentally touching. One muttered into his phone and the other texted. Both had a lot of tattoos for someone barely eighteen. Neither looked at me.

I didn't want to face the end of the world with them either. I did, however, want to steal their phones.

A woman who looked to be around my mom's age sat quietly with a pile of canvas shopping bags on either seat beside her. As if feeling my gaze, she glanced up and smiled. I smiled back at her and looked away, guilt rushing through me.

I didn't know anything about these people. Maybe they were all pros at handling stress and disaster. If the bus rolled over, the teens might be nimble. The mom might know how to solve problems and multitask. The woman with the groceries might have first-aid skills.

What would I have to offer?

"This is your stop, ma'am," the driver said.

I pulled myself up, palm slippery against the metal pole. "Thank you."

An empty parking lot and a quiet, summer-shuttered school lay before me. At home, our schools weren't flat like this expanse of one-story buildings and open-air hallways. My elementary school had been tall and enclosed against nasty winter weather.

The elementary school near the McKenzies' was a misshapen rectangle on my map. I turned slowly, orienting myself to the spiderweb of roads I'd drawn but forgotten to label.

I only had forty-five minutes to get back to the marina. It was now or never.

Already woozy in the heat, I set off at a light jog. That lasted about seventeen seconds. My jog became a brisk walk. And my brisk walk became a dazed shuffle. My brain began to remind me how reckless this was. What a tremendous betrayal it was to my dad. He thought I was nearby. And at the very least in air-conditioning.

I drew in a ragged breath and shielded my eyes, determined to keep the inevitable meltdown at bay as long as I could. I owed Skylar that.

All the houses looked exactly the same—pastel shades and vaguely Spanish architecture with pink and white roof tiles. I'd never seen so many palm trees in my life. Squat, spikey ones with dark-green fronds. Tall, smooth ones with pale, wispy fronds. Some towered above the power lines, impossibly skinny and straight.

A flock of pale-green parrots soared overhead, and I debated whether or not they were a mirage or fever hallucination. They squawked like car alarms, settling high in the branches of a towering oak that provided shade for a full two driveways, as I trudged toward my destination.

My map didn't have much in the way of accurate measurements. It had looked like a mile or so, but I wasn't sure now as I followed the winding sidewalk. Sweat poured into my eyes, stinging.

I passed a huge chunk of limestone marking the edge of a driveway and sat heavily. The uneven surface poked me through my jean shorts. Giving up on the horrible rock, I sprawled out in the spongy, thick grass. We had soft grass at home. This grass looked aggressive, like it would climb up and choke you if it could.

"Excuse me. Are you all right?"

"I'm in the grass," I said, looking up at the mottled canopy of oak and hairy moss hanging from the branches. The sun twinkled through the dense limbs and dark-green leaves. I liked the way it looked. This was the perfect place for a nap.

Footsteps squeaked in the grass beside me, and a face entered my line of vision, backlit by flashes of sunlight through the tree. "Can I call someone for you?"

I sat up as quickly as I could, panic giving me one last burst of reason. If this person called my dad, he'd come and get me. Then he'd immediately kill me for lying to him and clearly trying to find Skylar McKenzie's house. He'd call my mom and they'd discuss what a screwup I was, and I'd be confined to the bowels of *Brynn's Tide* for the rest of the summer.

"No. I'm on a walk. Like, on purpose."

"You look like you have heatstroke." It was a woman's voice. She crouched beside me, a thin frame in a polo shirt and pastel shorts, a newscaster bob shining with a plasticky layer of hairspray.

My breath stuttered.

Patricia McKenzie, the real estate agent.

"I could use a drink of water, actually." I didn't have to fake the meekness in my voice.

My heart buzzed and thudded like a fly trapped beneath a glass.

She offered me a skinny hand and hefted me up with surprising strength. Her Audi idled on the side of the road. After holding my elbow for a few steps to make sure I didn't fall down, she opened the passenger door. "Will your mom mind if you get a ride with a stranger?"

"I rode the bus with a lot of strangers."

Patricia gave me an odd look. "All right. I suppose she won't mind then."

The air-conditioning in the car was even colder than the bus had been. I let my slick forehead rest against the window, and I stared at the sleek dashboard, shiny instruments, and wood paneling. The car smelled new, like she'd just driven it off the lot.

My mom's car reeked no matter how hard we tried to keep it clean. French fries always ended up under the seats and milkshake lids toppled onto the floor. A layer of schoolwork and shopping bags and books accumulated in the back seat, taking on the musty smell of a used bookstore.

Patricia had probably never eaten a fry in her life.

I'd been closer to my goal than I'd thought. We only passed about ten houses before we pulled into her circular driveway. I stared at the big house with a set of dramatic stairs leading to double glass doors etched with frosted herons.

This is what Skylar had come home to every day. A house that looked like a resort.

"I can wait outside," I said hoarsely, daunted by the stairs—and the idea of walking exactly where Skylar had walked. Her bedroom was in this house, possibly with a closet still full of her clothes. Her books. Her underwear. The things she'd touched.

My vision swam, and I fought the spots soaring like leaping fish at the edge of my vision. I was screwed for sure if I passed out on Patricia McKenzie's driveway.

"Absolutely not," she was saying, her voice a pleasant drone. "Let's get you cooled off, and you can call your mom and have her pick you up."

"Sure." Mom could jump on a plane, fly down here, and double-ground me. No biggie.

The brisk air-conditioning chilled my sweaty skin, focusing my mind just enough to keep one foot in front of the next without keeling over.

A huge tile foyer greeted me, cold and completely devoid of personality. Patricia said something I wasn't listening to, her voice swept away by the high ceiling and the echo of a floor with no carpeting.

Two cream-colored miniature poodles dashed toward us, nails clicking against the tile. They orbited Patricia's feet, bobbed tails wagging and paws polite on the floor. I blinked down at them, unfamiliar with the notion of a well-behaved lapdog. Every tiny dog I'd ever met acted like a ferret on steroids.

Skylar had been allergic to dogs.

"This is Amelia, and this is Rochester," Patricia said, briefly bending to pat each on the head as if I cared which was which. I followed her into an open kitchen with gleaming countertops. A picture-window showed off the massive pool and a canal. I spotted mangroves in the distance.

Patricia handed me water in a heavy glass. I sat on a stool at the breakfast bar and drank it slowly. I'd read somewhere that drinking too quickly when you were hot and dehydrated led to puking, and the last thing I wanted to do was puke in front of another nice Floridian.

Halfway through the water, I thought about Paula and my stomach twisted. I should have written down her phone number. If Patricia had to call someone, I'd have a better chance convincing Paula not to freak out.

The glass clinked musically when I set it down. One of the dogs watched me, and Patricia watched me too. She wore a lot of makeup. It made her look pretty and very profes-

new what I should say, and I knew exactly what I
n't say.

brain was fried. My head ached. I'd gone this far. I
do what I'd come here to do.

m . . . I was wondering about Skylar."

athan's mouth clicked shut and lips whitened. Fine
e the ones around Patricia's eyes formed, hard and
ving. But he didn't seem surprised—only weary.
ry. It wasn't the first time someone had asked him
tion, and he didn't like hearing it.

cia was looking away from me, watching her hands.
yed against the black granite like she was trying to
hase there. Her nails were bright-cherry red. Her
mbled.

t were you wondering?" Patricia asked softly.

Jonathan reached for me but came short of
my arm. His gaze flickered toward the foyer. I had
e'd wrap his hand around my wrist and tug me to
I didn't move soon.

s weren't going to move even if I wanted them
de me leaden. As soon as the words had left my
wanted to snatch them out of the air and swallow
was too much. It wasn't a game at the library.
mystery. These were the real, sad-eyed, broken
o had spent a few helpless days thinking their
ter was only lost. They'd dared to hope despite
d their hopes had been dashed when my dad
heir daughter—their little girl. Now they were

sional, like someone in a commercial. The tired lines around
her eyes were caked with it, accentuated by the folds of foun-
dation and concealer.

She still looked sad.

My bus ride backstory might work. Cousins down the
street. Lost because I wasn't used to the hot weather. But how
was I going to ask about Skylar? I should have come up with
a better plan on the bus instead of spacing out.

I began to blurt something about pretend cousins
knowing Skylar, when heavy footsteps sounded. I turned
in my chair. Jonathan McKenzie walked down a gleaming
wood staircase, his hair shower-damp. He wore gym clothes,
but there was no mistaking the fancy-lawyer face and haircut
from the pictures in the paper. When he saw me, he flinched.
I saw that he looked decades older, as if he'd aged a lifetime
in just five years.

"More Girl Scout cookies?" he asked.

I looked down at myself. A baggy T-shirt, cut-off shorts
with a fraying hem. Flip-flops and brutally peeling thighs.
The tops of my feet were so pink they looked like pigskin. If
this was how Girl Scouts operated these days, the organiza-
tion was going seriously downhill.

Patricia laughed, in on a joke between them. He kissed
her on the cheek, and they both looked at me expectantly. I
wanted to vomit. I was going to repay this woman's kindness
with a reminder that her daughter was gone. If I could figure
out how to bring it up.

"Cool dogs," I blurted, immediately cringing. "My dad has a dog. She's pretty cool too."

Patricia's brow knit the way my mom's did when she was worried about me. Looking down at my knees, I let out an involuntary, blustery sigh. I couldn't go one goddamned day without someone worrying about me.

"Are you in trouble, honey?"

"No." I met her gaze, looking for Skylar in it. The wariness in her cool blue eyes was a tired mirror of Skylar's. "I mean, I am in trouble. But for the summer, like, grounded from my phone. That's why I don't have my phone. But I'm not, like, being abused or something. If that's what you're worried about. Although I guess that's what I'd say if I was, and I was covering for my parents. But I'm not."

After a long pause, Patricia said, "You should finish that water."

I sipped some more awkward little sloshes, watching them over the rim of the heavy glass. They exchanged a look that clearly communicated something along the lines of *should we call the police*?

If I didn't say something soon, I'd never have a chance. As it was, there was no way I was getting back to the marina on time. Dad was probably going to quit his job and spend the rest of the summer staring at me at this rate.

Jonathan held himself stiffly, obviously bugged out by my presence in his home. Patricia watched me with fluttering concern that I desperately wanted to soothe so I wouldn't feel like such a giant asshole.

I set the water down. "Thanks
of woozy in the sun. I'm from Ohi
break with my dad. He let me expl
to see the water, but I guess there a

"The beaches are on the ot
smiled faintly, but it was like
the clouds compared to her inc
"We're on the bay side. All man
I suppose you're not used to the

"It's hot in Ohio too. But n

"Do you know how to get
should we call your father to g

Do it, Brynn. Say somethin

"Oh, I know how to get b
deal. He's at work until after c
him."

Patricia opened a kitch
cate pink pen and paper illu
down a phone number an
script. "Would you do me
you're home? Otherwise I'

Jonathan gave her a sh
an angry look, but someth
cut himself. And then I
passing second, every h
Worried sick.

"Sure." I folded the p
my back pocket. "I will."

smaller, weathered with grief, living in an empty funeral home of a house that Skylar would never return to.

I had no right to be here.

I couldn't stop now. I wouldn't have another chance to get back here. I couldn't give up on Skylar, even if it meant hurting her parents.

"Someone." I cleared my throat, found my voice. Her voice. "Someone told me she was murdered."

"Enough." Jonathan's voice boomed. I jumped. The barstool spun absurdly with the momentum of it, twisting me to face away from them.

Skylar smiled at me from a portrait on the wall, her shoulders sun-freckled and bare, wrapped in a silly black blouse for senior portraits. She wore her hair down, and it curled loosely around her face, blond and perfect and . . . dry. A pearl necklace shone at her collar. One dimple etched into her cheek, her smile slightly lopsided. Happy. Real.

Whatever shred of doubt was left in me whistled out with a squeak of breath.

I pressed my hand against my mouth to stifle a horrified sob.

"I told you," Patricia was saying. Not to me. "Kids talk. People talk. They need to know the truth."

"Yes." The truth. The breath caught in my chest, hoarse and wet. I didn't want to look at her picture anymore. It wouldn't go away.

They had to tell me the truth. Skylar wanted me to know. She needed me to know.

Patricia spun my barstool back around, her hand ice-cold at my elbow. Her narrow chest heaved with a ragged breath. I held mine, ready to know—ready to find out.

We stared at each other, fear and pain like static electricity between our bodies. Anticipation stole the oxygen from my lungs. I leaned closer, waiting for her confession, for a path to the truth that would set Skylar free from her watery purgatory.

But Patricia's lashes fluttered. She closed her eyes and turned away. "You need to leave."

I choked. "But—"

Jonathan's hands shook. He tightened them into fists and gestured vaguely toward the door. "You goth kids—or whatever you are. It's disgusting what you do to her memory. You have no right coming here and saying these things. These—horrible things!"

Was he the bad guy? Blustering and angry, guilty. I could picture it. He'd lost his temper and pushed her, and she hit her head on the dock. It had been an accident, but no one would have believed him so he faked her suicide, set her body adrift in the murky canal.

How would I know? I wasn't a real detective. I was scared silly, and I couldn't stop shaking. Tears fell down my face. Snot gathered at my upper lip and I wiped it on the inside of my arm and nodded, mumbling an incoherent apology.

He was right to be angry. Beyond right. *Righteous*. What I'd done was unspeakably terrible. Invading their home,

Skylar's home. Dragging death and awkwardness along with me, like I did everywhere.

"She's upset." Patricia wiped her eyes swiftly. "Don't yell at her."

"She should be upset!" Jonathan hadn't been yelling before, but he yelled now. His voice frightened Alabaster and Persnickety—or whatever the dogs' names were—away in a flurry of clicking nails.

"I'm sorry," I choked out.

I shuffled off the barstool and caught myself against the wall below Skylar's portrait, struggling to keep my balance with my knees weak. Patricia touched my elbow again, her hand as cold as Skylar's, and I swallowed another sob and shook my head, willing her to go away. Willing myself back to Dad's boat, back to the bayou, back into Skylar's soggy arms.

"She's hysterical." Patricia sounded worried.

"I'm calling the police," Jonathan said.

"No." I waved my hand. "No. I'm leaving. I'm sorry. I'm leaving." I met Patricia's eyes. They looked even more like Skylar's like this, full of tears. I followed the wall and shuffled toward the light and the two herons. The McKenzies walked behind me. The dogs were nowhere to be seen. I wanted to run like that, to become small and invisible. An afterthought instead of another horrific bruise on their lives.

"I'm really sorry," I repeated, voice stronger now that I was closer to escaping this place and protecting them from my disastrous sleuthing.

Still, Patricia's words lingered on my skin. *The truth.*

She held the door open for me. I opened my mouth, but no sound would come out. I stumbled onto the terrace and turned my attention to walking down the stairs without rolling like a clown.

The door closed and Jonathan raised his voice, but the sound was muffled, like the bass from a car in the distance.

I only made it to the bottom step before my legs gave out entirely and the sobs came, loud and hiccupping, wild with grief for my dead friend and her broken parents.

CHAPTER THIRTEEN

THE PAIN OF AN acute crying-headache was already pounding through my sinuses when someone put a hand on my shoulder. I yelped out a wretched sound and shrugged away from the touch, the fingers so cold I could feel the chill through my sun-warmed T-shirt.

When I spun, fully expecting *more* dead people, Patricia McKenzie sat on the steps beside me, eyes big, mouth parted in surprise. She scooted away a few inches, her body hunched up like a child's and her face lined with pain that made her look decades older than the pictures in the paper—as old as a grandmother.

Maybe she was old enough to be a grandmother. Maybe she would have been one by now.

"I never got your name." Patricia carried a tote bag, as if she'd walked out the front door planning to go some-where. As she spoke, she dug into it with shaking hands and retrieved a pack of cigarettes.

I watched her light one with less finesse than the kids who smoked at the racquetball courts near our school. I'd never smoked, and I didn't plan on it—smoking caused enough side effects to leave me sleepless and trembling at night worrying about secondhand smoke. Patricia fumbled with the lighter again. It didn't seem like she was a regular smoker.

Then she coughed on the first puff, confirming my suspicions.

I smiled and scrubbed my hands at my eyes and nose, and then wiped them on my jean shorts. "Do you want my name so you can call the police?"

Patricia's eyebrows were pencil thin and perfectly shaded. When she frowned they became squiggly lines. "Should I be calling the police?"

"I don't know. I figured that's what people who live in houses like this"—I pointed at the frosted herons—"do when they're mad."

"Who told you that our daughter was murdered?"

Skylar did. She was alone. And she was lonely. Lonely enough to hang out with me.

My cheeks burned. The truth felt so absurd. So unfair. "A kid. At that seafood restaurant on the bayou."

She blew smoke away from me and swatted at it. "There are a lot of seafood restaurants around here."

"My name is Brynn," I offered, hoping to push her in front of a different train of thought.

"You care about this a lot, Brynn. I can see it on your face. Are the girls at school still talking about her? Starting rumors? I was a teenager once. I know how urban legends go."

I shook my head. "I really am from out of town. I'm so sorry." My heart beat a wild rhythm in my chest, and I needed to direct her away from this line of questioning before I panicked myself into a fit. So I told her something I never told random adults. "I have an anxiety disorder. Sometimes I get fixated on things. Mostly death. I'm, um. I see a doctor and everything. I'm working on it."

"That's good that you're doing that. Getting help. Talking about it. Not suffering alone." Patricia ground the cigarette on one of the pale-pink pavers, then tossed it into a thatch of spiky, tiny palm trees. The act was so brazenly careless that I smiled again. She was a rebellious kid with no one to rebel against. She owned the house. She made the rules.

Unless . . .

"Your husband doesn't want you out here talking to me," I said.

She gave me a long look. "He worries about his career. About the neighbors. This isn't a big city. People talk."

I swallowed against the sour taste behind my teeth. "What is he scared they'll talk about?"

Murder? How he has a bad temper? How maybe there was more to Skylar's death than the papers said?

Patricia watched me, measuring. "He's worried that people will say we let her down."

My stomach gave a slow, sad swoop. "Oh," I mumbled, hating how much that made sense.

She leaned back on her hands and tilted her head, and I saw more of Skylar, more of the girl Patricia had been. Wild once, not yet worn down with grief. She sat so still and quiet for so long that I was sure we were done, that she'd found me undeserving of the truth she and Jonathan had kept locked up in their cookie-cutter mansion.

"Here," Patricia said, digging a yearbook out of her tote. It was dark blue with a fancy crest on the cover. "Her school gave me a bunch of extras. I want you to have this."

I took the heavy yearbook with trembling hands. "Why?"

"I want you to know more of my daughter than what kids gossip about."

"She sounded really great," I choked out.

Patricia smiled through a wet laugh. "Yes, she was really great."

Clutching the yearbook, I couldn't help pushing just a little more. "Um. It sounds like a lot of people cared about her. But did Skylar have any enemies? Anyone who might have wanted to hurt her?"

Patricia sighed once, and then said, "Brynn. She died by suicide."

The word hammered at me, rattling my brain. "But—"

Patricia leaned closer, watching my face, and told me exactly what happened. I couldn't look away. She was crying—tears skimming down her face—but her words were even, measured. Memorized. A police report or a speech, something she'd played over and over in her head until the words didn't mean anything anymore.

I held on to the yearbook like a lifeline. It was hard to hear my own voice over the buzzing in my ears. When Patricia finished speaking, I asked, "What if someone just wanted it to look like that? Why did you believe what they told you?"

If Skylar's own parents didn't dig deeper, how could I prove that she was murdered? How could I save her?

"Brynn, I know—I knew—my own child."

"You're wrong," I whispered.

I saw my mom. I saw her crying. I saw her terrified, shaking her phone at me, showing me the screenshot. She'd trusted me, she sobbed. She'd trusted me to talk to her. She'd thought she knew me.

I didn't know me.

I didn't know anything.

It was too big. It was too much.

Too close.

Patricia had her hands on my arms. Her mouth moved rapidly, but I couldn't hear her over the sound of blood rushing in my ears. A little warning bell somewhere in the last rational crevice of my brain alerted me to the fact that I was having a panic attack. A big one. But the rest of me was certain that I was going to die here on the McKenzies' front steps, and I'd traumatize this poor lady even more.

Her movements became more frantic, and she looked over her shoulder, shouting. Jonathan poured out the door, angry at first, but then paling when he saw me there. I must have looked like a beached fish flopping and desperately mouthing for more breath.

She'd died like that. Scared. Gasping for breath. Vision going spotty. Lungs on fire. She'd reached for the surface, for the sunlight singing on the surface. And then she'd taken that last involuntary breath, water filling her fragile lungs, and she'd died alone in the dark. Murdered.

Now I knew what the killer had done to her. And I could never un-know. No wonder her spirit lingered there waiting for someone to pay for the terrible violence they'd done.

Jonathan was on the phone. He held my hand, and Patricia fanned my face. I was breathing too fast. I coughed on a quick, frustrated sigh, cursed with a split second of clarity, long enough to know that my dumb brain was screwing me over in the most major of ways and that someone was going to get ahold of my dad and that was going to break him.

Then I passed out.

~

The paramedics and an entire fire truck got there before Dad did. I climbed out of a brief flirtation with oblivion to find myself flat on my back on the McKenzies' driveway with a small army of uniformed men and women crouching around me.

It was sunny, but a patch of high palm trees shaded me, waving fronds black against the forever-blue sky.

A young man with a huge tablet asked Jonathan and Patricia questions: Had I fallen? Was I on medication? Did I have an existing medical condition?

The McKenzies sat on the steps beside me, squished together and probably hating every second of having to talk to first responders. I'd only seen it on TV shows about detectives, but I assumed a couple of cops had shown up at their door to tell them their daughter's body had been found.

I squinted. A middle-aged, round woman with thick-rimmed glasses and spiked, short hair caught my eye. The patch on her shirt said she was with the paramedic company, not the fire department. She smiled.

"Back with us?" she asked softly, only for me.

She knew. People with anxiety had a way of sniffing each other out. In this case, I had panic-induced body odor. So maybe it was that.

"Am I in trouble?" My voice sounded tiny, and it wobbled, dangerously close to tears. The conversations around me quieted, and it was Patricia who answered.

"No, honey."

"That's debatable." I closed my eyes at the sound of my dad's voice.

Other than right after I'd asked him about Skylar, he'd never raised his voice at me. He wasn't a scary guy. But this wasn't a minor disobedience. I'd lied, and I'd done something spectacularly, painfully wrong and super harmful to the grieving parents holding hands on their front steps. There was no way Dad wasn't going to lose his mind at me.

No one said anything. I peered out of one eye, and then the other, and then pushed up onto my elbows. Dad was watching the McKenzies, face pale and stricken. Their expressions mirrored his.

Their pictures had smiled next to each other in the papers—their professional headshots and a candid of my dad at the golf course. But they'd probably never met after Dad found Skylar in the bayou. After he'd seen her decomposing and ruined.

"I'm so sorry," my dad said. It wasn't clear what he was sorry for. Their dead daughter. His idiot daughter.

Jonathan gave a quick, tense nod, and Patricia nodded several times in a row, sniffling and bobbleheaded.

"I'm her father," Dad said to the paramedics. "Hunter Costa."

The low buzz of medical chatter started up again, the questions about my health history now directed toward Dad. The firefighters had him sign something, then climbed back into their rig. It idled loudly in the street, and a few neighbors and kids on bikes gathered at a distance, watching.

How many of them knew the McKenzies' story? Were they wondering what tragedy had befallen them now?

They'd find out soon that it wasn't a tragedy—just a tragically foolish girl chasing ghosts across Tampa Bay.

Dad filled in the paramedics on my health history and medications, rattling off diagnoses as surefire as Mom did. I wondered how he knew the words so well, if he'd rehearsed or if he and Mom talked more often than I thought. My heart fluttered, not uncomfortably, but with a rush of warmth. He cared about me enough to know the difficult parts of me, to speak about them confidently, without stuttering or making excuses.

"Do you use a rescue medication?" Glasses asked. The other paramedics were still faceless to me, ambiguously good-looking, strong people. But she kept her eyes on me, and her stern mouth betrayed quiet sympathy.

"Yes."

"Do you have it with you all the time?"

"No."

"You might want to reconsider that. And check in with your doctor to let them know what happened too."

"Yes, ma'am," I said, not sure how else to address her.

She snorted once and finished taking my blood pressure.

Dad promised to take me directly to the children's hospital downtown if I showed any more symptoms, and they had him sign a few other things that gave them permission to leave without hauling me off in an ambulance. It didn't take that long. Disappointment flared in my chest when they gathered their bags, rolled the unused gurney off, and piled back into their boxy ambulance. Without the buffer of a bunch of strangers, I'd have to face my dad and the McKenzies head-on.

He walked over to the driver's side of the ambulance and spoke too softly for me to hear, the engine purring and exhaling a diesel scent that masked the honey-sweet smell of the jasmine climbing all over the low fence around the yard.

I glanced at Patricia, and she gestured for me to sit beside her, the motion so surprisingly kind I settled next to her without thinking. She put her hand on my knee and patted it once. Her breath gave a little sob-shudder, but she wasn't crying. I could smell the faint, musty scent of cigarette smoke over her cloying perfume.

She placed the yearbook in my lap. I must have dropped it when I keeled over.

There was something protective about the way she huddled close to me. From the way I'd acted, maybe she thought Dad was going to walk up and slap me silly for what I'd done. I wanted to reassure her, but that would only make me sound more like an abused child.

"You ready to go home?" Dad asked. The ambulance pulled away behind him, neighbor kids and rubberneckers scattering like ants from a smashed pile.

I wasn't. "Yeah."

He stood there, arms rigid at his sides.

"We're not going to talk about this?" My voice was jerky and too loud.

Dad frowned. "We can talk in the car."

Patricia fumbled in her purse, and for a moment I thought she was going for her cigarettes again, too traumatized to bother hiding them. But she pulled out a plastic container of gum and shook one piece into her palm and another into mine, as she whispered, "If you need anything. If you need to talk. Give me a call. Please. I wrote down a suicide hotline number in the yearbook too."

Her words hit me with a hollow thud, reverberating through my belly like the time I'd flown off the monkey bars and flopped on the dirt, my breath whooshing out so hard I thought I'd horked up my lungs.

She thought I was suicidal.

I looked back at Dad, horrified that he might have heard her, but his gaze was still stormy with a cold cocktail of fear and anger. When I stood, my legs shook, but I wasn't going to throw up—despite the creeping realization that my dad also thought I'd do something to hurt myself.

I couldn't bring myself to reassure either of them, and that scared me the most. A phantom cinder block tugged at my middle. I didn't want to die. I didn't have suicidal ideations. Not really. But there had been times—plenty of times—when I'd hated my broken brain enough to wish I didn't have to go one more day wondering what normal, everyday thing was going to lock me up in my own mind.

That's what Jordan had sent my mom. A post about not wanting to go on like this: Having bouts of diarrhea before biology class. Avoiding birthday parties and pep rallies because crowds gave me anxiety. Cataloging all the ways the people I loved could die. Never being able to turn any of it off.

Death loomed over me all the time, so why not get it over with?

I hadn't meant it. Not in a serious way. I knew the criteria. I didn't have a plan, and I didn't fantasize about particular ways to die. But it had been serious enough for Mom to cut me off from my friends and ship me down here to find some new reason for living.

I had. I'd found something to face my fears for, and she was fucking dead. And her poor parents thought she'd drowned on purpose.

A wave of icy chills crept through me. Whoever had done that, that brutal thing, was still around. Maybe still in Tampa Bay. Maybe in this neighborhood watching us.

I hadn't thought about *that* part yet.

"Brynn?" Dad watched me impatiently. He'd been talking, and I'd been ignoring him. Everyone was staring at me.

"I'll call you if I need you," I told Patricia. "I promise."

She looked like Skylar right then, when she smiled. And I knew I wasn't lying.

⌇

Dad had the doors off his Jeep. I leaned toward the center, gripping my seat belt so tightly the edges of the worn nylon dug at my palms. We were only going about forty miles per hour, but the road whizzing by right beside me looked like the edge of a chainsaw waiting to tear the skin off my body if I tumbled from my seat.

"I didn't have time to put the doors back on." Dad watched me as he slowed at a stop sign. He looked like he needed to throw up. "I didn't know how bad it was."

Guilt pooled behind my belly button. I coughed once, but I couldn't shake the thick chill. "It's okay," I said. "The doors, I mean. It's fine."

Even if the doors were on, I'd worry about the Jeep rolling over and crushing our skulls. Or I'd think about getting T-boned at an intersection.

My nerves were on high alert, and that wasn't going to stop anytime soon. A woman walked a huge silver husky on the sidewalk beside us, and I pictured the dog getting free and dashing out in front of us and sending us careening into a fire hydrant. The water would spray sky-high, and the engine would hiss and smoke, and then it would explode in a fireball seen for miles. We wouldn't have time to contemplate our deaths, only blink-fast concern for the dog before our lives were cut short.

I flung my hand out and turned up the radio. It was talk radio, which I hated—someone was always interrupting to announce a disaster. My disinterest in world news plagued me, a character flaw. I was old enough to show an interest in the world around me but too weak to handle it.

A few frantic turns of the dial landed me on an easy-listening station. Someone crooned about sitting on a dock. I took a deliberate, slow breath. And then another.

It isn't a character flaw.

I almost said it out loud, following my therapist's orders to combat negative self-talk by literally talking out loud. But Dad wouldn't appreciate me bringing him in on the thoughts rattling around in my head.

Being delicate or scared wasn't a character flaw. I cared about the news. I cared about the world. It wasn't disinterest. I just had to protect myself—nibble on knowledge at my own pace, place a barrier between myself and the hurt that knifed through me so keenly when I opened myself up to the enormity of pain and loss in the world.

Pain like Skylar's. Like her parents'.

I choked and wiped my eyes, getting tangled deeper, hating that Dad wasn't saying anything. He'd left me here drowning in the passenger seat, analyzing my faults and fears and the courage and gratitude I should have had but couldn't feel, even with a beautiful summer sun beating down on my freckled, peeling shoulders. I was reasonably healthy. My parents loved me in their own ways.

I was alive, and Skylar wasn't.

Dad pulled over at a dead end by the water and got out of the Jeep. I swallowed a terrified sound, wondering what I'd do if he left me here and never came back.

He walked around the front of the car and pulled me out of the passenger side, gentle but strong, easing me to the ground and wrapping me in a trembling hug. He held me like I was made of glass, and I hugged him back extra hard so he'd know it was okay, that I didn't mind being squeezed—that I needed it.

A low, muffled sound vibrated against me. I realized with a sobbing gasp that Dad was crying. Crying hard. Hunched over and snuffling into my hair.

"I love you, Dad," I said, as loud as I could with my throat closing up around more tears.

"I love you too, sweetie." His voice was hoarse, wet with tears but still strong—still Dad-like. He wasn't yelling at me or walking away or throwing me out or sending me home. He was scared.

We were scared together. And that was so much better than being scared alone.

CHAPTER FOURTEEN

AFTER WE'D BOTH CRIED ourselves silly, Dad and I climbed back into the Jeep and headed to a frozen yogurt place. Dad didn't say anything else about the McKenzies or the yearbook in my lap, to my relief. Also relieving? Shoving my face full of frozen yogurt and marshmallows and hot fudge (and walnuts and shaved coconut and caramel and strawberries and mochi bites).

I shuffled from the car to the dock, every cell in my body weary. The McKenzies' insistence that Skylar had died by suicide itched at the edges of my awareness. I wanted to pick at it like my peeling sunburn. I believed Patricia, but what if she didn't know the truth? What if her own husband had tricked her?

I doggedly shoved my questions away for now. I owed my dad that much.

I'd never forget the way he sounded crying.

The tide lapped against the lower step on the dock, splashing up through the cracks every time a boat went by and sending rippling waves crashing at me. Black, square crabs ambled up the pilings to get away from the water and scurried away from my shadow when I came close. The air smelled like salt and evening wind. If the smell had a color, it would be pale blue, and soft like a big blanket washed nearly threadbare. I turned my face to it and took a deep breath. It hitched an echo of crying, and I blew it out with a stubborn sigh.

Dad patted my shoulder.

I opened my eyes. "Why's the tide so high?"

"You can tell, huh?" Dad asked proudly.

I smiled and pushed my hair behind my ears, glad he'd noticed. Little by little I was starting to get the hang of this weird Florida stuff.

"I dunno. It's higher than I've seen it."

"About that . . ."

His tone would have sent a shock of dread through me if I hadn't been tapped out, worn to nothing, and ready to nap away the fullness in my belly. My frayed nerves had gone on overdrive and beyond. All I was capable of was hibernating. This exhausted sort of numbness was one of my favorite moods, right next to the random days when my brain forgot to alarm me about everything that could go terribly wrong.

So I didn't react much when Dad went on. "That storm, Alonzo. It's a hurricane in the gulf now. We'll know by tomorrow what it's up to."

"Up to?"

"As in, hitting the panhandle or heading our way."

"What happens if it heads our way?"

"Well, we may need to evacuate. But don't worry, I have a plan."

Then I couldn't put off finding Skylar. I had to do it tonight.

Dad tossed his work duffel into the boat. He pointed to the bow, and I jumped on board, untied the lines, and held on to the piling, scaring another little flock of crabs away.

When the engine came to life, Dad nodded a signal and I pushed off hard. With the sun setting, the water was ink-black. I hated the way I couldn't see the bottom. It could be miles deep for all I could tell. I held the yearbook close to my chest, afraid of dropping it into the water. It was my only real clue.

We didn't go full speed. Maybe Dad felt the same weird reluctance I did—the sense that going home was never going to be the same now. Not when we'd hugged and cried together, and I'd screwed up royally, and we were both as raw as a fillet of fish.

He sped up a little when Leia started barking her head off, dashing from one end of her little yard to the other.

"Will she jump in?" I asked.

"No, thankfully." Dad watched her. "I had a dog before her who jumped in every time he saw a boat or a dolphin or a manatee."

I didn't ask why the jumpy dog was already in past tense. Thankfully my obsession with death didn't extend to making my dad recount the fate of slightly stupid pets.

Leia did leap right into the boat when we slowed beside the dock. Dogs, for all their barking and slobbering and goofiness, were pretty intuitive. She had lots of licks and wags and she distributed them evenly as Dad and I tied up the boat.

The sun hadn't even set by the time I finished with showering, dealing with my contacts, and brushing my teeth, but I curled up on my bunk with the yearbook tucked under the pillow. Dad opened the door a crack to let Leia in. She jumped up on the bed with me, huge and snuffly. I gave my dad a tired smile, hoping it conveyed how grateful I was. For Leia in my bed. For the lack of a lecture on the way home. For the frozen yogurt. For knowing exactly what to say to the paramedics. For the hug.

For everything.

He rumpled my hair and Leia's ears. "Good night, kiddo."

As tired as I was, I knew I couldn't sleep. Not when I needed to talk to Skylar. While I waited for Dad to fall asleep, I thumbed through Skylar's yearbook. Dozens of people had signed it. My stomach lurched when I realized Skylar's parents must have passed it around after she'd died.

I wish we'd gotten to know each other better. —Avery

We never really hung out, but you always seemed really cool. —Colin

Rest in peace, pretty girl. ♡ *Kayla*

I'M SORRY.

The last one was small, neat handwriting in all caps with no signature. I stared at it, wishing I knew something about handwriting analysis. The handful of letters told me nothing.

I ran my fingers across the notes. They were all in blue ink with the same shiny finish of a ballpoint pen. There was no way everyone had the same pen. The McKenzies must have had people sign the yearbook at a memorial service. There were no stories of time spent together. Just a wistful sort of acknowledgment that no one had really known this girl—and no one ever would.

No one but me.

What would I write in there? *Thanks for the manatees*? *Have a great summer trapped between life and death!*

Swallowing back tears, I crammed the yearbook back under my pillow. I'd read it cover to cover later.

Once Dad's snores sounded like a yeti being slowly murdered, I tiptoed across the room and carefully snuck out the sliding door onto the deck.

A full, high moon and the floodlight on the back deck made it easy to slip out onto the floating dock without worrying about stepping on some wayward alligator or water snake. I rolled my pajama pants up to my knees and sat on the edge of the dock with my legs crossed, not quite willing to stick my feet in the dark water.

The air had a strange stillness to it, as if the whole world had stopped breathing. I could hear every distant splash, every noisy birdcall. This was how horror movies started.

Even creeped out by the dark water, I could tell she was there. Her sadness pressed on me like a tension headache.

"Skylar," I hissed. "Skylar!"

She surfaced more quickly than I expected, her eyes eerie in the moonlight. Shivering, I tried not to think about her legs in the dark, her toes skimming the grassy bottom below. Instead, I considered the depressing yearbook and my nearly nonexistent list of suspects. Logan's older brother? Skylar's dad? It seemed unlikely to me that a total stranger would have been able to trick everyone into thinking she'd done it on purpose. But I couldn't rule out some random killer.

"Hello?" she said, tilting her head and peering at me. "Are you sleepwalking?"

"No." I rubbed my tired eyes. It kind of felt like it. "Did you see who hurt you? Do you remember anything?"

"Wow, cutting right to the chase." Skylar looked disappointed, as if she'd been expecting us to do something fun in the middle of the night. "No. I don't remember anything."

So much for helpful clues.

"Did anyone dislike you? I mean, did you have mortal enemies?"

"What kind of teenager has mortal enemies?"

"Look—I don't have a lot to work with here!" A ragged sigh erupted from my chest. "I should have gotten Logan's number."

"Logan? Lonnie's baby brother?" Skylar asked, looking baffled.

"Yeah. I guess? He said his brother dated you."

Skylar sounded annoyed. "Is he even old enough to have a phone?"

"Yes. Also, he's hot. Also, did his brother kill you?"

"What?" She sputtered a little spray of water. "Come on. I dated Lonnie for like a month our freshman year, and we broke up and didn't get back together. I don't know if Logan told you this, but Lonnie is perfect. Straight As. Cross-country star. I'm sure he got a scholarship and he's, like, in med school or something now. It didn't make sense for him to date someone like me."

"What do you mean, *someone like you*?"

"I couldn't be—" Skylar started. She scowled at the surface of water, and I got the sense that she was looking in a mirror, hating what she saw. It made me feel funny inside. A little sick. "I couldn't, you know, get my head in the game."

I don't think I'd heard Skylar say that much at one time before. I held my breath, hoping she'd go on, but she seemed to realize how bitter she'd sounded, and she sank in the water until it covered her mouth.

"I don't get awesome grades," I offered.

Skylar surfaced to mutter, "I got awesome grades."

She didn't sound particularly happy about that.

"Was it hard, though?" I asked, plucking at the nylon grass on the floating dock.

"Everything was hard," Skylar whispered.

Something nagged at my gut. Probably an ulcer forming. I brushed it aside and shifted onto my knees to lean closer to her. "Can you think of anyone at all who might have wanted to hurt you?"

Skylar looked up at the moon for a long time. I imagined hearing her breathing, but all I really heard was the gentle nudge of water against the dock and the night sounds that made the hair on my arms stand on end. Abruptly, she let out a brittle laugh.

"What?" I asked.

"Nothing," she said, reaching out of the water and resting her cold hands on my knees. "You should stop this. It's dangerous."

"Dangerous because the person who killed you is dangerous?" I asked in a whisper, trying not to look over my shoulder. There was no one else out here but my snoring dad. Still, I couldn't help feeling like a killer might creep up on me at any second, bash my head in, and dump me in the bayou.

Especially since I'd caused such a scene at the McKenzies' house. What if the killer had seen all the ambulances and followed me and Dad back to the marina?

"Skylar," I pressed. "Is someone going to try to kill me?"

Skylar shook her head, infuriatingly silent again. I hated this puzzle. I hated that she couldn't just tell me the truth. I knew she wouldn't lie to me, but the way she refused to give me the information I needed felt almost as bad.

"Fine. At least tell me something about yourself," I said, quiet and pleading.

She frowned, eyes wetter in the pale light. "Why do you even care?"

"Because I care about you. I don't know why. It doesn't matter why. I wish I could have known you. We would have been friends."

"We wouldn't have been friends," Skylar snapped. "I wouldn't have had time for you. I would have been busy studying or practicing or trying to be fucking perfect, and I didn't have time for people who would drag me down. You're fucked up. You said so yourself."

Her words gutted me, but I recognized the specific shape of her cruelty. I'd said things like this to my mom. To myself. I said these kinds of things when the pain inside me got so big, all I could do was let it leech out and hurt everyone around me. Choking back tears that welled up anyway, I shook my head at her. "You're wrong. We would have found each other. Just like you found me out here. You see me. I know you see me."

Tears flowed down her face. It was like watching ice melt. "You see me too," she said, voice thick with a muddy sob. "You shouldn't. You shouldn't bother."

"No." I wiggled out of my pajamas, knowing there was no way I'd be able to hide a pile of soaking-wet laundry from my dad. As Skylar stared, looking startled, I shucked off my shirt and bra and climbed down the ladder into the water in my underwear.

I was terrified.

"What are you doing?" she asked, breathless, half laughing and half crying. "You're insane."

"You already knew that. Oh my God, it's dark in the water. Please tell me you have the power to feel sharks approaching."

Stubborn and shivering, I treaded water in front of her, keeping one hand on the ladder in case the tide tried to whisk me away into the dark. Without the sun on my shoulders, the bayou felt miserably cold. "Now. Tell me something about yourself."

Skylar closed her eyes. Her lashes were wet and clumpy. They looked sharp. But she looked sad. "I had a cat stuffed animal," she whispered. "His name was Gee Whiskers. I hope . . . I hope they let me keep him when they—"

"Stop," I choked. That was too much. I could not think about her in a casket, in a grave, in the ground. Somewhere rotting, maybe only miles away. I couldn't think about her parents laying her to rest with something she'd loved since she was little.

If I had a panic attack in the water, I'd sink to the dark bottom.

"Brynn. Hey. I'm sorry. I'm sorry. Take a deep breath."

"Tell me something better," I hissed, trying to make my vision stop acting all spotty and terrible.

"Your boobs look great."

I laughed, wet and miserable. My toe brushed against her cold shin. "For real, Skylar."

"I didn't know who I was or what I was supposed to be. I don't know what was me and what was me just trying to be a good daughter and a good student and you know, get into college and make money."

"Capitalism is a scam."

She snorted and wiped her nose. I guess ghosts could have snot too. "I hated people who seemed so comfortable being weird or being different. Kids with colored hair or whatever."

"Theater kids?" I offered.

Skylar laughed softly. "Yeah. Just everyone."

"You hated everyone?"

She let out a soft whuff of a sound, like an agitated horse. "Aren't there people you hate?"

"Mostly just me," I said, grinning.

Skylar surged at me in the water, crowding me against the ladder—somehow without touching me at all. Suddenly, her voice sounded like thunder, like it came from inside my own chest. "Don't say that."

"Okay," I said shakily. "Jeez."

She drifted back, as if a wave had carried her away from me. Now, I could hear her breath. It was ragged and scared. "Don't say that," she repeated in a whisper.

I was suddenly so, so tired of trying to be normal. Being a person was exhausting. "All right. Hey. I was just kidding."

It didn't feel right to tell her how often I did hate myself. It wasn't like I didn't know how screwed up that was.

When she didn't answer, I sighed softly. "I just want to fix this. I want to find out who hurt you, and I want to set you free."

"What if you can't?" she asked, even farther away now. I couldn't hear her small sounds of distress anymore.

"I will."

I had the yearbook, at least. In the morning, I'd read the whole thing. Clearly Skylar wasn't going to be helpful on her own. With shaking legs, I climbed out of the water and shook off like a dog, not caring if Skylar or fish or night birds could see me trying to jiggle water off my chest.

When I was mostly just damp, I struggled back into my pajamas. I could feel her there in the dark, no longer close but not gone either. With my back to the water, I bowed my head. "I won't stop trying."

Tomorrow, I'd figure out who she'd been close to, and I'd figure out how to find them and talk to them. Even if Skylar didn't know who she'd been, who she was, I knew the people who'd cared about her would. People from her school did a memorial run for her. She'd mattered.

"Oh," I gasped, straightening. "Shit!"

"What?" Skylar was right behind me in the water again, worried.

The memorial run at Skylar's school. Paula had said it was later this month, and that had been a week ago. It had to be soon. If I went, I could find dozens of people who knew her there. Someone was bound to know something about the day she'd disappeared.

"Nothing," I said. "I thought I saw a water snake, but it was my shadow."

"I know what a lie sounds like," Skylar said.

I stared at the dock, hoping I was right when I answered, "Me too."

CHAPTER FIFTEEN

AFTER I SNUCK BACK inside, I slept like a brick, dreamless and completely out. When I woke to gentle shaking, I mumbled something about dumbass dogs moving around in the bed.

"Brynn. Come on. I need you to wake up."

I sat up quickly and hit my head on the bunk above me. "Ow!"

"Sorry, sweetie." Dad flicked on the light. "We need to leave quickly. Alonzo changed track and picked up speed." I pulled on my glasses, and his blur of a face sharpened to concern—and sadness.

My heart sank. How long did hurricanes last? Would the memorial run be canceled?

Then I woke up a little more and clocked the vague despair in my dad's eyes.

"Oh no." I grabbed on to the blankets as if I could protect them. "You won't have time to move *Brynn's Tide* somewhere safe."

Dad shook his head tightly. "No. It takes me about three hours to get her ready to move, and half an hour to steam in."

We'd have to abandon her to whatever the hurricane brought.

And she wouldn't be the only one alone on the water when the storm came.

I swallowed against a sour taste and hurried into a pair of jeans, a tank top, and a soft hoodie. It was still the middle of the night, but the wind whispered the way it did before the afternoon thunderstorms. No lightning lit the sky, and no thunder rumbled. The devastation was out there on the gulf, churning toward us silently.

Had Skylar known?

Leia whined.

Animals were nature's forecasters. People must have relied on them centuries ago, before they'd had any other way to know what was coming. I thought about our ancestors a lot, the cave people who couldn't afford to be sidelined by anxiety. I'd have been woolly mammoth fodder for sure, back then.

I plopped my contacts in, dumped my bathroom stuff into my bag, and packed my suitcase. I carefully tucked the yearbook into my backpack. It only took a couple of minutes. I hadn't slept enough, and muzzy exhaustion lingered in my bones, warring with the jittery tension that radiated off my dad. He carried a duffel out onto the deck and moved around like a pirate in the rigging of a ship. The wind tossed his hair as he climbed around the outside rails, chucking three extra anchors out into the water and securing them to cleats on each side of the boat.

He powered down the generator, grabbed a dry box, and loaded up the little boat while I stood with my luggage, trembling. "Ready?" he asked.

I didn't know what I was supposed to be ready for, so I didn't answer. I followed him onto the boat and sat on my luggage, clutching Leia's collar while Dad handled shoving us off. The moon shone down from behind the watery filter of a layer of clouds. It barely illuminated the houseboat, and in a few minutes, I couldn't see *Brynn's Tide* at all. As we approached the dock, I spotted a line of cars heading toward the bridge we'd crossed from the airport. It wasn't even dawn, but the traffic already moved at a rush-hour crawl, hundreds of angry red taillights trailing into the distance.

"Evacuations," Dad said. "Almost all of this part of St. Pete is in Zone A."

"We have to evacuate?" The reality of the storm cracked through the haze of disoriented sleepiness.

"That's what we're doing, sweetie."

I climbed out of the boat and stood with our stuff, bewildered, as Dad hooked his Jeep to a boat trailer and backed it down a sloped ramp near the dock. He gestured for me, and I jogged to him.

"Stand here," he said, pointing to the junction between the trailer and the Jeep. "When I drive the boat up onto the trailer, I'll toss you the rope. Tie it off here."

I didn't think my rope holding skills would help much. But it gave me something to do instead of looking for Skylar in the water, which was starting to get choppy. Dad aimed the boat at the trailer and gunned the engine at the last second, beaching it onto a cradle of carpet-covered rungs. The dark sky hovered, ominous weather too thick and too close for comfort. I shivered.

Water rained down from the boat, leaving a wet trail in the gravel. The jon boat seemed so tiny on dry land. It didn't even look seaworthy.

As Dad finished strapping the boat to the trailer, I studied the bayou. The wind had taken on the forceful push of a storm front, beautifully threatening, and somehow different from the usual storms. Maybe it was the lack of lightning or the cooler temperature. Clouds blanketed the stars. I was in a snow globe about to be shaken up by a giant's unforgiving palm.

"Skylar. Be safe." I swallowed, my throat tickling with embarrassment. It was such a waste of energy to worry about her. Storms lashed her every single day. And it wasn't like anything could hurt her. But I kept talking anyway, my voice soft and only for her. I couldn't shake the thought of the tempest pulling her out into the bay—out to sea—away forever. "Stay under the water or whatever you do. I'll be back soon."

They'd have to reschedule the run. Wouldn't they? They had to.

"Brynn!" Dad's shout startled me. I whirled around and ran to help him carry the luggage to the Jeep. Leia sat next to one tire, her big body pressed close to the Jeep, her tongue hanging out with nervous pants. Dad secured the tarp and put the doors on, hurrying through the process and narrating it too quickly for me to understand or follow. I tried to help, but I mostly got in the way.

My skin prickled. I tried to ignore how out of breath Dad was, and how bad the traffic was getting, and how many people had to get out over that one little bridge before Alonzo unleashed its fury.

As soon as the sun started to rise, Dad called my mom to let her know we were evacuating and safe. I pretended to be dozing so I wouldn't have to hear the worry in her voice.

"I know you're awake," Dad said gently when he hung up.

I shrugged. It was too early to get into it.

It took us an hour to get halfway across the bridge. I drummed my feet and tapped my thighs. The water looked like frosting in the gray dawn light, lit up all over with white-caps. Plastic bags and debris tumbled along the highway, moving a lot faster than the gridlocked traffic.

All I wanted to do was take a better look at the yearbook, but I didn't feel right doing it in front of Dad.

"We're hours away from the hotel," Dad said gently, for the third time.

Hours used to mean nothing. When I was online, there was always something to distract me, someone to talk to.

Now I was alone with my thoughts, Leia's panting, and some podcast about the interstate system that none of us were listening to.

The atmosphere squeezed closer. Hurricanes had something to do with pressure, and I could feel it. My lungs were too tight, and my head pounded.

Waves were starting to crest into fluffy white tips. If we got stuck on the bridge and the storm tide came up, it would wash us into the bay.

"Do you have one of those things to break car windows open?" I asked.

"Brynn. It's a Jeep. This whole thing comes apart."

I crossed my arms. My pits were beyond sweaty. "That isn't reassuring."

Dad reached over and scratched me behind the ear, and Leia made a jealous sort of sound from the back seat. "Put your window down a crack for now. We could both use the fresh air anyway."

I rolled it down and inhaled the salty-wet smell of the storm and the morning. With the window cracked, the sound of the waves crashing against the bridge whispered. Powerful. Frightening.

My heart rate started to climb.

"I don't like this." My voice wavered.

What if I had to go to the bathroom? Where would I go? What if I had to go on the side of the road and a car careened into me? Would I die right then, or would I get knocked over the side into the water, too broken to swim?

Dad's voice cut through my violent thoughts. "Thirty more minutes and we'll be back on land."

My next breath didn't make it in all the way. I fumbled for the backpack at my feet and tore it open, frantically searching around for my makeup bag, where I kept my bottle of Xanax. A tendril of shame wrapped around me, even as I recognized it as unnecessary and misplaced.

Be compassionate.

My therapist told me to care about myself the same way I cared about others. I wasn't a dick, so I'd never judge someone for taking medication. But I wasn't very good at not being a dick to myself.

"You all right, sweetie?"

Dad knew my history and knew how to talk about it. But that wasn't the same as having to wrench open a bottle of water and swallow anxiety medication like my life depended on it. I shut my eyes and waited for the little pill to do its work.

Most of the time I felt better before the meds had reasonable time to kick in. Because I knew it would work—it always worked. A reliable blanket fort, no matter how reluctant I was to crawl inside it.

I'd been worried about taking it the first time, afraid I'd get high or feel out of control. But it had only made me feel okay. Normal. Not ruled by my body going on a fight-or-flight mission for no reason.

Like needing Tylenol for a headache. Or chemo for cancer. No different.

I closed the bottle of water and tucked it between my thighs. Dad stayed silent, either because he didn't know what to say or knew better than to say anything. Little by little, I regained my footing. My breathing evened out. My nerves remained, jarring in my belly, but more of an uncomfortable flutter than an all-out riot.

We crept along the highway.

I watched a pelican fight the wind, brown feathers ruffling defiantly as it swooped and cut hard angles through the sky. I wondered how hard the wind would be when the hurricane reached us.

Up in Ohio, we occasionally dealt with tornadoes. I'd never personally seen one, but I'd huddled in the bathroom a few times. During one close call, Dad had still been at home. He'd taken the mattress off my twin bed and propped it up like a tent in the hallway, and the three of us had pressed close beneath it. Small, I'd squeezed between my parents, my face against my mom's warm ribs and my butt tucked against my dad's hip. I'd been little enough to find it exciting.

Half an hour passed, and the sky went from a creepy nighttime gray to a slightly less creepy daytime gray. I sighed involuntarily and slumped with relief when I noticed that my lungs filled and emptied all the way.

We'd made it over the bridge.

We idled in traffic on the outskirts of Tampa, having only made it that far in two hours. Tall pine trees and a low scrub of spiky palms lined the long stretch of dull highway. It was windy, but not even as windy as it'd been before the thunderstorm on Skylar's beach.

Every fleeting thought of Skylar tried to become bigger—tried to drag me into thinking about Patricia's sad eyes and Jonathan's anger and how I'd hurt them. I blew out a breath and forced myself to stare out the window. The yearbook was right there in my backpack. If I opened it, I'd find her smiling photo. I wasn't sure if it would be comforting or frightening.

A field of fat black cows interrupted the line of boring trees on the side of the road. They would have been a blur if we'd been going more than ten miles per hour.

"Cows," I said reflexively. Mom always did that on road trips.

Dad huffed a quiet laugh.

While the air still buzzed with the promise of the oncoming storm, it wasn't anything like the flash-bang arrival of a tornado. I stuck my bare feet out the window and slumped in the passenger seat. The easy-listening station I'd flipped to the day before had gone patchy. I hoped that meant we were getting far enough from the water to be safe.

"How far do we have to go?" I asked, craving a bed to catch up on the sleep I'd missed hauling ass away from the houseboat.

"The storm's as big as the whole state. There's really no outrunning it."

I plucked a snag in my jeans and braced myself for a wave of anxiety that didn't come. Maybe I had too many other things to be anxious over. "Wow. So we're screwed."

"Nah, we're out of the flood zone now." Dad let out a sigh as we ground to a full stop. "But I'd like to get a little further inland. Storms lose strength without the water feeding them."

"That sounds like magic." My voice came easily, no longer thinned with panic. Being super tired worked wonders.

Dad glanced at me and smiled, eyes mirroring the exhaustion in my bones. "I always thought so too." He waved his hand in a circle. "Especially because they have names. Alonzo's up there pulling the magic out of the gulf to get stronger and faster."

I grinned back at him. Rain pattered the windshield from another light band at the front of the storm. The weather had been like this since the sun came up—lightly windy and occasionally rainy. Hurricanes were like giant, slow-motion tornadoes, sending tendrils of mildly shitty weather out before the real show started.

They also spawned baby tornadoes. I crossed my arms, as if I could ward off the twinge of sneaky dread. "Well, I hope he chills out."

Dad's eyes shadowed. He turned his gaze back to the road as we began our crawling pace again, and I knew he was thinking about the houseboat. The yearbook was starting to feel like more of a necessity. I couldn't just sit there perceiving Dad's sadness.

His phone lit up in the cup holder on the dashboard. Paula's face smiled from the caller ID notification. He picked it up.

"How are you doing?" he asked, warm and tense all at once.

I heard the gentle sound of her voice but couldn't make out her words. She'd already called once to let Dad know she was volunteering with a nursing home to help with patient transport. They were in a van only a few miles behind us. Dad obviously didn't like being even that far away from her with the storm approaching. My tummy fluttered with a mix of jealousy and happiness that I couldn't even begin to unpack. She wasn't a threat to me at all, and it was good that Dad was this serious about somebody in his life—somebody as cool as Paula.

Beneath all that weirdness, I worried about her too. It was just worry, though. Not anxiety. I'd tried to explain the difference to Mom many times, but she didn't understand it. No one did, unless they had anxiety too. Because it wasn't like a gnaw of concern or a whiplash moment of fear. Anxiety grabbed me by the lungs and the throat and drove its fingers into my intestines and shouted at me until all I could hear were its lies.

Worry I could deal with, and I latched on to that reasonable response to a deadly storm, relieved that I hadn't felt more than a little ripple of intense dread since taking my meds. Maybe my brain knew I needed to keep it together in case we faced an actual, for-real life-and-death situation.

My tongue went dry and I swallowed, turning my attention back to Dad before I managed to trigger another freak-out.

"I don't think we'll make it much farther before this really picks up," he told Paula. "I'm getting off at the next exit and taking back roads."

He laughed a huffed-breath of a sound at something Paula said.

"Do you want to try to meet us at the hotel?" Dad had called ahead the moment we'd gotten in the Jeep, securing us a pet-friendly room at a motel off the interstate.

He frowned as he listened to the calm lilt of her voice. "Okay. Be safe. Love you." His gaze darted to me like he'd gotten caught doing something wrong, and I offered him a smile to try to say that it was all right—he was allowed to care about his girlfriend.

Even though love sounded very, very serious.

"Are we there yet?" I asked playfully, but not entirely insincerely.

"It's still several parsecs to the next exit."

"Oh my God, Dad. That's it." Overcome with cringe and boredom, I finally got out the yearbook. It was too big to hide from Dad, but he didn't react when I started thumbing through it. He was probably busy chuckling to himself about embarrassing me.

I'd never bought a yearbook before. It had sounded old-fashioned. And what did I want to remember? I hated school.

I doubted Skylar had hated school the same way. I imagined seeing her in every spread. But I only found her in two places—her official photo and the volleyball team photo. Convinced I'd somehow missed her, I went back through every page, scanning the pics of groups of kids posing candidly in the hallways and in the cafeteria and out on a lawn. Skylar was never part of the groups of girls who posed, arms around one another's shoulders, smiling.

"Dad?" I asked abruptly.

He let out a startled sound and responded, "Yeah, baby?"

My throat felt dry. I wasn't sure what I'd wanted to ask him. "Did people sign your yearbook when you were in school?"

"Um, a little. Honestly, most of the signatures were accompanied by crude drawings and thinly veiled references to parties."

"But people, like, knew you."

"Of course. I mean, yeah. People know you too," he said, obviously trying to sound reassuring. That wasn't what I needed reassurance about.

"Yeah," I said absently, closing the yearbook. Feeling unsettled and adrift, I put it away in my backpack. The yearbook didn't line up with the picture of Skylar I'd put together in my mind. My Skylar had been popular. Envied. Active. Magnetic. Surrounded by adoring friends.

If I was so wrong about that, how would I ever figure out who had hurt her?

I needed this jerk hurricane to get itself over with so I could ask Skylar to give me tips on who to talk to from her yearbook. And maybe she'd recognize the handwriting of the person who had written that they were sorry.

Maybe *someone* could tell me how she'd spent her last days.

Her last day.

We broke out of traffic on a four-lane road lined with produce stands and tiny motels. Most of them were boarded up, and all of them had amazing old signs with mermaids and gators and pirates on them. Homesickness stuck in my throat as we drove by an antique stand, where a small crowd of old people were carrying odds and ends from a display near the road into a shed that didn't look like it would stand up to a thunderstorm, let alone a hurricane. This neighborhood looked like Ohio.

"Is everyone going to be okay?" I don't know why I asked such a childish question.

Dad patted my leg. "I hope so, sweetie. It doesn't help that it changed course overnight, but people got moving. It's the ones who don't have the means to move that are in the most danger." He tripped up on the word and glanced at me nervously, probably concerned that the wrong thing could set me off at any moment. Which wasn't really an unfounded concern.

"Like old people?"

"And people without cars. People who live in trailer parks."

"Won't someone help them?" I asked, thinking of Paula stuck in a van full of sick, frail, old people. I didn't really like being around super elderly people. Their spotted, shaking hands and milky eyes set my nerves on edge, and made me feel like a complete dick for feeling equal parts fear and empathy.

"This area hasn't seen a big storm in over three decades. Most folks don't have any firsthand experience with hurricanes. I don't think there were enough evacuation processes in place." He turned the music up. A woman crooned about saying good night, her voice punctuated by static. It sounded like radio broadcasting from the edge of the world, and it didn't do much to soothe my concern for the people left behind in St. Pete. "Anyway, the weather people exaggerate sometimes to get people moving. Maybe it won't be as bad as it sounds."

He didn't sound very hopeful.

We stopped at a red light. I scanned a cluster of hotels—each identical to the next except for a few colors in the logo. Sleep Well. Comfort Place. Nite Inn. Every single one of them looked sturdy and clean. The light turned green, and we passed them. I craned my neck to look back longingly. "We're not staying there?"

"They only take pets under thirty pounds. Leia's about half a billion pounds." Dad reached into the back seat to ruffle her fur. "Aren't you, girl?"

The oaks and pines and palms alongside the road swished and swayed. I cracked the window to listen to the sound of the wind in the leaves, and the pressure made my ears pop. The rain had stopped again, but everything was wet and the sky was gray. The street was already littered with leaves and fronds and small sticks blown down from the trees.

My heartbeat turned up a few notches. Healthy worry leaned a little toward the squeeze-tight embrace of panic. "We're almost there, though?"

Dad ruffled my hair just like he'd ruffled the dog's fur. "One more mile. We did it! The drive is the exciting part, trust me. After this, we sit around and stare at each other."

I didn't believe him. There was no way riding out a hurricane would be boring, even if we were in a hotel with nothing to do but wonder if a tree would impale the entire room, crushing us instantly.

Fortunately, our hotel was in the middle of a wide parking lot with no big trees nearby to become deadly projectiles. It wasn't a shack, like I'd expected, but it was only two stories tall. I wasn't sure if that made it sturdier in a hurricane or at greater risk of whatever hurricanes did to mess things up.

"I don't like those big windows," Dad said, his eyebrows creasing with a furry frown. Each window faced the outside instead of an interior hallway. Sunlight streamed through the glass. He saw my face. "I don't see any big trees around. It'll be fine."

I waited in the Jeep with Leia, stroking the wrinkles between her ears idly while Dad checked us in. My thoughts shook around restlessly. I needed to ask Skylar who she'd been friends with. Why wasn't she in any pictures?

She was so far away now. Back in the water. Like something I'd only imagined.

Dad showed up at his door, startling me. He flashed me two key cards and a parking tag for the rearview mirror. "I'm going to get you and Leia settled in and then head to the pharmacy across the street to see if they have any more water."

"We already brought like six gallons." My voice hit an embarrassing whiny tone.

What I meant was that I didn't want Dad to leave me alone with the storm lurking.

"Why don't you come along with me and get some snacks?" he asked.

"I need tampons anyway." Which was true. My period hadn't arrived yet, but it grumbled in my lower belly, warning me of another impending storm.

Dad didn't flinch or anything. "Sounds good."

I climbed out of the Jeep and helped him unload the luggage and boxes crammed around Leia in the back seat. We made a few trips from the car to the room on the first floor. It smelled strongly of bleach, which hopefully meant it was very clean and not the recent scene of a gory murder. The flat-screen TV beckoned me, the promise of my first exposure to cable in weeks. I wasn't sure what I wanted to watch first—a juicy reality show or one of those wonderfully soothing science shows about how pencils and refrigerators and makeup were made.

I found a spot near the bathroom to shove my suitcase and backpack while Dad got Leia settled on a dog bed between the double beds in the room. Excitement fluttered through me. Mom and I rarely stayed in hotels. We'd gone to Niagara Falls once, and we'd driven down to Tennessee to go hiking another time. Both had been trips for fun, adventures away from home and school. When we weren't at home taking care of our everyday things, Mom softened and became a person who laughed more easily. She cheated on her diet and stayed up late watching the shows I liked, and she didn't stress about damp towels left on the floor.

We got along better on adventures.

I associated plain white sheets, ugly paintings, and uglier bedspreads with adventures, and even though this wasn't exactly an adventure, my heart tripped with excitement. I took Dad's hand when we walked out the door. He glanced down at me—wearing surprise openly—and squeezed my hand back and smiled.

The wind was so strong it felt like we could lean into it and fly away. It whipped my tank top against my body and slicked my curls back from my face. "Whoa."

Dad's low laugh rumbled. "*Whoa* is right. Let's hurry up."

We dashed across the street as rain began to pelt us. In the pharmacy, everyone jogged around as if we were about to be struck by a tidal wave. Trying not to get swept up in the jittery energy, I grabbed barbecue potato chips and beef jerky, candy, and a loaf of bread. Dad grabbed canned meat, swearing that it wasn't the worst thing ever on sandwiches.

I told myself we were playing house, supplementing Dad's huge hurricane kit with tasty road-trip goods. When Dad led me to the water aisle, only three bottles of sparkling water remained on the whole shelf. I stopped short, my grip tight on the little blue pharmacy shopping cart.

The excitement of checking into a hotel room snuffed out.

I'd never seen an empty store shelf before.

This wasn't a game.

Dad loaded up the cart with the remaining water and nudged my shoulder. "Better get going."

I grabbed some ibuprofen, tampons, and wet wipes. The travel section caught my attention, and I picked up travel shampoos and conditioners since I'd forgotten mine in Dad's shower. Also because I couldn't resist the cuteness of tiny shampoo bottles.

The adorable little bottles weren't enough to kick-start the excitement I'd felt before. This was scary. Water-shortage scary. People-rushing-around scary.

After Dad checked out, we divvied up the bags and headed out into the wilds of the pharmacy parking lot. With the wind at our backs, we ran across the road. My hair slapped my face. I sneezed and nearly dropped my bags.

Someone honked relentlessly at the intersection as we crossed. Angry lines of tension marred the driver's face as he screamed at the car in front of him. Across the street, twenty cars lined up at the gas station, and half the pumps had bags over the handles. Uneasy, I huddled closer to Dad and followed him like a duckling back to the relative safety of our hotel room.

Dad sat on the bed, checking the batteries in a bunch of flashlights. A weather radio droned beside him. He tossed me the TV remote. "Better watch what you can before the power goes out."

I shivered and put on the worst reality show I could find, hoping Dad was exaggerating about the power outage being inevitable. Leia jumped up on the bed and settled her big, warm body beside me, and the wind began to howl.

CHAPTER SIXTEEN

MY MOM HAD A thing about weather reports during the winter. She kept the TV on nonstop to try to predict how much her commute would suck and what she needed to dress us in. The quiet instrumentals and calmly concerned forecasters were the soundtrack of my crappy weeknights.

Curled up in a scratchy floral comforter, I watched red and orange blobs move in from the Gulf of Mexico to Tampa Bay and up the coast, to where we hid in our inland hotel room. They wobbled like video-game clouds, the same as all the weather reports I'd ignored while doing my homework on the dining room table. Dad sat on the bed by the window, messing around on his phone and occasionally glancing at the screen.

For the past week or so, I hadn't thought about Jordan as much as I'd expected to. Skylar and the bayou had pulled me away from the constant nagging sensation that I needed to talk to my best friend. Now the loss of phone and Internet access ached keenly. Being trapped in a hotel room was the perfect occasion to chat with Jordan. I had so much to catch them up on, I didn't even know where I'd start.

Of course, I'd have to tell Jordan that Skylar was a real girl. A living girl. Jordan and I had made a pact to always call each other out on worrisome shit, and if they'd texted me about talking to a ghost I'd probably invoke the dreaded parental heads-up.

Which is what Jordan had done to me at the end of the school year.

Did they wonder if I was still mad?

I wasn't.

Now it was only a lingering ache. A hitch in my breath.

I picked at a frayed cuticle. Leia snored in her sleep.

The summer was only going to last so long. Every hour I spent here in the middle of nowhere was an hour I could be spending trying to understand how Skylar had died.

The hurricane felt like a waste of time. It was leaning toward more disappointing than exciting, and even acknowledging that as a half-baked thought made me feel like a tremendous tool. If the storm fizzled out, it meant people wouldn't lose their homes or their lives. It didn't mean I was being cheated out of an interesting life experience.

Besides, nothing was going to get much more interesting than being marooned on a mangrove island in a full-blown summer thunderstorm. With a dead girl.

I sighed, and then smiled weakly at Dad when he glanced up at me. *It's fine, Dad. I'm thinking about whether my dead buddy, Skylar, is able to stay under the water or if she has to go to the surface to ghost-breathe.* That would go over well.

It was true. When I let my mind drift, it filled with ugly images: The calm bay gone stormy. The dark waves choking her and pushing her onto the sharp shell-covered shore, where the mangrove buds spiked all around. Limbs falling from trees and the rain going sideways in the furious wind. Skylar unable to get away from any of it.

I was more concerned about someone who'd already died in those unforgiving waters than I was about the people who might have gotten stuck on the shoreline, unable to evacuate on time. I wasn't scoring very many karma points.

My belly sloshed with the two liters of Sprite Dad and I had shared before it got warm. I climbed up to pee, groaning at the cramping sensation of my full bladder.

When I set my foot down on the thin carpet, the window to our hotel room shattered.

The booming sound cut through me, and I registered the shock as pain at first, certain that I'd been sliced into pieces by flying glass.

I screamed and dove between the bed and the wall. Leia leaped down there after me, and we landed in a tangle of limbs and paws. She barked and I yelped out senseless noises. I realized I wasn't cut or bleeding, but the terror-shock of the crash and the rainy wind blasting into our hotel room paralyzed me.

Fear took the wheel. I couldn't see or think. I couldn't move.

Neither of us stopped making terrified sounds until Dad leaned over us, yelling something about *be quiet for five seconds*. Sheepish and sniffling, I determined that he was fine. I was also fine. We weren't actively dying. Leia ducked her head and planted her wet snout into my armpit.

Dad shook his head. "Good to know I can trust you two in a crisis."

I wiped my nose.

"An empty trash can blew across the parking lot and hit our window. I'm going to prop one mattress against the window for now just in case, but I don't think we'll be unlucky enough to be hit by another random thing. Got it?"

I didn't think Dad should be pushing his luck making assumptions like that, but I nodded and helped him move the mattress. My legs shook so hard I stumbled. He didn't need my awkward assistance, but I needed to move to make sure my body would listen to me.

The adrenaline of the boom-crash and diving away from it sent waves of buzzing weakness through my limbs. I'd never really understood how any of that worked. According to my biology textbook, adrenaline was supposed to be make me faster and more responsive to danger—sort of like a quick shot of superpower skills. But it only made me feel disoriented and a little like I needed to poop.

Dad and I made a noise of disgust at the same time. Where the mattress had been, the box spring displayed an array of loose change, shiny foil condom wrappers, and enough multicolored stains to make it a work of modern art.

He threw the spare comforter over it, but that only sent a handful of wrappers scattering onto the floor.

"There are no words," I said.

"Hey, it's a sixty-dollar hotel room. What do you expect?"

"That seems like a lot of money for being exposed to someone else's potentially life-threatening germs."

My bladder reminded me how fortunate I'd been not to piss my pants when the window shattered. I hurried to the bathroom the way I did on an airplane, certain that turbulence would send me crashing off the toilet, only to be discovered later, unconscious and pants-less. I scrubbed my hands hard with the too-small bar of smelly hotel soap. As I was soaping up to my elbows like a surgeon on TV, eager to get the hotel germs off, the power went out with a quick pop and a high squeak.

Actually, the squeak was me, screaming again—but too startled to get the whole sound out. The water continued to pulse, and I splashed the soap off my arms in a rush. Hot tears sprang down my cheeks. Dad came up behind me with two flashlights and wrapped his arms around me.

"It's okay, sweetie. The power lines are aboveground around here. It's completely normal for the power to go out."

It was only early evening, but the mattress over the window blocked the light. I turned and hid my face against Dad's chest until I could get ahold of the tears. He was right; there was nothing to be scared of. It was only dark. I could hear the wind, and it was the same as before. Howling and scary, but nothing like the freight-train sound my mom had always warned me tornadoes sounded like. We'd be fine. We weren't going to get sucked into the sky and dropped onto the concrete, broken and dead before we hit the ground. Probably.

"This is the really, really boring part, that's all," Dad said. He pulled me to the floor, and we sat between the bed and the wall—both of us too big for the space. Leia rolled onto her side on the bed, probably using her unfair night-vision advantage to laugh at us.

The narrow space cradled me in a tight hug. Dad's even breathing and the constant whoosh of wind lulled me into a light doze. I curled against him, my knees pulled to my chest—squishing my boobs—and let my brain go into that woozy mode that preceded sleep. My thoughts circled like water going down a drain. Logan and the library; his friend's appraising gaze. The McKenzies and all their huge windows and the big trees in their neighborhood. Paula and her old people. Empty yearbook messages. *Brynn's Tide* alone on the water. Mom worrying.

Until the storm passed, Mom would be freaking out. Her stress was always my fault. The post that had gotten me sent here in the first place. The doctor's appointments that ended with long lists of questions and the quiet scratch of her pen against the notebook she carried around in her purse—the notebook full of anecdotal evidence of my issues.

Mom tried to be neutral when she talked about me, but I'd heard her out on the porch talking to her friends. *It isn't normal.*

I wasn't normal. Mom told me again and again that it wasn't a bad thing, that deep down no one was normal and everyone had their stuff. But my stuff made my mom's life harder, and I hated that more than anything else. I could handle navigating the ways my brain made it a little harder to do regular, everyday things. But my mom didn't sign up for that crap. She had enough on her plate.

"What is it?" Dad asked softly.

I realized I'd sighed. "Do you ever wish you didn't have a kid?"

He stiffened. "Sweetie. No. Not ever."

"But you went away," I said. I'd meant to say something else, but the words crept right out of my throat. I was powerless against their escape. "You left me."

Dad breathed in slowly. He shifted his arm to hug me more tightly. "I did. I ran away from my responsibilities, and I regret it every day. I thought I'd see you more often, but it didn't work out that way."

"That's a shitty excuse, Dad."

"I know." His bristly beard poked my forehead when he kissed my hairline. "But I never wished you weren't around. Not ever."

"Even when you found out I was crazy?"

"Listen, kiddo. You know better than to use that kind of language." His stern tone made my throat ache, especially because he was right. I was using my words to hurt him, but the shots ricocheted right back at me.

I sucked in a breath. My voice broke. "Don't you wish you had a normal kid?"

"You're not abnormal. You're atypical. And typical would be boring."

"You think hanging out in a hurricane is boring," I said, squinting at him.

"I don't think you're boring." Dad cleared his throat, his voice suspiciously thick. "Your mom sent me your website with the little music videos you make."

My face heated. It was bad enough that Jordan had sent my post to my mom. I had no idea Mom had shared it with my dad.

Tumblr wasn't for my parents. I posted my fanvids, role-played with my friends, shitposted and reblogged memes, responded to asks, and curated sexy photos—men and women that made my stomach flip-flop and my girl parts ache. They weren't Dad-friendly posts, especially when I tagged photos with stream-of-consciousness thoughts about exactly what I'd like to experiment with, physically speaking.

Worse than that, I posted snippets of Jordan's poetry laid out on graphics and collages. I wasn't great at art or coding, but that was my sandbox, my safe place. I missed collaborating so much that I couldn't let myself think about it or the hurt and emptiness would crumble me.

Sharing what I created was like standing in the middle of the street naked with a sign inviting strangers to critique me. It pushed me, and sometimes it hurt me, but I knew it wasn't ruining me or isolating me or enabling me or any of the things Mom blamed on the Internet.

It was easier for Mom to make my problems about what my online friends were doing to me, I guess. She was wrong. All those broken parts were me. Pure Brynn. No one had taught me to feel the things I felt.

I didn't need to be fixed.

I braced myself for Dad to echo the things Mom had said—that I was dabbling in things too grown-up for me, that I was being melodramatic online, that Internet people weren't real friends, that it was too much escapism and not enough confronting the real challenges in my life.

"Your videos are amazing," Dad said. "The way you match the cuts to the music. And the art you do. Do you write the poetry or is it from somewhere else? I don't really . . . I don't know what it's all called."

"Amazing?" I asked in a whisper, still stuck on that part. The word exploded below my heart. I pressed my hand against my belly.

"Well, you know me, I can't even make a stick figure, and I have a Yahoo email address I only check at work. I don't understand technology the way you do. Or art. I think it's great stuff. You need to make me a Star Wars one."

"Okay." I sobbed and laughed at the same time, and it sounded like a sneeze. So much so that Dad mumbled out, "Bless you."

"That was my private stuff, you know." Dad's pride wasn't quite enough to erase the betrayal of my parents creeping on my social media.

"I told your mother that. We don't always see eye to eye. She . . . Well I'm sure you know she was a bit of a problem child at your age. She's scared you'll make the same mistakes she made."

"Wait. Mom was a bad kid?"

Dad laughed like a low roll of thunder. "Oh my God. Don't tell her I said that. She wasn't a bad kid. She . . . She drank a little too much, smoked too much pot. Um. Got caught shoplifting once or twice. Her parents had to send her to a strict private school for high school, and that straightened her out, more or less. I'm going to deeply regret this conversation."

"Mom. My mom. The lady I live with. Smoked weed?"

"She wasn't always a mom." Dad wiggled his nose. "Are you going to rat me out?"

"And lose my source of secret information? No way." My mind reeled. Mom took supplements and had wheatgrass smoothies and frequently lectured me on the dangers of toxins according to infographics she'd seen on Instagram. The most irresponsible thing she did was eat pizza-flavored Combos on road trips. I couldn't picture her breaking the law or getting high. "She thinks I'd do those things?"

"I don't know. Would it be so terrible if you did?"

"Are you advising me to try getting high?"

Dad let out another laugh that tickled my ribs until I smiled too. "No. I'm not. You're a teenager, though. There's certain things kids do. If you get a little crazy with friends, that wouldn't be the end of the world."

He wanted me to hang out with friends. As if I'd never done that before.

My smile faded. "So you don't think my online friends count either."

A little Jordan-shaped place in me hurt like a bruise.

"Now, I didn't say that." Dad sighed. "I don't exactly understand it, but I'm not too worried about it. It's not like you never have contact with other kids. You're smart and funny and confident, and it looks like you dress like other kids your age, and you practice basic hygiene. All that, on top of making art and reading lots of books and putting extra effort into having crushes. Why should I be concerned?"

"Because of the other stuff."

"Because you're awesome, despite struggling with stuff that kneecaps you once in a while?" Dad shifted around and took my chin gently. The flashlight cast Halloween shadows on his face. I decided not to tell him he looked slightly more terrifying than loving. "Your mom feels helpless when she can't make life easier for you, but she's never once complained about you. I mean, she's complained about you hogging the bandwidth on your Wi-Fi. And she said you used all her expensive conditioner once. And when you were a kid, you pooped on the living room floor the first day we tried to potty train you."

A glow of hope formed, but my anxiety squashed it right back down. I struggled to speak around the tightness of it. "She doesn't complain about me being—having all my stuff?"

Dad let go of my chin. His eyes were brighter now, and I looked away, startled by his tears. "Why would she?" he asked.

The question hit me like a crashing wave.

"Would you complain about somebody for having anxiety and needing support?" Dad prompted gently.

I shook my head quickly.

"Do you think if you had a kid someday, you'd be mad at that kid for needing your love and support?"

I blinked, crying for what felt like the billionth time this week. I didn't bother wiping the tears away. "No."

"Do you think your mom's an asshole?"

My jaw dropped. "Wh-what?"

"You heard me," Dad said, firm and gentle all at once. He wasn't kidding.

"No, I don't. Mom's great." The wrongness of his question rang in my ears.

"I'm not going to tell you how to live your life, but next time you start thinking that your mom complains about you or that you annoy her or anything like that, I want you to remember that your mom isn't an asshole. If she works hard to help you, it's because she loves you, and if she has a shitty day, it's because life is hard sometimes. For everyone. For you; for your mom. God, Brynn." He let out a noisy breath. "We want you to be happy, and she's been there for you. She didn't run away."

"I don't think you're an asshole either," I said in a small voice.

Dad choked and dropped his face to my hair. "Thank you."

"Will you tell Mom to give me my computer back when I get home?"

In the silence after my question, the word *home* echoed back at me. This wasn't my home. Dad was never going to be my mom. The word had barbs on it, and I swallowed back my guilt. Maybe we were all meant to hurt each other a little bit, all the time. Maybe the pain kept us honest.

The pain made the weight of Dad's arms on my shoulders warmer and more solid, made me crave the sound of Mom's voice on the phone. "That's up to her. I have to tell her about the McKenzies, that you're still thinking about—"

"I'm not!" The words burst out of me, a hoarse yell that made him jump. Everything had seemed so close to okay again, and now Dad had to rip me open and act like I'd done something bad when I'd only been trying to help Skylar. Disappointment and shame snaked through me, wild and hungry for more pain to gnaw on. And, tired and still a little scared, I fed the hurt. I raised my voice. "I never wanted to kill myself! Neither did Skylar!"

Dad's breath went reedy. I couldn't tell if he was trying not to cry or trying not to shout at me. I had no reason to think he'd yell at me in a scary way, but panic frizzled up my spine. Tensing up, I moved to inch away and he let me squirm out of his arms without protest.

"Brynn. I wanted to give you space, but we have to talk about this. Skylar McKenzie died by suicide. She had depression. I know that's different from what you're going through, but—"

"No." Blood thundered in my ears, louder than the wind outside. I thought about all the happy photos in the yearbook, how Skylar wasn't in any of them. But Skylar wouldn't lie to me. "You don't understand. You have to believe me, Dad. Somebody hurt her and made it look like she did it on purpose. It's true. She—"

She told me.

The breath rushed out of his lungs. The angry sound didn't match the softness of his voice. "Brynn . . ."

I wasn't going to shatter. He could yell at me. He didn't have to murmur like I was an animal about to bolt. "Don't—fucking do that." My breath caught on a snarl of a sob. "You don't believe me. Fine. But I'm going to figure out what happened to her."

"No one hurt her!" he roared.

Fear stole my breath. Leia whined as I scrambled over her warm body, into the empty darkness of the room. Away from his rage.

Even though I knew. I knew.

He wouldn't hurt me.

"She wrote a note, Brynn. It was on her kayak. I found it first, called the cops, idled through the channel. I thought I could save her. I thought I'd get there fast enough, and she'd be all right."

Dad choked between every word, fighting tears that sounded thick and painful. But I couldn't move. I couldn't help him.

"She was only a few years older than you, and that's all I could think. Somebody's daughter. Somebody's little girl. Her handwriting looked like a kid's. She wrote, 'I love you. I'm sorry.' It had been three days. She'd been gone so long already. I stayed with her until the coast guard got there."

Fissures of doubt ran through my body, cracking me open, lighting me up with sorrow unlike any I'd ever known. I thought my bones would shatter like the hotel room window, that I'd blow away, broken into pieces.

I wanted to believe him.

I wanted to believe Skylar.

I didn't remember deciding to move—or moving at all. I was choking one moment and in his arms the next, burrowing against him as if I could retreat from the storm outside and the raging wind inside me. The howl of hurt and confusion.

Had she lied to me?

Had she really hurt so badly, she'd thought she had no other choice, hurt—hurt—

Dad calmed down quickly, shuddering and catching his breath like it strengthened him to have me right there close by, solid and not dead. But the calmer he got, the more I felt like my body would break apart, incandescent with pain and confusion and something else that was harder to touch and name.

I couldn't bear to think that Skylar was carrying broken parts like mine, broken parts that might have lied to her and told her she had no other way to go on.

"I'm sorry," I whispered. To Skylar. To Dad. To the McKenzies. And Mom.

I didn't know what was real anymore. I didn't know what to believe.

I had to talk to Skylar.

Skylar had to tell me the truth.

My muscles burned from being jammed up between the wall and the mattress box and Dad and the dog. I tried to focus on that tangible hurt, anchor myself to it. But the storm inside me churned, bigger than thoughts or sensations. Too big. Too much.

Shivering, I hid my face against my arm and let Dad stroke my hair until rawness gave way to a numb chill. I wasn't going to be able to think my way around this.

I couldn't cry anymore. My throat burned, and my eyelids were gummy.

She was alone in the water.

She'd been alone in the water.

I wanted to rewind the world, to put her back on that kayak and float her to safety. I wanted to tell her to stay inside that day. No matter what had happened, if she'd just stayed inside she'd still be here.

My bones itched. My lungs were heavy in my chest. I gritted my teeth until pain reverberated through my jaw and into my skull.

I needed to scream and thrash, but I held still for Dad.

I held still until my heartbeat evened out and the hurt became heaviness. It occurred to me, like a reflection in a foggy mirror, that I hadn't done a very good job reassuring him.

I didn't have the words to.

"I love you," he finally said, exhaling the words like it taxed him to form them.

My breath whistled through my stuffy nose. "I know."

The storm sang, a torrent of rain and wind that screamed the way I longed to—wild and raw. Without any thunder to startle me, I slowly forgot to be frightened of the weather. The angry hum became white noise.

I extricated myself from Dad's arms and stretched. Too hollowed out to be scared, I learned how to change a tampon in total darkness, which I considered a vague win. Hopefully the skill would never be needed again, but if it did, I'd be set. One tiny victory in the face of too much to wrap my mind around.

I sprawled out on the musty carpet like a snow angel. As the sound of the hurricane faded from a roar to a yawn, the broken window lit up and I spent several seconds thinking aliens were after us.

Aliens wouldn't be *that* much weirder than Skylar.

Heart beating wobbly-fast, I followed Dad to the door, creeping along the wall like backup in a detective movie. The light wasn't aliens. It was headlights. We opened the door to Paula, soaking wet and laughing—dropped off by a taxi with bats inexplicably painted on the side.

I struggled with a brief, strong urge to push her away. Dad and I were surely puffy-eyed and ragged. She was an intruder, an outsider.

Dad ushered her in. I closed the door behind her and leaned against it, watching the glass glitter beneath the window as the taxi pulled away. As quickly as it had risen, my resistance to her presence melted away. Maybe what Dad and I needed was a buffer, for a little while, so we could learn to talk to each other again and pretend we'd never discussed the dead girl in the bayou.

Paula changed in the dark, borrowing one of Dad's shirts and a pair of his boxers. I curled up in the bed facing the mattress-covered window, cheeks heating at the way they giggled softly together while she got dressed. They weren't doing anything shady, but it still sounded so intimate to me. A boyfriend-girlfriend thing. I tried not to think about them taking their clothes off together in other situations.

"Brynn, do you mind sharing the bed with Paula?" Dad asked in a normal way, as if we hadn't yelled at each other and cried forever.

I scooted to one side and patted the sheets. "As long as Paula doesn't mind knowing what's under this mattress."

"What I don't know can't hurt me," she said.

I didn't realize how hungry I was until we had a picnic of water and Spam by the light of Paula's cell-phone screen. A full belly went a long way toward convincing my body that it was time to stop feeling feelings and start sleeping. I crawled to my spot on the bed and pressed my face to the pillow. Exploding with emotions exhausted me in strange places. My cheekbones hurt. The roof of my mouth ached.

Dad slept on the floor with Leia. Paula rustled beside me, her breath never quite evening out. I sent her a mental fist-bump, figuring she was wound up from rescuing her old people and taking a cab all by herself to wherever the hell we were.

But I must have fallen asleep, because the next time I rolled over the morning sun shone around the barrier of the mattress against the window, and my bladder yelled at me to stumble to the bathroom.

A week might as well have gone by. Or a hundred years. Still tired and sore, I wandered around outside, arms stretched out to air briefly free of humidity. Alonzo had sucked it all up and carried it across Florida. Now it was dumping it out into the Atlantic while we licked our wounds.

The parking lot looked the way I felt inside, cluttered with broken palm fronds and wet leaves. I took slow, crunching steps across the waste of it, imagining a world where people stopped existing and plant life took over, sprouting up through the cracks in the pavement and climbing up the walls. When I looked back, civilization hadn't ended. Dad and Paula loaded up the Jeep with our stuff and Leia padded around after them, her great big tail wagging itself into a blur.

A few cars whooshed by, tires noisy against the wet road. I picked out a few broken windows like the one in our hotel room. The buildings still had roofs on them. It wasn't total devastation—just a lot of debris and the streetlights blinking endless yellow. No one had any power yet, but the radio said it was safe to head back to St. Pete. We weren't going to spend another second in the stuffy hotel room with no air-conditioning or electricity or anything to do but gnaw on our feelings.

I wanted to leave everything we'd said here in the ugly room, but going back to St. Pete would mean confronting reality—and Skylar. Dread tickled my intestines. Would I fail some mystical test if I didn't believe what she'd told me?

"Cramps?" Paula asked, gesturing to where I'd pressed my palms against my middle.

I couldn't decide if she looked older or younger with circles under her eyes and her scrubs wrinkled. "Yeah. They're not too bad, though."

"Well, let me know if you need some ibuprofen." She pushed a wisp of hair back into her messy bun. "Are you ready to go?"

I climbed into the cramped back seat with Leia. Even with the windows open, the smell of sweaty, gross bodies thickened the air. Leia was even worse, reeking like a wet rug left in the basement too long.

I rubbed my nose and leaned forward to catch Paula's eye. "Were you scared?

Paula turned in the passenger seat as Dad navigated around a smattering of plastic dumpsters that had blown across the parking lot. "In the storm?"

"With the old people. What if they'd died in the van?"

"I would have felt very helpless. But not scared."

"If you're not scared of old people dying, what are you scared of?"

A strange look crossed her features, brow creasing like a fluttering wing. "I'm scared of failing people. I'm scared of fire-ant nests." She licked her chapped lips. "I'm scared of tidal waves. What about you, Hunter?"

Dad made a humming sound. "What?"

Paula and I exchanged a look. "What are you afraid of?" she asked.

"I'm afraid of losing my daughter," he said, slow and weary. I watched him turn the radio up. His hands looked older than I remembered.

After that, none of us said anything. The tires sang against the pavement, and I draped my body across Leia's back. I'd read somewhere that dogs are warmer than people, and I believed that as her fever-hot body cradled me and I dozed restlessly, my insides twisted up in knots with too many feelings to name. Before I talked to anyone else, before I kept digging and searching and hoping, I had to find Skylar.

She had to tell me the truth.

CHAPTER SEVENTEEN

THE HURRICANE HAD WEAKENED dramatically before hitting land, but the storm surge combined with a high tide had still swamped all the coastal areas of St. Pete. We listened to announcements on the radio. Inch by inch, the high water seeped back into the gulf.

When an hour passed and we were still forty-five miles from home, a guilty twinge in my belly prompted me to dig through my bag. I still hadn't called Mom, mostly because talking to her with Dad and Paula in earshot made me vaguely uncomfortable in ways I couldn't figure out.

I'd forgotten to pack the charger for my shitty flip phone when we'd left. "Can I use your phone to call Mom?" I asked Dad.

Mom picked up halfway through the first ring. "Brynn?"

"We're heading back home now," I said, before she could ask me anything. "I'm fine. It wasn't really that bad. Just long. We haven't seen anything crazy on the drive home. Just a few spots where little tornadoes went through." I yawned. It sounded fake, but it wasn't.

Mom's silence on the other end told me she thought the yawn was fake, and I frowned. It wasn't my fault we'd ridden out a hurricane, but Mom was already mad at me, as if Alonzo had been a delinquent kid from school I'd snuck into my bedroom to dry hump. She made me go from zero to ashamed in the span of a breath. I didn't know who I hated more in that moment—her or me.

"Well. If you're fine, I'll let you go." Her hurt snapped at my skin. I'd blown her off before, faking yawns and deliberately trailing off into carefully cultivated boredom. But this time I really wanted to talk to her, and she'd already thrown up an icy shield between us.

She told me she loved me, and I echoed it back like a robot, dizzy trying to figure out how a short conversation had gone sour that quickly.

I handed Dad his phone. He dropped it in the console, and it jangled against the loose change. We got stuck in traffic again. He sighed and fiddled with the radio stations. When a sports car in front of us stopped suddenly, he pounded on the steering wheel and yelled, "Goddamn it! Watch the fucking road!"

"Hunter."

"She's heard worse at school," he said, voice cutting. Tired.

Paula shifted and looked out the window, nearly putting her back to my dad.

The flare of Dad's temper didn't scare me. Even if it did, I deserved it. He was like this because of me. Because I'd kept him up all night thinking about a horrible thing. Because he worried about me.

All the time.

I stared out the window. We were on the bridge we'd crossed the first day I'd come to Florida. I watched the water, scanning for blue-black dolphin fins.

And flashes of yellow.

My chest gave a pang deeper than the rumble of hunger in my belly.

I missed her.

Digging out the yearbook, I found her school picture and traced the tiny square. She was far too much to be contained by one photo.

Longing ached in my finger joints and my sternum and where the underwire of my bra dug into my chest, sore from sleeping with it on. All this time, Mom had begged me to make a local friend, and now I could see why. Skylar's wicked smile coaxed joy out of places I'd never tapped into before. She pulled me out of my head and pushed me through my choppy fears to the calmer waters beyond. I wanted to touch her—not in a sexy way. I wanted to feel the solid strength of her body.

Even if it was cold.

Skylar made me stronger. It didn't seem fair. The water had taken her. Kept her. Was there really nothing I could do to help?

The sky was gray-white with low, cottony cloud cover. I leaned my head against the window.

We weren't far from the bayou. I could see the squat industrial buildings in the distance, where the bridge hit the land. My eyes drifted closed, and I pictured Skylar with shimmering mermaid scales and a tail. Her hair flowed in watery swirls around her smiling face.

Even in my mind, the water wouldn't clear up. Mud and seagrass swirled around her. I swam toward her, reaching for her hand. It wasn't wrinkled, but mine was swollen and waterlogged. The current pulled me away and the darkness grew between us, and I called her name.

"Brynn."

The water went down my throat when I screamed for her. I looked up, trying to find the dappled-sun surface. The bubbles from my nose went down, not up. I choked.

"Brynn!"

Dad was patting my face, his eyes close and worried. I blinked at him, and the water receded as if someone had pulled a drain in a bathtub the size of the world. I'd fallen asleep again in the back seat.

"Where's Paula?"

"We dropped her off. You were really out. You were talking in your sleep." He looked at me funny.

I got my tonsils out when I was twelve, and my biggest fear had been coming out of anesthesia without any control over my words. I'd been so worried about it I'd asked every nurse and tech who came near me to make sure I had the lowest dose of sedation possible, and to keep my mom away while I was getting up. It was the first year of my raging, brand-new hormones, and I'd already started spending night after night with my hands shoved in a karate chop between my thighs, my mind volleying between all my crushes. I was terrified I'd say something sexual and my mom would hear.

I hadn't thought about that day in a long time. Nothing weird had come out of my mouth when I'd woken up. I'd only cried, voice hoarse and eyes gummy from whatever drops they'd put in there while I'd been out.

The way Dad looked at me was exactly how I'd been afraid my mom would look at me—like I had something to be ashamed of. I pushed him out of the way, extracted myself from the back seat, and lost my footing. Dad caught my arm and kept me from jamming my knees against the gravel.

I stared at the lot where Dad kept the Jeep.

All the boats on trailers were jumbled up against one another along the far fence, stacked like toys. Broken toys. Fiberglass peeked from cracked hulls, pink as flesh. Blue and white coolers and orange life vests dotted the ground. With a low gasp, I spotted our little boat upside down, the trailer mangled beside it.

"We should have taken the boat with us," Dad said very quietly, as if talking to himself. "I don't know what I was thinking. The surge lifted everything." The tired lines around his eyes deepened. He scrubbed his hand across his beard.

I looked out at the water and didn't want to say a word. Not a single word. I wanted to pause time forever, even if it meant being stuck in this funhouse of a gravel lot next to the carcasses of sheds and boats and battered, waterlogged cars.

Dad must have seen the way my expression changed. He whirled around, following my gaze, and saw her out there on the horizon, peeking out from behind the closest mangrove island.

It wasn't fair.

"Dad." I grabbed his hand and tried to turn him away. He'd already done this once before—scanned the surface, saw something *wrong*. Had it felt like this before? The drop-drop-drop of realization. The horror.

Brynn's Tide was on her side, the slide and rail protruding from the water. Alonzo had unmoored her and tossed her through the bayou. She'd lost the battle, coming to rest on the mushy bottom near the marina. All Dad's stuff—his books and his clothes and the guitar propped in the corner collecting dust. The paddleboards and Leia's dock and her bowl and her toys. All the things I hadn't picked through and asked about because I'd been too busy hating being there to ask my dad what he cared about. All of it was gone.

He must have known all along that *Brynn's Tide* wouldn't make it through the storm.

I looked away, closed my eyes, pressed my face to my dad's back, and shivered, too tired and woozy from sleep to cry. This was a bad dream, as warped and gummy eyed as the nightmare bayou and Skylar swimming away from me, a flash of shimmering green scales.

"Fuck this," I said, finding power in the shock-hurt of anger that made me want to shoot a torpedo at the houseboat and finish the job. Obliterate every sign of our life out there on the water.

Dad's shoulders shook. When he turned, I saw that he was laughing with wet eyes and a rueful twist of his mouth.

He pushed his hands into my hopelessly tangled hair until they got stuck, and he smooched the top of my head. "You got that right," he said.

We walked down the street to a convenience store and bought cans of SpaghettiOs and warm sodas with cash, while we waited for one of Dad's friends to come by with another boat on a trailer. I ate bite after tangy bite like I'd never eaten before.

A plan brewed behind my eyes, no matter how much I tried to unthink it. I couldn't be this close to the water and not do something, especially when our waterfront property was at the bottom of the bayou. For all I knew, we wouldn't be staying anywhere near Skylar from now on.

I'd only have a small window of opportunity.

"You okay?" Dad asked. He bumped against me, sending an aftershock of guilt through my body. I should have been the one asking him—after all, he'd just lost his home.

I forced a smile. "It's already getting hot."

"We don't get much of a reprieve this time of year."

Speeding cars skittered pebbles at our ankles as we walked along the side of the road back to the boatyard.

I wrinkled my nose. "Ew! Is that smell dead fish?"

Dad laughed. "It's probably seaweed. Maybe some dead fish. The storm surge washed a lot of crap up past the tide line."

I pictured Skylar washed up onto land and reminded myself that she was a ghost, not a fish. She'd walk her fine ghost self right back into the bayou, probably.

Skylar.

Dad was going to kill me for this.

While he and his friend put a small, undamaged speedboat in the water, I climbed around in the wreckage. Sweat soaked my shirt at my armpits. The rotting smell that lingered all over wasn't enough to mask the stink of a nervous teen girl who hadn't showered in two days. My shoes slid against the hull of a flipped boat as I climbed over it, scanning all the flotsam and jetsam for exactly the right shape.

Dad called out to me to be careful like I was five, not fifteen, and I called back to him that I was fine. He was busy enough not to look too closely, so he didn't see me when I found exactly what I was looking for.

I jogged back over to the boat ramp. "Dad, I'm going to stay here," I said. "I don't want to see the boat all messed up. If that's okay." It was half true, at least.

"Are you sure?" He wiped his eyes and squinted. The afternoon sun had grown relentless. "Want Paula to come pick you up?"

"Nah. That's okay." I had a thought. "But can you leave your phone here with me? In case Mom calls."

He brought me the phone, handed me five dollars for water if I got thirsty, and told me to stay by the Jeep. I wasn't sure why he had to go out and see *Brynn's Tide*. The way it rested in the water, I doubted he'd find anything salvageable.

As soon as Dad took off, I sprinted to the wreckage and began dragging the canoe out from where it was wedged between two boats. It had a tiny hole in the hull, but it was up high—past the waterline. I was pretty sure it would stay afloat. And I didn't have far to go.

In theory, my plan didn't require a boat. But the last thing I needed was someone jumping in after me if they saw me diving off the dock and swimming out into the bayou aimlessly.

I stopped short, my palms raw against the rough metal rim of the canoe. I hadn't dragged it far, and my arms and back already ached. What if the water held dangerous, sunken wreckage from the storm? If this many boats had ended up beached in the lot and the houseboat had rolled over, who was to say other boats—big boats—weren't right there in the dark water. The canoe might hit one and get a bigger hole, and then it would sink. I'd cut my feet on something unseen and waterlogged, and I might bleed to death or get stuck and drown.

Self-loathing welled up inside me. I couldn't do anything. I was useless. What was the point of anything if I couldn't make my brain shut up?

The only thing that kept me moving was helpless anger at my fear. I kept dragging the canoe until I reached the boat ramp. I didn't have a paddle. All I had was a desperate need to know the truth. It was a tiny sliver bigger than my terror.

So I climbed into the canoe.

The whole thing wobbled precariously each time I reached over the side to paddle with my hand like a one-legged duck.

I couldn't see Dad's little boat out in the distance, which meant he was on the other side of the houseboat, probably tied up to it and climbing around the wreck. Hopefully not inside it, where he could be trapped if it rolled over.

"You're more of a flibbertigibbet than usual," Skylar said.

I wasn't more than fifteen feet from the dock. She watched me warily, as if she already knew what I was going to ask her.

"Are you kidding me?" The canoe nearly tipped because I stood up. Standing made me feel powerful, like a cat with a ruffle of furious fur bristling up all around me. "You could get this close to the dock and you made me paddle out here to talk to you?"

"It was funny!" She treaded water, smiling, her hair pooling around her shoulders, her teeth and eyes bright, and all of her so good to see. "I wanted to see how far you'd get, but then I got bored."

"Bored!" I caught myself shrieking and lowered my voice to a hysterical growl. "Bored?"

I glanced at the boatyard beyond the empty dock. The handful of men picking through the rubble paid me no attention, but that would change if I started screaming at the water. Especially if I was the only one who could see Skylar there *being a dick*.

A million things bubbled through me and got caught in a traffic jam in my throat. All that came out of me was a guttural sound and wheezing breath through my nostrils. Skylar shrugged one pretty, freckled shoulder.

I knew her sadness was there, like grime beneath my feet, but I was too fired up with rage to pay attention to it, to care about what it meant. I waved my hand wildly, as if I could erase her from the bayou. From this summer. From my life.

"Tell me the truth," I spat out. "My dad said he found a note. A note you wrote. A suicide note."

"Your dad found it?" Skylar asked, looking horrified.

My fingers sank into my hair. I felt like ripping it out. I felt like dissolving. "Why are you asking me that?" My voice was a hollow, scraping sound. "Skylar, did you lie to me?"

Skylar's mouth opened and closed silently.

I hated everything so much. I started to cry so hard I thought I'd choke to death. "I believed you. Why would you lie to me?"

The canoe tilted sharply. I jammed my foot back to catch my balance, which tilted it more. It flipped hard, thrashing me into the water. Pain flared by my ear, hotter than my rage.

"Brynn." Skylar swam up to me. Her eyes were wild. Two little storms. "Grab the canoe."

"You can't tell me what to do! You're a liar! You tricked me! I made a fool out of myself. I hurt my dad! That's not even the worst part." I was howling, crying like a little kid. "The w-worst part is—you didn't trust me. You didn't trust me. Nobody trusts me."

"Grab the canoe!"

She yelled it, the sound of her voice echoing not across the water but in my ears, the way God spoke to people in movies. Startled into silence, I grabbed the canoe and wiped my eyes with my free hand. My fingers came away red.

"You cut your head, you idiot! You're bleeding all over. Take the canoe and swim back to the boat ramp. Right now. Right now, Brynn! You can't touch the bottom here."

Only a little anger seeped out of me. Here I was, probably mortally injured, definitely in danger of a shark attack, likely seconds from passing out and drowning, and for once I didn't think about death chasing me through my life.

"But I trusted you." My voice sounded like a croaking frog. "I tried to help you, to solve your—your fucking fake murder. After you lied to me."

"I didn't want you to know the truth." Skylar's eyes shone. She looked pale all over, like my anger was washing her away. "I didn't want you to hate me."

"I don't hate you," I sobbed out. I wanted to hate her, and I couldn't. I never would.

"Keep swimming, Brynn." The water rippled around her. Her voice got softer, smaller. "Kick your feet."

My head hurt. I swam, clutching the side of the canoe, and tried to remember all the things I needed to know. The empty photos. Her empty smile. "Your mom gave me your yearbook."

"My mom?" Skylar's eyes widened. She was there one moment and out of reach feet away the next, blinking through the water.

I sucked in a breath and tightened my grip on the canoe. Had I lost time for a second? Or was Skylar bringing out all the dead girl tricks now that I knew the truth? She had nothing to lose—the friendship we'd forged out on the beach was nothing but disappointment and lies.

"Yes." I licked my lips and tasted the blood running down my face from my hairline. "I talked to your mom, and I didn't *believe* her until my dad told me about your note. And you're a giant asshole. Do you have any idea what you did to them?"

Her face changed, stricken with guilt and sadness. A small part of me recognized that what I was saying was terribly wrong—a tremendous betrayal. It was cruel to let her believe that her parents held her pain against her, but the words had been satisfying.

Even if they felt like rusting anchors now.

She blinked away again, farther, until she looked like one of the white crab-trap floaties that dotted the bayou.

Like something you might mistake for a person.

Maybe that's all she'd ever been.

My heartbeat roared in my ears, and my vision tilted. The water was black. Black black black.

A thought cut through the murkiness. *I don't want to die.*

I started swimming awkwardly, kicking my feet, my shoes heavy. My hand slipped from the canoe, and when I reached back up it was out of reach.

I went under.

This was her home. Her mermaid home. Her dead girl, dead fish home in the dark. Skylar's bayou and Brynn's tide. I loved to swim. I was so good at it, at cutting through the water, pretending to be a graceful thing.

I sank, and the water stung my scalp.

One time after a swim meet, our coach dumped a giant cooler full of ice into the pool on top of us. I swam through it, each cube stinging against my skin. Like Skylar's icy skin when she pushed at me from below, shoving me to the surface and shouting at me to *open my goddamned eyes and swim*.

She was cold, and it hurt. Her eyes sharpened like a knife's edge. Icicles of worry prodded me out of my tired, dizzy fog. I kept kicking listlessly.

My face broke the surface. I breathed the hot summer air. I didn't slip into the quiet dark until my face rested against the rough concrete boat ramp and Skylar was behind me in the water, in the waves, sobbing, "I'm sorry, I'm sorry, I'm sorry."

CHAPTER EIGHTEEN

PAIN WASHED OVER ME in slow, steady waves. Groaning, I opened my eyes and froze, every sensation hitting me at once. The smell of tangy soap and gummy bandages. A low, faraway chime. Something beeped over and over. Thin sheets scraped at my bare feet, and I didn't have a bra on.

That was the worst part. Most nights I slept with a sports bra on, more comfortable with the support than trying to figure out how to heft my big boobs around. Whatever was happening, someone had stolen my bra, and that was not cool.

I lifted my hands and saw an IV taped to the back of one. *Shit.*

I was in a hospital. And I'd screwed up. Big-time.

Bigger than ever before.

Dad's fingers caught my free hand. His face wobbled into my vision, his eyes bloodshot and his hair uncombed.

"Brynn?" he asked, soft and scared.

This was probably the part where people on TV said, "Who am I?" And maybe that's what Dad was so scared of.

Unfortunately, I still knew exactly who I was. "Hey, Dad."

He sat down on the edge of my bed and folded over me, shaking silently. I dropped my hand into his hair and took that time to observe my surroundings. The walls were covered in a mural with dancing bears, and a fancy TV mounted over the bed played *SpongeBob SquarePants*. Not only had I landed myself in a hospital—I was in a children's hospital.

A nurse bustled in, wheeling a cart with a spiral cord and a small computer screen. She didn't even spare Dad a glance. I knew just enough about children's hospitals to know she saw awful things every single day and wouldn't think twice about a big, bearded dad quietly crying on his daughter's ridiculously tiny hospital bed.

I managed to catch her eye. "Hi."

"Hi. I'm Anne." She smiled at me. It was forced but still warm. Her bangs were curled in a way I'd only seen in pictures of the eighties online. "Can you tell me your name?"

"Brynn Costa," I said.

"What's your pain level?" Anne asked, pointing to a poster with numbered stick figures ranging from happy to super distressed.

"Five," I said, picking the one with a squiggly, unhappy mouth.

"I'm going to give you some acetaminophen, but if that doesn't help, we'll bump it up to something else. Can you tell me your birth date?" She took my wrist gently and checked what I said against the plastic band there.

My head ached wickedly. The liquid painkiller tasted like grape candy.

Dad ducked away and busied himself at the small sink along the wall, blowing his nose noisily and washing his face while the nurse took my blood pressure and temperature.

"Um." My stomach rumbled. I considered asking for food first, but the question gnawed at me more than my hunger. "What happened?"

Anne and Dad both looked at me like I'd developed a spotted purple rash. I rolled my eyes. "Specifically, what are my injuries. I know I fell out of the canoe and hit my head."

Dad's shoulders slumped, and Anne gave me another tight, professional smile. "You have a mild concussion, and we gave you eleven stitches." She made the same face my therapist made at my mom right before she asked her to speak in private, and a wave of nausea-freak-out crashed into my ribs. "We had to shave part of your hair."

I wasn't obsessed with my hair or anything, but shaving was a little on the extreme side. My hand jerked to my hairline, and sure enough the bandage there was surrounded by a patch of stubble.

"Holy shit," I said.

Anne sat on the side of the bed where Dad had been. The other side sported a bright-blue rail, like I was a kid in a crib. "The good news is those haircuts seem popular with girls right now. When you're healed you could even have them shave little lines in it. I hear chevrons are in."

I wasn't about to take style advice from a lady with a perm and hair-sprayed bangs, but she wasn't incorrect. I liked undercuts, and there was no way my mom was ever going to give me permission to get one. I'd stumbled onto the perfect back door to a haircut ninety percent cooler than I was.

My tentative haircut thrill screeched to a halt, cut off by a thought more unpleasant than my drumming headache.

My mom.

I had bigger concerns than whether she'd hate my haircut. She was going to absolutely lose it over me getting myself hospitalized. When I glanced at Dad, his mouth had tightened into a flat line like on an emoji. I guess we were on the same page.

"I'm flying you back as soon as you can go." His words lanced me. *Back. Go.*

Leave.

I'd done enough to mess up his life and worry him. He wanted me out of here, back to Cincinnati, back to being a birthday card and a Christmas card and an occasional stilted phone conversation. I nodded and picked gunk out of the corner of my eye, blaming my tears on the dryness.

"Sweetie . . ."

Anne made herself invisible again, back in nurse mode, punching things in on her computer.

"It's fine," I said.

"No one means that when they say it." Dad took my hand but didn't sit. The bed wasn't high enough, and he hunched over like a puppet with its strings broken to reach me. "You don't have to be fine."

"And you don't have to want me to be here."

"Brynn." My gaze snapped up at the sound of his voice, the same way it sounded when he told Leia to sit. "You're going home because your mom is frantic. It took all my negotiation skills to keep her from jumping on a plane immediately. First, a hurricane, and then a head wound? This is not the summer vacation she had in mind for you. For either of you."

"I shouldn't have to go because Mom's wigging out." I sounded sullen and childish, and I blamed it on the continued angry buzz of my empty stomach. "That's not fair."

"It's not fair that you got hurt, but that's how it is." He watched me until I looked away, knowing I hadn't imagined the emphasis on *got hurt*. He either thought I did it on purpose, or understandably thought I was the world's dumbest teenager for managing to get a concussion by falling out of a stationary canoe.

As if she could hear the sound of my flesh attempting to eat itself, Anne dropped a single-serving tub of peanut butter and a package of graham crackers on the rolling tray table and pushed it to me. She hit a button on my bed, and it slowly transformed, sitting me up. "Apple juice, sports drink, or water?"

Mom didn't buy juice. She'd cited articles about added sugars causing hyperactivity, so we stuck with water and almond milk at home. I had juice at the school cafeteria sometimes, every sip tasting like sweet rebellion. "Apple juice," I said. It didn't come across as defiantly as I'd hoped.

Anne dropped a little juice box with a tiny plastic straw next to the snacks.

Dad grabbed it and opened it for me. Secretly grateful, I took it and drank the whole thing down in several long gulps, my fingers clumsy with sleep and the bulky tape all over my hand.

Anne walked out of the room and left the door open slightly. Light shone in between the cracks in the blinds on the window, and I wondered how much time had passed—if it was still the same day. Hopefully they hadn't cut my clothes off my body. I really liked those jeans.

"What were you doing?" Dad pulled up the guest chair and sat beside me.

Oh, just having a giant fight with my dead friend.

I stared at my lap.

"Brynn."

"I wasn't trying to kill myself."

"I didn't suggest that you were," he said, each word clipped and upset.

"Dad, I'm serious."

"Were you trying to get to the boat?"

The truth was phlegm in my throat, and I wanted so badly to spit it out. *I was trying to find Skylar. I wanted her to tell me the truth. I wanted to tell her that she ruined my summer and kissing her had been a good kiss, a kiss I'd remember forever, even if she was a liar and didn't like girls and didn't like me and wasn't alive.*

"Yes," I said. "I freaked out, thinking you'd get trapped inside it and drown, and I was trying to get out there and help you."

Dad took a long, slow breath, like he hadn't breathed in fully in hours. "That makes sense," he said softly—to himself.

Parents were easy to lie to if you told them what they wanted to hear.

I didn't feel guilty this time. The truth would hurt him more. And it would also get me evaluated by a children's hospital psychologist. The past few days had been crappy enough without dredging up my entire medical history in an effort to prove I didn't normally see dead people and wasn't interested in becoming a dead person.

"I'm sorry things are so scary for you," Dad said absently. He stroked my forearm with his thumb and watched the monitor attached to a little clip on my pointer finger.

"This isn't scary. Look. There's a bear mural. No one's allowed to be scared in the presence of dancing animals."

He laughed once. "Those bears are the scariest thing here."

They were slightly demented now that I looked more closely. No one was that excited about balloons.

"I mean . . . everything." Dad's voice was gentle, bordering on pitying. I hated that the most—almost as much as when the anxiety got so bad, I couldn't remember what it was like to be unafraid. Pity reminded me that even when I felt okay I'd feel bad again later, that I wasn't normal.

"I'm not scared of everything." I consciously unclenched my jaw. "Will you open the peanut butter for me?"

"I know that. Here."

I ignored him for the minute and a half it took to lick the contents of the entire peanut butter container like a dog with a treat. There was absolutely no shame in my game. Peanut butter was full of protein, probably.

Mouth sticky and voice thick with sugar, I turned my attention back to my dad, who was still chuckling weakly at my peanut-butter binge. "You don't know, though. I mean, that's all right. I wouldn't want you to know. But you don't really know."

He sobered. "Then tell me. I want to understand."

The plastic peanut-butter container crinkled in my hand when I made a fist. He wasn't asking me the way my therapist did, well meaning but clinical in her approach. He asked me like he was a kid watching subtitles flicker by too quickly, unable to read them—unable to keep up.

"It's me I'm scared of," I said. "When I think about my broken parts, it's like I summon them. When I get butterflies in my stomach, they feel like a car crash in my intestines because I go hard at everything. It's never like . . . oh, I'm kind of worried or I'm kind of excited." I looked away from him and stared at a smear of peanut butter on my finger. "I'm scared I'll get stuck thinking about death and bad things. When I do, I have to think about all the bad things and all the ways I might die or you might or Mom might. Because . . . when awful things happen to people, you know they weren't thinking about it the second before. Some lady getting hit by a tractor trailer wasn't worrying about getting hit by a truck. Right?" I'd gone a little breathless, but I kept going. "We're all going to die. That's the only part I can't outthink. Even if I can outthink the horrible ways it'll happen, it's still going to happen. It'll happen, and it'll be forever. What if we can feel it? What if we feel ourselves being nothing for all eternity—not just a long time but forever, Dad. Forever goes forever. And sometimes I'm scared that's what I'll want. That I'll give up."

"Brynn. Brynn." He caught his arms around me as I gasped for breath. One of the monitors in the room chirped with concern, and Anne bustled in. Dad waved her off with one arm, and I moaned, miserable and embarrassed—but free. The words were out there, all my stuff on the table, and Dad wasn't telling me I was wrong and he hadn't told me not to worry or not to think about it.

He held me.

And I cried.

And cried.

I was origami, folding in on myself over and over, weeping and hot faced and safe in my dad's arms. It took a long time to settle down, and even when the long, keening noises stopped, I couldn't stop shaking and shuddering, my breaths like beats on a snare drum.

"My head hurts," I said, sniffling and pitiful.

"Well, you tried to crack it open yesterday, so that doesn't surprise me." Dad eased me back and grabbed the remote control with a nurse button and a bunch of arrows. He found the one for the TV and SpongeBob's horrible-yet-awesome voice filled the room. I took a deep breath, and it went all the way down to my belly, filling me up, rushing out of me, and taking so much bad with it. I yawned, wiped my nose, and smiled at my dad.

"Can you open those graham crackers?"

⌒

Once I got discharged the next morning, the first thing we did was drive to a barber shop near the hospital, where a tall woman with a vintage pinup bob and arms covered in colorful tattoos of cats gave me a proper undercut. She offered to shave a design into the short, dark hair. I asked for two lines of waves.

When she turned me to look at the mirror, my hair looked . . . cool. Wild curls high on my head cascaded to one side. The shocking fuzz of the undercut above my ear gave way to the even more shocking sight of a bright-white bandage covering my stitches. The circles under my eyes didn't look as cool, unless I was going for insomniac chic. Having a shaved bit of hair made me feel harder, stronger. Even if my slightly upturned nose still made me look like a kid.

"Gonna tell people you got in a bar fight?" Her name was Suzette, and I wondered if she'd been in a real bar fight. Or if that was something that even happened outside of cowboy movies. Thick black eyeliner ringed her eyes, coming to flawless, symmetrical, catlike points at the corner of each eye.

So cool. So unattainable. I couldn't even write my name neatly.

"No way," I said. "Underground cage fighting. I mean, that's what really happened."

She laughed, her voice deep and husky. She was probably fifteen years older than me, but a blush still crawled up my throat. After she scrunched some styling cream into my hair and told me how to air-dry it so the curls stood out more, Dad paid her and we climbed back into his Jeep.

I didn't even know what day it was, and I was wearing pajama pants—the first thing I'd found when digging into my suitcase.

Unlike most of Dad's stuff, my belongings were safe in my luggage in the Jeep. And back in Ohio.

We checked into a motel a few blocks from the dock. Our room smelled like stale cigarettes, but Dad didn't seem to notice and I wasn't going to complain to him. About anything. Ever again. In my entire life.

Dad walked differently, as if the sky was pressing down on him or gravity had shifted. I spotted a particularly thick patch of gray hair at his temple and couldn't remember if it had been there before—or if it had spontaneously turned white when he'd seen me facedown in the water with my bleeding head resting on a boat ramp. He carried my luggage and his bag inside, refusing to let me help.

"I'm going to pick Paula up in a few minutes to run to the grocery store," Dad said hesitantly.

"Why aren't we staying with her?" I cleared my throat. "I mean, the room is fine. I just wondered."

"She lives across town, and I need to be close to work and the boatyard right now."

I suspected I wasn't the only person bending the truth, but I nodded. "Okay."

"Would you like to come with us?" he asked.

"I'm feeling pretty run-down. Is it okay if I stay here and nap?"

"Can I trust you by yourself?" He gave me a lingering look and my heart skipped several beats, hammering me with a reminder that I was the worst person on the planet for what I was about to do.

"You're welcome to watch me nap if you need to," I responded, as sweetly as I could.

He rolled his eyes. "I'm the one who needs a nap, you know."

"You asked if I wanted to come! If you don't want me to stay and nap, I won't stay and nap."

"It's fine," he said, rubbing his temples. "You're right. You need to rest."

When he went to the bathroom, I dug into my luggage again. I found the folded sparrow paper I'd tucked in there with my underwear and covered with a bunch of tampons, as Dad-proof as I could get.

Patricia McKenzie's phone number.

Luckily, Dad didn't take his phone with him to take a dump, so I grabbed it and opened the door as quietly as I could. An old man sitting in a bright-green Adirondack chair smoked a cigar on the front stoop next to me. He saluted me and I saluted back, making sure to show him my tough side—the bristly hair and badass bandage. No one was going to mess with me.

He chuckled and turned his attention back to the traffic whooshing by.

My fingers trembled as I tapped out Patricia's phone number. I kept my back to the door so that I'd feel it the second Dad came out. I already had a plan—burst into tears and tell him I was calling Mom to tell her I missed her. Then fumble with the phone, delete Patricia from the call history, and talk about cramps.

"Hello?" Patricia answered suspiciously, like she expected me to be a telemarketer.

"Um," I said. "Hi."

"Brynn?" Patricia sounded so much like my mom that I almost dropped the phone. I forgot to respond until she called my name again, more frantically.

"Mrs. McKenzie, can you meet me? I need to talk to you. Only for a little while."

"Can it be over the phone? I hate to do this, but we have an inspector coming out this afternoon to evaluate the flood damage."

The hurricane. I hadn't thought about their proximity to the water. "It can't be over the phone. I'm sorry. I wouldn't ask you if it wasn't important."

She breathed noisily for several long seconds. "Aren't you living on a houseboat?"

"I can meet you on the dock," I said. "Next door to The Oasis."

"Does your dad know you're calling me?"

"He doesn't. This is his phone. Please don't call him back."

Patricia let out a long sigh. I held my breath until she said, "All right. When?"

I squinted at the screen on the phone. "Three o'clock?" That would give both of us half an hour to get to the dock. It was a short walk for me and a shortish drive for her.

"I can do that. Brynn, do you need anything? Can I bring you anything?"

I wondered what she had in mind, what she thought I might ask for. "No. Just you," I said, smiling so my voice would sound happy.

"All right."

I didn't habitually consult with the universe or pray to any deities, but I made a silent promise to stop fucking up once I got this last thing over with. "Thank you, Mrs. McKenzie. Seriously."

"It's no problem." The edge to her voice suggested the opposite.

I hung up, erased the call, and crept back into the room. Dad was still in the bathroom, so I quickly put the phone back where I found it. By the time he came out, I was curled up under a musty blanket with my eyes half closed.

Dad wrote his cell number down on the pad next to the phone—the regular hotel room phone I hadn't even noticed. Because I'd never used a regular phone in my life.

"Call me if you need anything. Anything at all, okay?"

The second adult in a matter of minutes to ask me what I needed. On any other day, I would have come up with something. Some brownies. A soda. A hug.

Nothing came to mind. I didn't want anything but to somehow pull this off.

"I will. Thanks, Dad."

I watched the digital clock on the nightstand, waiting for three minutes to pass before I threw off the covers. Sitting up quickly sent a searing throb of pain through my head. The hospital had advised me not to do anything strenuous for three days. Hopefully that didn't mean walking a quarter of a mile to meet my dead buddy's mom.

I expected the air to smell like low tide and rotting fish, but a strong breeze carried the fresh, bright scent of clean salt water. I'd read somewhere that salt water made things more buoyant. Despite the knot of dread behind my belly button, the breeze carried me along, pulling me on a gentle tide toward the last place I'd seen my friend—the last place I'd ever see her.

CHAPTER NINETEEN

THE TIDE MADE LIP-SMACKING sounds against the bottom of the dock. I kicked my shoes off and lined them up neatly beside me, adjusting them for a full minute until the heel and toe were even.

My anxiety had manifested as compulsions when I was little. I only knew because Mom talked about it sometimes, tired-fondly telling me how I'd have to arrange my stuffed animals in a specific order along the foot of my bed before I went to sleep. One of my first therapists had helped my parents figure out what to make of that, and they'd done some little-kid version of cognitive behavior therapy. For the most part, I'd grown out of arranging things. But at times like this, times when I could feel my bones and muscles and tendons snapping like live wires under my skin, those tendencies rippled to the surface.

"I see you," I told my perfect shoe arrangement. No judgment. Just recognition. If my brain told me I needed to arrange things to keep bad things from happening, I'd go with the flow.

Or maybe I'd flip out about it later. But right now, I had something important to do.

The warm water embraced my feet, hugging my ankles, turning my feet the color of iced tea. I leaned back, bracing myself with my palms, and turned my face to the cloudless sky above. The steady *beep-beep-beep* of a reversing forklift cut into the water sounds of the bayou. A small crew was righting the boats that had been tossed around the gravel lot during Alonzo. None of them had acknowledged me when I'd picked my way across the lot to the dock, but I felt their eyes on my back. I'd tell Dad, when it was time to explain, that adults had been watching me. That I hadn't been by myself.

"I'm sorry I said the shitty things I said," I told the empty water. "They weren't true. I was mad, and that doesn't make it right. You don't have to forgive me."

And then, because I wanted her to know that she'd left marks on me, good ones, ones that would last forever, I whispered, "I love you."

I heard Patricia's car and didn't turn around. The tires snapped against the gravel, and the engine made an expensive-sounding purr. I pictured her dressed in a tennis outfit—a short skirt revealing strong legs like Skylar's, and a pale-pink polo shirt looking like it had never been worn.

She dropped a pair of flip-flops next to my shoes and made a pained sound as she lowered herself to the edge of the dock beside me. "It gets a little harder to sit down on the ground when you're my age," she said.

Her newscaster hair was limp and dull, pushed behind her ears. She didn't wear any makeup at all, and age spots dotted her cheeks. She had a scar on her nose, like she'd had some skin cancer taken off. She wore a pair of baggy shorts and a paint-stained plain T-shirt, and I wanted to apologize for making her a cartoon character in my head. She was a person. A sad person.

"What happened to your head?" she asked.

"I fell out of a canoe." I pointed at the boat ramp. "Over there."

"After a hurricane? You're having quite an eventful summer."

She had no idea. I kicked my feet at the water gently, making tiny waves that rippled away across the calm bayou. Nothing broke the surface.

"Earlier this year I said something on my Tumblr—on my blog. I wrote about wanting to die."

Patricia didn't react. I thanked her silently.

"My mom freaked out," I said with a humorless laugh. "She won't let me go online anymore, for now. And she sent me down here to hang out with Dad and get my shit together."

"She's afraid." Patricia stretched her legs out. Water dripped from her heels. "She doesn't know how to help you, and she's scared she'll miss the one thing she was supposed to catch. She's your mom. She's supposed to know you better than anyone else."

I'd brought it up to get her on the subject of Skylar, and I hadn't expected her to say these things. Things that mattered to me.

I went still, struggling to catch a full breath. I looked down at my arms and saw the fine hair standing on end across a field of little goose bumps. I closed my eyes, and I was back at the airport with Mom's arms around me, her breath hitching as she told me she loved me and to call her as much as I could, to have fun. I hadn't heard the backbeat behind those words or noticed the fear in her eyes, but I could see it now. She'd put me on that plane wondering if I'd ever come back to Ohio. If she'd ever see her kid again.

"She knows me pretty well." I choked up and cleared my throat. I had to focus. "Can I ask you something?"

"Of course."

My breath rattled. I watched the water. "Are you mad at Skylar for what she did?"

Patricia made a sound like laughter underwater. "Of course I am."

I clenched my jaw, my teeth snapping together. This wasn't going the right way. "How can you be mad at her? She was hurting. She had to have been. Right? She wouldn't have done that if she wasn't hurting—if it hadn't seemed like the only thing she could do."

And I'd yelled at her and sent her away and made her feel terrible about her parents. She might not ever come back now because I'd been so mean to her, when all she'd wanted, probably, was a friend. I wanted to be her friend.

"Brynn, people can have more than one feeling at a time. Haven't you ever been angry with someone you love?"

I nodded, sucking in a sniffly breath. Patricia scooted closer and took my hand in hers. Her fingers were ice-cold, and for a hysterical moment I wondered if she was dead too. But she wasn't. She was upset. Because of me.

"Some days I'm angry, but most days I'm grieving. I'm very sad, and I miss my little girl. Her dad . . . Everyone grieves in their own way, but he isn't angry as often as I am."

"I feel like a giant asshole for making my mom and dad worry."

And for saying hateful things to Skylar because I felt those hateful things about myself. Worthless, shameful, ugly, a burden, a waste of space. In my rage, I'd wanted her to feel the way I did when it was the worst.

Skylar, come back.

"Would you feel like that if you had cancer? Would you feel like a giant asshole?"

It was my turn to let out a watery, weak laugh. "Yes."

Patricia laughed too and squeezed my hand harder. "Would you think that was a reasonable response to being sick?"

"No."

"My daughter was sick. She had depression. She died of depression. She died of a disease the same as those kids I see on Facebook, the ones with pages about them and hashtags and people saying 'fuck cancer.'" Patricia made a nervous sound and looked back over her shoulder, as if the guys with the forklifts would rat her out for swearing. Or maybe rat her out for hating on memorials for dead kids.

I kind of loved her.

And I saw my in.

"What would you tell her right now if you could?"

"Oh gosh," Patricia said. She closed her eyes. Tears ran down her face, silent, ignored. "I'd tell her this wasn't her fault, that she didn't do anything wrong. And I'd tell her I'm trying not to blame myself, but I'm not there yet. I don't know if I'll ever stop trying to figure out what I could have done better or if I could have done more for her. I'd tell her that I'm angry that I have to keep going without her." She let out a sob, low and guttural, and this time I squeezed her hand. Squeezed it hard, like I'd fly off into the atmosphere if I lost that grip. "Oh, Brynn, I don't know what I'd tell her. I'd talk to her every single day. Jonathan always told me I couldn't be friends with my own kid, but I wanted to be her friend. I wanted to be there for her for her whole life, when she got married and had kids—not that she ever talked about wanting that. Maybe she never would have. I don't know what she would have done. I want to know. I miss her so much."

She twisted and fell into my arms, smaller than I expected, her shoulders narrow and her breath whistling between hiccupping, quiet sobs. "I'd tell her I'm so honored to be her mother. I'd tell her I love her, so much, every day, forever."

I cried too, for me. For Mom and Dad. For the McKenzies. For Skylar.

"No matter what." Patricia's words squeaked out between weeping breaths. "I'd tell her I love her no matter what."

Maybe she didn't hear the gentle splash over the sound of her anguish, but I did. And I felt strong hands grab on to my feet in the water. I felt a shaking body against my legs, wet with the bayou, trembling with tears, a forehead against my skin. I heard a gentle rustle of waves whispering warm, voiceless gratitude.

For the first time, I didn't feel sorrow or longing. My bones settled in place as if they'd been fractured all summer.

"It's okay," I said, intoxicated by the peace that washed over me. The relief and love. "It's gonna be okay."

I kept my eyes closed when Skylar went away, not releasing her grip, but ceasing to exist as if she'd never touched me at all.

Except her fingerprints were all over me, on my sore muscles and the knot on my head and my badass undercut and a fierce desire to *be*.

Knowing I wouldn't see anything on the surface of the water, I opened my eyes, wiped my tears on Patricia McKenzie's shirt, and held on to her until my dad pulled into the lot, spraying gravel and twisting to a stop like it was a getaway car.

I counted myself lucky that no paramedics were involved this time. Instead, my dad and Patricia spoke in tight, low tones near his Jeep while I dangled my toes in the water. I couldn't bring myself to worry about what they were saying. I couldn't stop smiling, even with the low buzz of a crying-headache and the deeper throb of the stitches at my hairline.

"Whoa, nice undercut," Paula said, her feet thudding on the dock as she approached. "A girl at work has one, but I'm terrified to get a trim. Let alone shave part of my head."

"Hi." I patted the spot next to me, where Patricia had been before she'd gotten up to wave off my dad's stormy approach. "I don't think I would have done it out of the blue."

"Crazy about the boat, isn't it?"

It took me a long moment to realize she meant *Brynn's Tide*, out on the water, capsized and beached on the shallows. I'd been so busy with Skylar I'd forgotten to look for it. Even the loss of Dad's home couldn't touch me right now. "Will Dad move in with you?"

"Ah." Paula let out a soft, nervous laugh. "Yes, I think so. Probably. We haven't talked about it, but I've thought about it a lot."

"Worried about it?"

"A little. I've been single for a few years. Bringing a guy into my space will be an adjustment, but he's worth it." She hummed. "Does that bother you?"

"No," I said easily, lightly. Happy-tired. "I'm glad he won't go live on another boat. I think he needs to let go of the bayou."

"Wise words." Paula offered me a sliver of her crooked-tooth smile. "Hunter said you're going back up to Cincinnati pretty soon. I hope you come back. I'd like to hang out with you more."

"Do you have a computer?"

She laughed brightly. "Yes, Brynn. I have a computer."

I shrugged, blushing. I don't know why I'd asked. This was the most unplugged I'd been since the first time I'd started banging on my mom's old laptop in preschool. "We could email. I guess text too, if I get my phone back."

"I'd like that, but I also want you to come back," she said with a significance that sunk in slowly, the way the clouds changed colors at sunset.

"For Dad."

"For both of us. We have book notes to compare."

"Oh my God." I looked back out at the water. "My library books sank in the hurricane."

A moment of silence stretched out between us, punctuated by the high whine of a Jet Ski engine, and then we both started laughing—not calm, quiet, familiar laughter but whooping, barking laughter that carried across the water.

"I'll drive you to the library to apologize," she said.

I wasn't going to say no to seeing Logan again. To carving out another reason to come back here next summer.

Two old men on a squat boat in the distance turned to look at us, too far for me to make out their expressions. But I pictured their wrinkled lips pressed into lines of disapproval, and that made me laugh harder. Paula leaned into me, and I leaned back into her, and we giggled ourselves silly. My head hurt just a little more from shaking with laughter. I forced myself to chill out before I ended up sick to my stomach from the pain. Even with the hurt there, I couldn't stop smiling.

CHAPTER TWENTY

DAD HAD THE DECENCY to wait outside the library while I ran in right when it opened. I literally ran—because we only had a ten-minute window before we had to get on the road to be at the airport on time for him to chaperone me back to Ohio.

I was breathless by the time I got to Logan's information desk. My nervous smile faded when a very old woman looked up from sorting a bin of books into neat stacks. "May I help you?" she asked.

"Um. No. Sorry. Is Logan here?"

She adjusted her glasses and pursed her lips. "I haven't seen him." Thin chains swung from each ear. I stared at them, lost in my disappointment.

"May I borrow a pen and some paper?"

A huge clock on the wall behind her ticked as she moved like a frail sloth, sifting through a messy junk drawer to find a yellow legal pad and a pen. I tried not to wrench them right out of her hand, wound up and hyperaware of each tick-tock-click. Dad had gone on and on about how bad traffic would get on the way to the airport if we left too late.

Hi, Logan. My dad's houseboat sank with your library books on them. I know they're not your actual library books. The library's books. Sorry. Paula said she'll pay for them. She's my dad's girlfriend. Please burn this note so that no one will ever witness this stream of awkwardness. I have some questions to ask you. But not in a weird way. Mostly. See you on Tumblr?

—Brynn

(we talked at the marina but also here one time)

As I reread my note, my guts shriveling up over my inability to backspace on the fly, a shadow crossed the paper. I twisted, terrified Dad would be there hovering over me and reading my screwy rambling.

It was Logan.

"Um," he said.

"Oh!" I shoved the yellow paper at him, crumbling it into a ball in the process. "Sorry—this isn't trash, it's a note. For you. I wrote you a note."

"Got it." The corner of his mouth quirked up, revealing a dimple.

"Well." I swallowed. "I won't spoil it. Bye!" Before a black hole opened up in the carpet and swallowed me, I pushed by him and started sprinting for the door.

"Brynn!" he called out.

I turned, bumped into a rolling cart of books, and barely managed to keep it from toppling over. "Yeah?"

Logan smiled broadly. "I sent you an ask."

No longer trusting my ability to communicate with other humans, I waved once and retreated. When I jumped up into the Jeep, Dad gave me a long look. "You're awfully flushed."

I grinned.

Dad fell asleep while we taxied on the runway. So much for keeping an eye on me.

Not that I was going to jettison myself from a plane to cause more trouble.

I pressed my sweaty forehead to the plastic window, grateful to have no audience and no one expecting me to talk.

My thoughts floated as the plane took off. If I was ever allowed back online, I planned on asking Logan about the notes in Skylar's yearbook. Hopefully he'd understand that talking about her wasn't bad. It was good. It was important.

The mangrove islands sprawled far below us as we climbed and banked sharply. Dark green and darker blue mottled like bruises at the edge of the peninsula city. I wiggled one finger against the smooth surface of the window in one last farewell to Skylar's bayou. A pang of sadness echoed the hiccup-hum of my ears popping and the sound of the jet engine roaring.

She'd always been gone. She'd never been mine. But I'd never see her again, and while I'd decided that her absence could only mean peace, I had grieving to catch up on now that she was normal-dead. Forever-dead.

Patricia had met us at the airport to give me one last hug and a sweatshirt that had belonged to Skylar. It smelled strongly of the kind of detergent my mom hated—the kind full of dyes and perfumes. I wore it now and tucked my nose against the inside of my elbow to inhale the strong, clean smell. She didn't tell me why she'd chosen to give me something of Skylar's. I didn't tell her that I'd spent my brief Florida summer with her dead daughter—that I already had something of Skylar's forever now, even if I couldn't put a name to it.

Dad didn't wake up when the flight attendant asked me what I wanted. I asked if I could get two packages of cookies, and he gave me three with a wink. I nibbled them and dipped them in a cup of coffee with so much cream and sugar it tasted like melted ice cream. As I finished up the last, sweet drops, the plane shuddered. I tucked the cookie wrappers into the Styrofoam cup, checked my seat belt, and lowered the plastic shade over the window. I glanced at Dad, and his mouth was parted in a quiet snore.

A seat belt wasn't going to help me if we went down. I knew that. I'd even gone online and looked at plane wreckage photos once. Content warnings always made me click—because I had to know if what I'd end up seeing was as bad as what my mind conjured up. So far, the photos were always worse than my imagination, which was really saying a lot considering the kind of carnage my brain was capable of serving. In the wreckage photos, people were still belted into their seats, or pieces of their seats. And their body parts weren't bloody or torn open but bent and crooked like broken dolls. We weren't going to survive a crash. If we were lucky, we'd black out from the force of the fall or the lack of oxygen.

I see you, I told the anxiety. It didn't make it go away, but it released some of the tight knot of anger that always piggybacked alongside the fear and tension. Anger at myself.

This part of me would never go away, but I didn't have to be mad about it. I didn't have to feel weak or broken.

When I'd looked at those horrible plane crash photos, I'd closed my browser and hidden in Mom's closet, where her longest dresses curtained my face. Deep down I knew that girls my age shouldn't be hiding in makeshift forts in a closet. That didn't stop me. And not believing in heaven and not understanding what the point of higher powers was didn't stop me from holding on to hope. I hoped that some benevolent force had put everyone on the plane to sleep before they had a chance to realize they weren't going to make it.

Anticipating death scared me as much as the forever of it, and that was one of the reasons I'd never understand how Skylar had been able to do what she'd done. It's why I knew I'd spend the rest of my life haunted by the thought of her final moments. When I had nightmares about death, it always came at me in slow motion. A plane spiraling unnaturally slowly toward a rocky landscape. A car spinning out toward a cliff. A fire blocking every exit from my home. A gun leveled at my chest.

But these thoughts weren't forever. They weren't always.

I took a slow, deep breath, feeling it fill my chest and belly.

"Turbulence," Dad muttered. He stretched his legs, and his knees hit the seat in front of him. "Oh man, I missed cookies?"

I closed my eyes tightly, endured another shimmy-shake of the plane, and turned my focus to Dad. "We tried to wake you up," I said, my voice wavering.

"You did not."

He looked worried, so I smirked. "I did, but you kept moaning something about Paula."

He stared at me for a long second before he punched my thigh lightly and started laughing. "Nice try. See if I snag you extra cookies."

When the flight attendant came back with Dad's diet soda, Dad asked for more cookies, and we shared a package of them, trying to see who could guess the most ingredients before we read them off the wrapper.

Dad won.

The plane shuddered again, rattling our tray tables.

"Want to know something I've never told anyone?" Dad asked quietly.

I leaned in, hoping he'd give me something as juicy as the revelation that Mom had been a wild kid in high school.

"I used to think I saw her in the water," he murmured. "Swimming around, I mean. Alive. I almost talked to my doctor about it, but I'm not as brave as you are."

My mouth hung open, but I had the good sense to stay silent.

"Anyway," he went on with a sigh, "I have my stuff too. Just like your mom always says. Everybody does."

I chewed my sunburned bottom lip so I wouldn't burst into tears—happy to have another story about my friend. "I know."

We made it through the turbulence.

My nerves were eating each other like piranhas by the time we made it out of the terminal and into the area where families and drivers with signs waited for arrivals. Mom and I had never been apart this long, and it was the opposite of what people said about rubber bands connecting their hearts or strings connecting their souls. I was farther from her than ever before, disconnected and peering across an endless chasm.

Or maybe the airplane coffee was churning up an endless chasm of angst in my belly.

I hadn't expected to see Mom in the crowd, not when she knew Dad would be trailing behind me. When I saw her, my gaze had already tripped over to the next face before I realized who it was. Her expression was so pinched, I'd written her off as a stranger. Mom wasn't exactly calm on the best of days, but she was usually just stressed—not unhappy or afraid. This woman hesitating to approach me was scared. She flinched when our eyes met.

I stumbled to a halt. "Mom."

Dad bumped into my back, chuckled something about both of us still being asleep, and made a quiet, uncomfortable sound when he spotted Mom. We shuffled forward, and she took a few steps. We were trapped in quicksand, struggling. The waiting area was deserted by the time we met with the slow-motion, weighted momentum of every crash from my bad dreams.

"Brynn." She looked at my hair and not my eyes. Her hands fluttered out at me, not quite reaching. "Hunter. You guys look tired."

"Early flight," Dad said.

The mom-space in my brain had been occupied by white noise for the whole flight and the descent into the Kentucky airport near Cincinnati. With Mom right in front of me and Patricia's detergent tickling my nose, I was in a full-on vortex of mom-ness. My backpack slipped out of my hand. It thudded at my feet, muffled by the carpet that was as ugly here as it was back in Florida.

I tipped into her. Mom caught me like I'd lobbed a basketball, letting out a gentle *oof* and cupping my arms tenderly, carefully, before she pulled me into a gasping, tight embrace.

"Mom."

Her heart hammered against my chest. "You got taller," she said.

"Sorry about my hair."

She lifted her head, held me out, and exhaled a wet, gusting laugh. "Don't be sorry. It's very stylish. That actress—the one on the HBO show—she has that same haircut." She spoke too fast. People said they couldn't tell our voices apart.

I gave my head a little shake so my curls would bounce against the sensitive, fuzzy part of my undercut, where I still had stitches that needed to come out. At least they weren't covered by a big bandage anymore.

"Cool," I said. I wanted to say more words, but they hovered out of reach, somewhere behind the haze of unshed tears and the tightness in my throat.

"Let's get your bags so you ladies can head home," Dad said. He grabbed my backpack off the floor and walked ahead, and Mom and I followed next to each other.

Mom took my hand. "Are you okay?"

"Yeah." I squeezed her fingers gently. "Are you okay?"

"I am. I've been talking to someone while you've been away."

"Whoa. Like a guy?"

She laughed. "Like a new therapist. For me. I hadn't seen someone since the divorce, and it was time."

Something inside me crinkled up like paper at the thought of my mom feeling as bad as I did, needing someone to make her feel better. I stopped again, and Mom kept a tight grip on my hand, refusing to let go. "What is it?"

"It's my fault you had to go to therapy," I said, continuing to fold up, lips first, my chin flattening with the effort to hold back tears.

"Brynn Alice Costa, you're not the center of the entire universe."

I blinked.

"I'm an adult woman. I have plenty of reasons to talk to a professional about my emotional well-being." She gave me a gentle tug, and I continued following her. "I'm only telling you because my therapist helped me see that banning you from talking to Jordan and your other friends was about my feelings, not yours. And I thought you'd be happy to hear that."

It was vindicating, but being right wasn't much fun when Mom had to be wrong. Except—was she serious? "Wait. I can go online?"

"Yes," Mom said, eyes gleaming with amusement at my reaction. Her expression abruptly faltered. "I missed you." She cleared her throat, smiled tightly, and acted like she wasn't supposed to cry or be mom-shaped.

I'd spent all my time in Florida thinking about how much I made her life suck, and looking at her now, watching her try to rebuild herself into someone who didn't need me, who didn't need us, I realized she was probably doing the same thing. Thinking she made me embarrassed or uncomfortable or unhappy. Thinking being online was escape from her, from our too-close, always-together relationship. From our little house and our dinners for two.

It had been, a little bit.

"Mom." Her eyes widened and her attention snapped to me fully. "Mom," I said again, careful and gentle. This time, when I hugged her, I rested my head on her shoulder and sighed out, "I love you. I missed you too."

We hugged for a long time. Mom kissed my hair, careful of the stitches, and wiped her eyes. She took my hand again and looked up when an announcer said something about a baggage belt change. Her hair fell against her face, and she reminded me of a cartoon dog, in a cute, complimentary way. I saw her younger, a little sillier. A girl. She looked back at me, and another layer of the fear I'd seen before peeled away, as if the tight grip of our hands allowed an exchange of energy and strength.

"So. My therapist also shared some fascinating research on the value of online friendships." She made a nervous sound, and I wondered if she'd rehearsed this speech. "I've thought about it a lot. I shouldn't distinguish between online friends and school friends or devalue those relationships."

At that point my jaw might as well have remained in Florida. "Uh."

Her steps became awkward for a few feet as she dug into her pocket and held out my phone. She tapped the home button. It was charged but still locked with the password I'd given it to keep her out of my stuff.

I stared at it as we walked, overwhelmed with the possibilities. She may as well have handed me the key to a spaceship.

"You don't have any restrictions as long as you keep your grades up in the fall and you sleep regularly, but . . . I'd appreciate your attention. And if you could wait until we're in the car . . ." She hesitated like I was the one in charge.

It occurred to me then that she'd probably been missing me for a lot longer than the past few weeks.

I tucked the phone in my back pocket and struggled to catch my breath. "Mom."

"What is it?"

She stopped walking when I stopped walking, and I hugged her again. "I missed you more than I missed my phone."

An older man walking by through the crowded hallway overheard me and laughed, and Mom and I laughed too, anchored against each other as the tide of tired travelers brushed by us. I looked over Mom's shoulder and saw Dad at the end of the hall, where it opened up to a sea of luggage belts and signs. He caught my eye and smiled, nodding almost imperceptibly. I didn't know what he meant, but I took it as permission to have a different relationship with Mom than I did with him. At least he'd agreed to spend one night before heading home, so he could see my room and we could have an awkward family dinner.

Dad would always be there, moving in with Paula, chasing alligators off the golf course, catching pinfish by channel markers, keeping a space for me in his life and a room for a summer trip. I loved him, and he understood me, but he was always going to drift in and out of my life. Mom was right here, locked into my gravitational pull.

Next time I was down in Florida it would be a vacation, not a banishment, and I'd bring my computer and my phone and I'd post pictures of the fat lizards and shady strip club signs and the osprey high on the summer breeze and the stacked-high thunderheads and the cute library boy.

I'd post pictures of Skylar's beach. *Our beach*.

"I'll get one if you show me how to use it," Mom said, as our laughter drifted into tired smiles. I'd almost forgotten what she was talking about. Her own space in my world, a new way for us to connect, a closed circuit between her grown-lady-mom life and my not-broken, growing-stronger path.

I couldn't hold back a big grin, imagining the kind of text posts she'd make between her occasional bubble baths and falling asleep. It wouldn't be funny—it'd be awesome. I had no idea what my mom really thought about, what she cared about.

And I wanted to know.

"So!" She tugged me toward the carousel of bags and the dwindling crowd rushing off to waiting cars, waiting lives. "Tell me what a hurricane is like!"

I did.

ACKNOWLEDGMENTS

THIS BOOK BEGAN as an awkward first date. Drifting on a borrowed paddleboard, I noticed an abandoned houseboat anchored in a quiet mangrove lagoon near Weedon Island Preserve. I started daydreaming about life on that boat, and that evening Brynn was born. Before bed, I sent the first chapter to a friend in an email with no subject line. I woke up to a text asking for more.

Writing close to the heart is an act of vulnerability, and I was so lucky to be surrounded by love and support while walking alongside Brynn and Skylar.

Early readers are so important to my messy process. Thank you to Megan for being the first person to meet my girls. Thank you to Tehlor Kay Mejia for helping me revise my earliest draft. Thank you to the Pitch Wars class of '15, who years later have continued to be a source of encouragement and camaraderie. Thank you to Linsey Miller for reminding me that I can do this. Thank you to the sensitivity readers who helped me shape the complexities of Brynn's interiority: Erin, Casey, Terra, and Azaleah. Thank you to Violet and Isla not only for reading but for being such deeply cool people. Every time I write a teenager I ask myself if I'm doing you justice.

To my brilliant agent, Erica Bauman—thank you for being my champion and sounding board and Brynn's unofficial big sister. Your belief in this story fueled me when I needed it most.

To my delightful editor, Ashley Hearn—thank you for seeing and loving Brynn. I treasure your perspective and have so much gratitude for getting to be part of your spectacular journey at Peachtree Teen. Every time I see a dolphin I think of you!

This book has had a powerful team behind it from the start. Thank you to my copy editor, Melissa Kavonic, for your grammar wizardry and patience. Thank you to J.A.W. Cooper for illustrating a cover that does Brynn and Skylar and their world so much justice, and thank you to Lily Steele for pulling the cover design together so beautifully. Thank you to the marketing and publicity team at Peachtree Teen for getting this book out in front of the world, and thank you to the booksellers and librarians who help teens connect with the stories they need.

My personal scaffolding deserves so much acknowledgment. Thank you to Dafna Pleban and Joyce Sun for listening, being vulnerable, and locating the best dumplings in Queens. Thank you to Diane Ashoff for keeping my writing process and wiggly brain company for so many years. Thank you to Emma Schwartz, Adrienne Browning, and Jace Covert for creating a professional environment that leaves room in my noggin for creative endeavors. Thank you to Kristen Quinley for believing in manatee superiority, always making space for us to be a lot together, and sending me restorative TikToks.

I grew up playing in the mangroves where Brynn found Skylar. Thank you to my mom for teaching me how and when to go to the water—and for opening my heart to what I might find there. Thank you to my family for showing up in ways that help me show up here on the page, especially to Katy for teaching me what every weird, wiggly creature is at the sandbar.

To my kids, Max and Simon: I love you and I'm proud of you, even when you're beating me at Mario Kart.

Lastly, thank you to my readers for keeping this and countless other stories alive. You are so powerful. I'm glad you're here.

MARIA INGRANDE MORA (THEY/SHE) is a content strategist and the author of the acclaimed young adult fantasy *Fragile Remedy* (Flux, March 2021), a Junior Library Guild Gold Standard Selection. Their love languages are snacks, queer joy, and live music. A graduate of the University of Florida, Maria lives near a wetlands preserve with two cats, two teenagers, and two billion mosquitoes.

MariaMora.net

Find Maria on Instagram @mariamorawrites.